This Just In . . .

Other books by Yolanda Joe

Bebe's by Golly Wow!

He Say, She Say

Falling Leaves of Ivy

This Just In . . .

a novel

Yolanda Joe

Doubleday

New York   London   Toronto   Sydney   Auckland

PUBLISHED BY DOUBLEDAY
a division of Random House, Inc.
1540 Broadway, New York, New York 10036

DOUBLEDAY and the portrayal of an anchor with a dolphin are trademarks of
Doubleday, a division of Random House, Inc.

Book design by Donna Sinisgalli

Library of Congress Cataloging-in-Publication Data

Joe, Yolanda.
This just in . . . : a novel / Yolanda Joe.—1st ed.
p.   cm.
1. Television broadcasting—United States—Fiction.   2. Women in television
broadcasting—Fiction.   3. Television broadcasting of news—Fiction.   I. Title.

PS3560.O242 T47 2000
813'.54—dc21

                                                                                99-088178

ISBN 0-385-49256-1

10   9   8   7   6   5   4   3   2   1

READER'S NOTE

This Just In . . . *is set up like an hour-long news broadcast!*

Headlines

Tease Breaks #s 1–9

Weather

Sports

Kicker

Bye-Bye

Closing Credits

Headlines

Dateline: Chicago. March 1998.

Coming Up Next on WKBA-TV:

First:

Holly Johnston—

Reporter/Anchor. Twenty-five years old. California pretty. Black Bourgeois. Considered a lightweight. Holly wants to prove her journalism skills to the WKBA newsroom. But how?

Then:

Alexandra Harbor—

The only black woman photographer. Thirty-six years old. A Chicago native. She battles sexism and racism. This broadcast veteran is talented, burned out, and volatile. She struggles to stay focused and afloat at WKBA.

And:

Kenya Adams—

An uprooted small-town Southern girl. Twenty-six years old. A print reporter at heart, she struggles to make the tough transition to writing and producing TV news. Kenya's drive to succeed jeopardizes her home life with her med school husband and toddler son.

Also:

Megan Rippley—

Nickname: Beans. Forty-four years old. The first woman to become a photographer at WKBA. White. Working class. Chicagoan. Slight stutterer. Manages problem by talking in phrases. Beans is also considered a sort of troop leader to the other women in the newsroom. But there are racism struggles. Will those struggles damage her respect and friendship with the black women at WKBA?

Plus:

Denise Mitzler—

A trailblazer. One of the first black women managers working for a network-owned station in a top-five market. Forty-one years old. Denise is scrappy. Reared on the East Coast and college-educated. Her sights are set on reaching the top. But Denise fights to find balance. Should she correct years of racism at WKBA? Should Denise rock the boat? When does fairness end and reverse racism begin?

All Those Stories and More.

This Just In . . .

Starts Right Now.

Holly
Reporter/Anchor

All eyes were on me.

I walked through the WKBA newsroom. It was a whirling hub of activity. In the large oval-shaped space with rectangular metal desks, my new coworkers sat up, stopped what they were doing, and openly stared.

All eyes were on me.

In whispers, my new colleagues debated my existence and my worth as though I weren't there. *Is that the new reporter? Yes that's her. Do you think she's pretty? In a common sort of way. Think she'll make it? Who knows? Who cares?* How ironic; I felt visible yet invisible.

All eyes were on me.

I was following my new boss's executive secretary, Vera. She's fifty-ish and petite. Vera has literally grown up at this station. Recently Vera celebrated her twenty-fifth year on the job. You could do that behind the scenes in a nondecision-making position, you could stay twenty to thirty years at one television station.

But it's not like that for reporters and anchors. For us, television stations have revolving doors. Broadcast news is a complicated game, it's a lot of stick and move.

I was coming from a tiny but well-respected station located in Palm Springs. In news, no one really tries to stay rooted at one particular station until they get to the big time—New York, Chicago, L.A. That's what WKBA/Chicago is—the big time. And I'm determined to stick.

I kept my diva face and accompanying strut going full throttle despite all the emotion churning inside of me. Who will my new friends be? Will I get off to a good start?

It wasn't that I hadn't been in WKBA's newsroom before. I had, actually, for a final interview with Kal Jimper, the vice president/general manager. He's the number-one guy.

I met with the news director too—Mitch Saleen. He's the number-two guy, responsible for the overall daily operations within the newsroom.

Then I was briefly introduced to Garth Ingalls, the executive producer, a tall man with steel blue eyes and a whiskey voice. I met Denise Mitzler too. She's managing editor. Denise is a classy sister with a no-nonsense demeanor.

But Kal Jimper and Mitch Saleen were the ones I had to win over. And I did win them over so here I am.

"You'll like Chicago," Vera chatted as we walked. "There's so much to do! Blues. Jazz. Theater. Great summer festivals in Grant Park. I've lived here all my life and I love it."

"You never thought about moving?"

"Once," she said. "My husband is a car salesman. He thought he could do better in Dallas. At the time my twin boys were babies. But we thought since my family is here, and his family is here, it wasn't worth going to a new place where we didn't know anyone."

I nodded—I was now in a strange new place where I didn't know anyone.

"Plus," Vera chatted on, "I ended up getting a better job at 'KBA. At first I was in the mailroom. I got to know everyone in the building. When people heard that I was thinking about leaving, the news director gave me a job as his secretary. That convinced us to stay."

"I hope I like it here as much as you do."

"You will." Vera smiled pleasantly. Now we had reached the last desk on the third row. "Well, Holly, here's your spot. I sit right around the corner there," Vera pointed, "outside Mitch's door. Holler if you need help."

"Thanks."

"That's good advice!" someone complimented as she walked away. "Vera's number one around here!"

"Rerack your tape, baby," a voice jackknifed through the air. *"Hazel Morriette is the top bitch around here and don't you forget it!"*

I turned to look at the woman who spoke with such cutting pride. Hazel Morriette was sitting across from my work space with her right arm draped across the back of her plaid desk chair. She gnawed at me with a hungry gaze that made me both uneasy and guarded. Hazel seductively snapped her wrists as she whipped the telephone chord around and around in the air. With a sly smile, she cooed, "My dear, you are in the presence of greatness. I am Hazel Morriette, senior anchor at WKBA."

Lucky me. Hazel was on vacation during my final interview at WKBA but I'd heard about her. Oh yes. I'd heard that Hazel was like radiation—the less exposure the better. Her story is a lesson in Journalism 101. Who: Hazel Morriette. What: 10 P.M. anchor. When: Since 1987. Where: WKBA Chicago. Why: Solid audience recognition and tight with network brass.

Hazel has glossy black hair that flows past her shoulders. A streak of gray adorns the sides of each temple. Hazel has stunning bone structure, from her sculpted eyes to a dimple that centers in her chin. But age has forced a heavy hand when it comes to Hazel's makeup. She's camouflaging wrinkles and a splatter of age spots. Hazel had on a Donna Karan dress and Gucci shoes. Be friendly, I thought. After all, what had I done to her? So I smiled at Hazel Morriette.

That's it. That's all.

Then this Hazel Morriette broke on me in a rude and crude manner. Hazel said, *"If you can cut it, you might make it here . . ."* She said, *"I'm just trying to figure out if your talent is in your* head *or in between your legs!"*

I was stunned and severely wounded. In my head I came back in my best California B-girl voice with, *"My talent is in the same place as yours—minus the wrinkles and the age spots!"*

But in reality I didn't say anything. I was new and I had no backup here. I held my tongue. But I stared Hazel Morriette down, refusing to cower.

That was just the beginning. By the end of my first week at WKBA, I learned that Hazel was nicknamed Dragon Diva and for a most appropriate reason. But there's more. By the end of my second week at WKBA I was wishing that I'd never come to Chicago at all. And stranger still, an incident shook me so badly, I literally packed my bags.

DENISE

MANAGING EDITOR/ACTING ASSISTANT NEWS DIRECTOR

TV news is not for people who bruise easily. And WKBA in Chicago will beat you up with a quickness.

I have two years in at this shop.

I'm careful.

How else can a black woman get ahead in this business? I've been in broadcasting eighteen years. Eighteen years. Twelve cities.

It's been tough.

It's been an uphill climb. I've dealt with slick ropes. Few footholds. With my talent and drive I should be a vice president/general manager at a network-owned station.

That's *three* rungs higher than I am right now!

I should be there. I was on the fast track ten years ago. But it happened.

The incident.

The incident stalled my career but taught me two important things. One: There is no room for error when you are black and in broadcasting.

And two: Be careful.

The incident didn't teach me to bend or kowtow. But it taught me to be careful about the battles I fight. Careful too how I fight them.

Be careful.

My phone rang. I answered it. There was something going on out in the newsroom. A commotion. Static. In short . . .

A fight.

The person on the line was tipping me off. There's a way that managers get information about what's *really* going on out in the newsroom. Sources. Unidentified sources.

A mole.

A mole is a friend who wants to help you. Or a mole is a suck-up who wants to cash in the favor later. Our motto: Never reveal a source.

Never ID a mole.

The mole said, "Dragon Diva is torching the new hire." The new hire? The victim had to be Holly Johnston. The attacker had to be Hazel Morriette. Nickname: Dragon Diva.

She's a bitch.

Long black hair. Long gray streaks. Long hot temper. Queen Bee. Ten o'clock anchor. In every city, the late night broadcast is the show of record. The benchmark.

The big stations go head to head.

In Chicago, the ten o'clock show is the show of record. That's the big prize. Bragging rights. The goal is to win ratings for the ten o'clock show.

Then you can win it all.

Dragon Diva anchors the ten o'clock. But recently ratings are way down. She's fiercely jealous. Dragon Diva slaughters anyone who looks like competition. As soon as they cross the threshold she lets them have it.

A broadcast drive-by.

Should I break up the fight? Or should I let Holly slug it out? Can she slug it out?

I want the sister to make it.

If I break it up, how will it look to the staffers in the newsroom? That's important. The Dragon/Holly fight is big news. The word will spread.

Boy, will it spread.

The news will go from WKBA reporters, to writers, to secretaries, to sales reps, to mail clerks, to technicians in the garage, outside to the competing reporters and cameramen on the street, then into their newsrooms.

How will it look?

It will look like I broke up the fight just because Holly is black. That's favoritism.

That's risky.

And the big boys in New York *love* Dragon Diva. I'd chance her holding a grudge. She'd be out to cut me off at the knees.

That's risky too.

Hmmmm, what should I do?

Beans

Photographer/Technician

This is how I got into the fight, a friend in the newsroom called me over in the garage across the street. My friend said, "Beans, there's a big fight going on in the newsroom between Dragon Diva and the new reporter, can you help?" I thought, Whoa, already?

So I decided to hustle over there to check it out, not because I get off on negative tension, although WKBA is famous across the country for its cutthroat atmosphere. No, I hustled over because I hate to see two women go at it and become enemies; women in TV need to stick together.

Like there was a time when I was the only woman technician WKBA had, and that was back in 1981. I started out in 1979 as a scheduling secretary in the technical department but I wanted a shot. I always loved photography, and I wanted a chance. When they needed more minorities, I stepped up. The black and Hispanic men they were hiring looked at me funny, but I'm a white woman, and I'm a minority too. There were no women on the technical side, period, and I got hired.

It was ugly back then, and for one reason. The good old boy network was running better than ever. Silence would have been welcomed, but instead a nasty group of men made a habit of meowing when I walked by, calling me a *you-know-what*. They taped sanitary napkins to my locker, and they meowed, and my male supervisor said, "Can't you take a joke?"

So I ignored the pranks and discouraging remarks every chance I got; other times when it was too much, I went into the bathroom to cry. But I was staying, had to stay, because who knows when they would give another woman a chance?

I was slow getting warmed up to the job because the camera was bulkier then, yeah, heavier, it was harder to hold. No one wanted women in this lion's den, but I was going to claw someone to death if I had to because like I said, I was staying.

The first reporter I worked with, who is now retired in New Mexico raising horses, was a moody SOB. He told me I talked too much without taking a breath, and that I didn't know beans about what I was doing, but I told that SOB, I wasn't giving up. After a few months of that, of me practically killing myself to learn and to hustle, that SOB started requesting me for his special shoots. He started saying, "Give me Beans!" and I've been Beans ever since.

That was the first word out of Hazel's mouth when she saw me striding across the newsroom in her direction. She said, with humor and authority, "Beans to the rescue!"

The new reporter turned around and looked at me and I could see the anger in her eyes, not meant for me, but meant for me to see. She's a pretty girl, about five seven, but very thin, so she looks lean and long. I would say that Holly looks like a darker version of Halle Berry, but with beautiful dark auburn hair that shags just above the shoulders. Holly is a dresser, spends a lot on her clothes; she looks expensive from the top of her head to the heels of her shoes.

I grabbed Hazel around the neck playfully, and joked out loud for everyone to hear, "What are you causing trouble for? Huh?" As usual, that made Hazel laugh. Hazel and I went back to her first days in the WKBA shop; back then I helped her get the lay of the land.

Holly was smart enough to retreat, to just walk away quietly toward the ladies' room. Later I found her there fixing her makeup, her eyes particularly, and they were red from crying. "Good thinking," I said. "Don't try to go head to head with Hazel. She can hold a nasty grudge, but buried deep down inside of her is a decent person."

"I doubt if the *Titanic* is buried down that deep."

"I hope you don't mind, but can I give you some advice, huh, Holly?"

"I could use it."

"Don't ever let them see you cry in the newsroom. I'm not saying that you won't cry in this business, but don't do it out in the open."

"Why?"

"Because, Holly, in a big-city newsroom it's cutthroat, and you have to maintain respect. You cry in the middle of that newsroom and *half* the people will feel sorry for you, and the other *half* will feel contempt for you, and *none* of them will respect you."

"Why did I come here?" Holly groaned, but it wasn't a give-up groan, but more like *I've got an uphill battle ahead* groan.

"Dues, kiddo, there are heavy dues in the big-city markets, but you've got friends here already."

"One," Holly said pleasantly, looking at me.

"Two . . . the friend who called and asked me to help you out, but see, don't ask me who it is, they don't want you to know." Then I laughed. "It's an exclusive."

After I told her that, I headed for the door, and Holly stopped me when she said, "Thanks, Beans. I appreciate it. I hope I can put this stupid fight behind me. Do you think it will get around and become a big deal?"

Alex
Photographer/Technician

Say what? Dragon Diva got it on with the new reporter? It's all over town now—going from newsroom to newsroom. Men are from Mars. Women are from Venus. Journalists are from Jupiter—we're always the biggest and the baddest, ruling the universe with all the inside scoop. A TV news jockey will call across the world to tell or learn about some dirt popping off in a newsroom.

That's how I got the 4-1-1 on the Dragon/Holly fight. I'm out in the burbs on a story. Just doing my natural-born thang. Me and a bunch of other photogs are there shooting background video, or b-roll as we call it. A cameraman from another station says, "Hey, Alex, heard Hazel Morriette kicked the new reporter's ass!"

That Dragon Diva ain't no good. But she's high on the newsroom power chain. Managers are top dogs on the power chain because they're running the TV station. Then there's talent—the on-air people. Then there's the writers/producers and after that the technicians—camera, audio, editors—then researchers, and the rest.

That's the way the power chain is hooked up pretty much but if a reporter or anchor gets *starlight-star bright?* Shit, he or she can run the place and take down *anybody*, including management. Dragon Diva's got game like that.

I heard her guardian angel was the president of network news. Heard she was screwing him. I also heard it was the owner himself, old Texas money bags Jeb Quincy. Heard she was screwing him. I'm not exactly sure *who's zoomin' who* but Dragon Diva gets away with mass murder. But hey—I ain't *that* mad at cha'—that's just how TV news goes sometimes.

I finished my shoot and jetted back over to my unit—a unit is the car or truck with your equipment, two-way radio, and phone in it. Before I could call in to get the lowdown on the throw-down, I got a call over the two-way.

It was the assignment desk. I cursed. The assignment desk is the hub of the newsroom. The person running it sits in what we call "the slot." That's the person who makes sure all the stories are covered. The job title is assignment editor. That means setting up the stories, sending a camera crew to shoot them, double checking facts, and making sure everything gets back "in house" (to the station) in time to make air.

And sitting in that damn slot is nothing to play with, baby. Usually I feel sorry for whoever it is—he or she gets yelled at by crews, reporters, and producers too. Being an assignment editor is a thankless gig with a lot of headaches. And damn dangerous too. If you miss a breaking story your behind is fertilizer.

But today the *butt* sitting on his butt is Stalerman Klein—nicknamed Stat. That's because he wants everything *right away, stat!* It could be a Simple Simon animal story like a giraffe born at the zoo and psycho Stat would bug you to death. *How much did you shoot? Hurry up and get back with the tape.*

And damn if today Stat wasn't bugging all the way out. Man, Stat always works the shit out of me when his boy Will is working my same shift. Will and Stat were interns together in South Bend, Indiana. Ten years ago, Will got hired at WKBA; then he helped Stat get a job. So Stat figures he owes him. Every time Will messes up because of his drinking, Stat covers for him. When Stat is in the slot, Will doesn't do jack. But girlfriend me? I feel like the Energizer Bunny! *I keep going and going and going. . . .*

Stat calls my unit over the two-way radio, "Sixteen-sixteen. Breaker. Fire at Thirty-ninth and Lake Park, copy?"

I said, "Stat, Will is closer, isn't he?"

"No. He's back in house. Don't fucking worry about what other people are doing. Just get going."

Ain't that nothing? Stat busted me out over the two-way. But Stat let his boy Will go back to the station while leaving me out on the street to pick my video cotton and his too. *Again.*

But what could I say right then? Not a thing. You can't refuse a breaking story. First, it's not ethical to me. Do your job—this is news.

Second, that could get you fired at WKBA. Check this shit out. You can sit in the middle of the newsroom and do blow and they have to send you to rehab *three times.*

You can threaten to break somebody's neck and they have to get you psychological counseling.

You can call someone a bunch of racial slurs and they'll send you to sensitivity classes.

But refuse to cover a breaking news story? A breaker? You can be fired on the spot. *You're out of there!*

Speaking of out of there, I was rolling toward the fire. I got a couple of blocks from the location and I could see the mustard yellow flames. A veil of smoke hung over the right corner of the building. I got out of the car. I strapped on my battery belt. I grabbed my camera, popped in a beta tape, and started doing my *natural-born thang*.

One side of me was getting that ice cold breeze off Lake Michigan. The other side of me was getting that microwave heat coming from the fire.

But I'm thinking, rock steady. Steady shot, girl. Pan shot . . . left to right and back again. *Forty pounds pulling down on my body with the battery belt and camera.* My knees hurt. My back hurts. Keep rolling. Never-ever-stop-rolling-till-you-got-the-story. And I had it.

I stopped shooting and ran back to my car, packed up, and headed for the expressway to make it back to the station for the noon show. *Keep on truckin', baby.*

I parked my unit in the garage. I made good time, I can drive my ass off in a pinch. I headed for the bathroom—and as usual I sucked air. For years Beans and I didn't have a bathroom—we had to go all the way across the street.

Then they built a new bathroom six years ago. Think it was for "us"? No! They built a big bathroom for the guys—then they gave the old one to Beans and me, promising to fix it up. Lying dogs hadn't done a thing. It still had a urinal in it—though it didn't work—and that ugly light blue color inside with one stall and the hazy, fluorescent light. We complained. Even the damn MEN sign was still on the door—all the guys knew it was our bathroom—but we wanted a new one like they had. We refused to pretty it up or remove that sign. But management never kept its promise.

I put my game face on in the mirror. Then I made my move. I grabbed all the beta tapes I'd shot. I left the garage and bolted over to the newsroom. I put the stack of tapes down right in front of Stat. I turned my gorgeous girlfriend mug to the right, and I asked, "Who do you see?"

"Alex!" Stat shrugged.

I turned left and asked again, "Who do you see?"

"Alex!"

"In no way shape or form do I look like Kizzy, do I? I'm not a slave so don't work me like one." Then I walked away.

"Whooooooo!" came the howl from the newsroom bleachers.

Just as I was about to get the details of the Dragon/Holly fight, the Godfather walked out into the newsroom with this sister. That's Mitch Saleen's nickname—the Godfather. That's because, excuse my Swahili, he's a ruthless motherfucker.

The sister he was walking with was new. She was young, twenty something, short, stocky, dark-skinned with braids. We don't have many blacks in this newsroom. There aren't many blacks behind the scenes period. So that left me wondering, Who is this sister?

KENYA
Writer/Producer

I'm a small-town Southern girl with a husband in med school, a rip-roarin' two-year-old son, an overdrawn checkin' account, and a sardine-can apartment. I'm also an experienced journalist in need of a job.

I'd taken a writer's test and was called back for a meetin' with WKBA's news director, Mitch Saleen. He's a good-lookin' man, about six feet tall, light brown hair cut close, dimples whittled into his cheeks, eyes as black as Texas tea, but his spirit is mean as a bull.

Mitch Saleen sat me down in his office and said magnolia sweet, "Kenya, I've got your writer's test here . . ."

Suddenly, my heart seemed to stop. Then my mind spun back on its own accord to how I came to be at a network-owned station in Chicago.

I'm a Texas girl and not from those city-side places like Dallas and Houston. I was raised in a town just a piece outside of Amarillo, called Honesty. That's where my parents, glory to God, were murdered when I was two years old. But I have lived all over the South, includin' Mississippi and Georgia.

I got here to Chicago, period, because of my husband Jarrett. He got accepted to the University of Chicago Medical School. Jarrett has wanted to be a doctor since he was a little boy livin' in Michigan. But Jarrett never got the chance till now.

We met in college at Vanderbilt in Nashville. After graduation Jarrett was headed to Meharry Med School but his mama was in poor health and had to move South. He decided to get a job to help her and his little brothers. That's the beauty bustin' inside of my Jarrett, he's a helpin' man.

But let's face the sunrise—you know how family can get to actin' crazy. Jarrett's youngest brother began courtin' trouble and Jarrett stayed 'round way too long in order to help straighten him out. By the time we got married and looked up, shoot y'all, it was two years later. Then I took another breath and by the time I exhaled I was pregnant with my bouncin' baby boy. I named him Jefferson, after my father and grandfather. Jeffie for short.

I was workin' at a small, but well-respected daily in Velmont, Georgia. Our paper was so good that folk from *The Atlanta Journal-Constitution*, the Louisville *Courier-Journal*, and even *The Washington Post* scouted it for talent.

But this school opportunity came up for Jarrett. He heard about a partial fellowship for minority students. Jarrett won it and the fellowship covered *most* but not all the costs. We didn't know how we were goin' to make it but I had to lay down the law. I said, "Jarrett, we go now or forever hold your peace." So we packed up two-year-old Jeffie and journeyed to Chicago.

I'd interviewed with both the *Sun-Times* and the *Tribune*. Both newspapers said they liked my clips—samples of the articles I'd written at my old job—and would keep me in mind in case an openin' came up.

With my head hangin' I went to a meetin' of the Chicago Association of Black Journalists at the NBC Tower on Columbus Drive. They announced that WKBA had a job openin' for a writer. Right there, I don't know why, my spirits perked up.

I never worked for a TV station before but we were dippin' in our savings like my aunt Rae dips snuff. We really needed some money comin' in so I decided to take a spin on the cotton gin as my auntie would say—I sent in my résumé and my clips to WKBA. I got the name of a black woman there named Denise Mitzler, called her. She said to send my stuff and she'd pass it on by hand.

Three weeks later, I was called in for a writer's test. Now, two days later, I'm sittin' in the news director's office hopin' that I've got the job.

I was in Mitch Saleen's office and he said again, "Kenya, I've got your writer's test here . . ."

I remember bein' given a stack of long newspaper articles. I was told to write as many "readers" as I could in one hour. I had to ask the secretary who got me started, nice woman named Vera, what a "reader" was. She called over one of the mornin' writers. He said a reader was a story with no videotape. The anchor stays on camera and reads the story. Readers are about twenty seconds long, that's three short graphs. Television stories are much quicker hits than newspapers. I banged out three readers in an hour.

Mitch Saleen had a serious look on his face now. "Kenya, you don't know shit about television. You only wrote three stories. We need people who can crank out at least five. Television news is about writing for the ear and writing fast."

Well, why did Mitch Saleen call me way down here then?

He walked from 'round his desk and sat on the corner of it. "Here's a story about a little boy who froze to death in a refrigerated car on a train."

I remember it bein' the last story I wrote and now I kicked myself for spendin' so much time on it. I could have written another story but that one needed a cotton touch.

"Kenya, here's how the story aired":

An eight-year-old boy froze to death after stowing away in a refrigerated car overnight. Marion Stevens was headed from Peoria to North Carolina to surprise his father on his fiftieth birthday. His parents were entangled in a bitter divorce and the boy had not seen his father in three months. Police say temperatures inside the steel car plunged well below zero. Funeral services for the little boy will be held Friday morning at Holy Mary Church.

"Now, Kenya, here's what you wrote":

It was a cold night in Peoria. A little boy bundled up, packed his bag, and braved the darkness with only one goal in mind— to get home to see his father. Divorce and distance had prevented eight-year-old Marion Stevens from seeing his father, who lived far away in North Carolina. Marion hopped a refrigerated freight car headed south. He fell asleep knowing when he woke up he'd be in North Carolina in time to surprise his father on his fiftieth birthday. But Marion never woke up. He froze to death inside that car, where overnight the temperatures fell below zero. Family and friends will lay him to rest Friday morning at Holy Mary Church.

Mitch Saleen tossed my test on the desk and stood up. "You don't know shit about TV but you know how to tell a story. I'm willing to take a chance that you can learn broadcasting on the fly."

I blinked twice before bustin' out in a grin. "I got the job?"

"Kenya, welcome to WKBA."

Holly
Reporter/Anchor

It was two weeks after my first day and my newsroom battle with Dragon Diva. I came to work for a meeting and got hit with a bombshell. Kal Jimper, the general manager—he and I had scheduled a meeting about the new four o'clock show. I'd been waiting for him to come back from New York. I was unprepared for the events that followed.

I got into the office around 1 P.M. because Kal had told me that I could use the mornings my first couple of weeks to look for an apartment. The rest of the time I spent wisely learning about the city, its history, and going out with a crew to get the lay of the land.

One of the directors was sitting at his desk. He was a friendly guy, fiftyish, jockey short, thin, shell brown hair, and large eyes. He loved to wear college football jerseys and was quick to get a game of catch going with a Nerf football he kept on his desk. He was reading scripts while he talked to me. "Holly, you're in late today. Reporter for the ten o'clock?" he asked.

"No. I was out looking for an apartment. I still haven't found anything. I stopped looking a bit early because I have a meeting with Kal Jimper and—"

I stopped talking because the next breath he drew was like a man being choked. Then he caught himself and gently said to me, "Holly, did you read The Column today?"

"What column?"

"You always read The Column," the director admonished kindly. "It's in the daily. The Column has all the latest stuff happening in media around the city. TV. Radio. Newspaper. Half of the damn time you'll find out about things going on right in this newsroom; sometimes The Column has it first."

"Interesting. I'll check it out later."

Then Dragon Diva walked by. She spoke lightheartedly. "I'd advise you to check it out now, *girlfriend!*"

I began an urgent hunt for a newspaper. I grabbed one off a coworker's desk, scanned the listings, and found the page for The Column. There was Kal Jimper's picture.

"WKBA GM OUSTED!" the headline read.

The Column said that Kal Jimper had traveled to New York thinking it was for a meeting about his idea to add a 4 P.M. newscast. Instead, the New York bosses blasted him for sagging ratings and fired him after they weren't satisfied with his new plan to turn the station around.

According to The Column, Jimper was heading back to his hometown of Toledo, Ohio, to start a consulting firm. The new 4 P.M. newscast was reportedly up in the air.

I slammed the newspaper on the desk. Then I strutted out the rear door and up to Kal Jimper's third-floor office. It was true. Kal Jimper's office was stripped bare. I kicked at one of the moving boxes; its corners were bent and its top was shiny with tape.

What about my contract? What about the 4 P.M. newscast? I was brought in to anchor it. Was it dead or just in limbo? Who would know? Who could I ask? Suddenly it occurred to me to go talk to Mitch. He's news director and will know what's going on. Mitch will know what the changes mean for me. I retraced my steps and headed straight for Mitch's office.

Vera said, "He's in a meeting."

My brow wrinkled, anxiety flushed my cheeks.

"What's wrong, Holly?"

There was something in Vera's eyes, a real sense of concern. I told Vera my anxiety about Kal Jimper's firing and how I wanted to talk to Mitch.

"Yeah, everybody's talking about it," Vera said. "Denise has been quiet all day today too." Vera began scanning her desk calendar with a pen. "Mitch is booked." Then she looked up at me and whispered, "But just hang around. I'll squeeze you in."

As I waited, questions continued to swirl around in my mind, among them, why did they fire Kal Jimper? I thought he was secure with the big guys in Corporate. What happened?

DENISE
MANAGING EDITOR/ACTING ASSISTANT NEWS DIRECTOR

Kal Jimper died by the book.

Nielsen has a rating system. It's used by the television industry to set advertising prices. Four times a year for one solid month. It's war. That's the system. It's a war. Who's number one?

It's called "Sweeps" or "the Book."

The months are February, May, July, and November. Our February ratings book was terrible. From sign-on to sign-off: WLS was #1, WMAQ was #2, WGN #3, WBBM and WFLD tied for #4, and

WKBA was #5. The New York powers saw the February ratings. They waited a few weeks. Called Jimper to New York. Then that was that.

Kal Jimper died by the book.

WKBA is owned by the Quincy Metro Broadcasting Network. The major stockholder is Jeb Quincy. Old Jeb's daddy, Hollis, made his money in Texas oil. Jeb inherited the money. Poured it into broadcasting.

The son doesn't always rise.

His heir apparent is Jeb Junior. Junior is hemorrhaging money. Hollywood starlets are his weakness. His twin sister Gina sets him up. She's a filmmaker. Jeb Junior launched a computer chip company two years ago. It failed.

Quincy Metro is losing money.

That's a big problem. Corporate is sending a message. It's clear. Mitch called me into the office. The ratings have got to come up.

And fast.

Corporate is laying down the threat. Ratings up or managers out. WKBA and the other owned-and-operated stations around the country have a mandate. We're called O&O's. That's short for *owned* and *operated*.

There's a rumor.

Word is that old Jeb Quincy wants to sell. He's tired. Wants out. And he doesn't want his "Hollywood twins" to ruin what he's built. That's the rumor. That could be good.

Or bad.

Suppose our network is bought by someone who knows what he's doing like say Ted Turner? Ted Turner knew what viewers wanted. Turner knew how to expand globally. He made CNN a household name.

That's a good thing.

Suppose our network is bought by someone with money like Rupert Murdoch? He spent a ton of money building up Fox. He outbid CBS for football. Fox is now a player.

That's a good thing.

Suppose our network is bought by a company that has its own big name? The two become a powerhouse. Case in point: Disney/ABC.

That's a good thing.

But suppose our network is bought by someone who does not know news and programming period. Maybe it's someone who wants to suck off profits? Or someone who wants to boost profits by cutting news budgets and selling off TV stations around the country?

That's a bad thing.

Broadcast news is a public service. News informs the public about what's happening. It's a checks and balances forum for our country.

But it's big bucks too.

A network news magazine show like *20/20* on a given night can pull a 12.0 rating. Nationally each rating point equals 980,000 households. The competing network programming is say a show like *ER*. Say *ER* pulls a 15.2 rating.

ER won.

Or did it? It costs less to put on *20/20* than it does *ER*. NBC pays more than $280 million a year for *ER*. One hit drama—$13 million per episode.

Break down the dollars.

With *20/20* you pay your talent and staff but it's not even close in the costs for a mega-hit sitcom or drama. But the ratings are still high. You can charge big fees for commercials. Plus hit shows die with viewers. Or sometimes cast members kill off the show to make other career moves. Like *Seinfeld*.

Not broadcast news.

A good news magazine show can run for years. Turn big profits. Think *60 Minutes—20/20*. Plus they add credibility to the network. That's priceless. CBS was often called the "Tiffany" Network because of high journalistic standards. News made the CBS network a cash cow.

Broadcast news is money.

A local television station in a large city can turn a 40 percent profit. The money is made in advertising dollars. The higher the ratings, the more the local station charges for commercial spots. An O&O—network-owned-and-operated station, can earn millions of dollars of profit for its parent network.

Broadcast news is money.

Now Mitch says that we're getting a new boss? Who will the new GM be? Mitch is nervous. He was Kal Jimper's hire. When the head goes, other body parts follow.

But Mitch may live.

Mitch is a killer but a kiss ass too. I'm okay. I've been here two years. I'm solid. I'm the only woman they have in management. And I'm the only black. They'll let me live. *This time.*

I just wish they'd let me thrive.

Holly
Reporter/Anchor

I went into Mitch's office, high strung and poised to ask hard-hitting questions. Mitch is a pack rat and this office is his hole.

On the shelving units bolted to the wall were stacks of broadcast trade magazines. Some of the magazines were six years old or more. There were scripts from old newscasts lying on top of the four television sets. Each set was tuned into a cable news network. CNN. MSNBC. FOX NEWS CHANNEL. CNBC.

There were a dozen ginger-colored mail bags scattered around Mitch's desk. Each had a beta tape sticking out of it. There were still more tapes stacked on the floor. These were the audition tapes of reporters who were WKBA wannabes.

The carpet was a distracting test pattern of teal and burgundy. The chairs were expensive, padded leather black with red wood trim. Mitch looked up at me and said, "Close the door and have a seat."

My knees were tight, toes pointed in, and I scooted the chair up two inches and anchored it there.

"Holly, Kal is no longer with us . . ."

"Yes, I was very surprised to hear the news."

"Holly, that's the nature of this business. Low ratings mean off with your head at a moment's notice. The ratings are sinking and Corporate doesn't like it. Do you realize that some ten years ago this particular TV station brought in more revenue than any of the other network stations across the country?"

"Really?"

"Really. More than New York, L.A., or Dallas. But it's been changing fast. Kal stayed here four years but there was no change. So New York management *changed* him. Anyway, I know you're wondering what this means for you."

"Absolutely," I said. "I want to do everything I can to bring up the ratings. As the anchor of the new four o'clock show—"

"There is no four P.M. show."

"Excuse me? Kal Jimper and I talked about it. Remember, Mitch? A half an hour show at four o'clock. You were there when we talked at breakfast. I was brought here to solo anchor the four o'clock newscast and to do feature reports."

Mitch picked up a contract and held it out to me. "I had Vera pull your deal . . ."

A trickle of sweat rolled down my right side.

". . . you signed a one-year contract for sixty-five thousand dollars, with an option for a second year."

Right but.

I had a letter of intent from Kal Jimper. We had talked about an anchor spot. I had a letter of intent that said I would get the 4 P.M. show that was starting in the fall. I would then get a three-year deal *starting* at $150,000. The $65,000 was just a beginning point to get me here— to get me on the books in New York, Kal Jimper said, so that I could move to Chicago faster and get up to speed quicker. Mitch dropped the contract on his desk. "Holly, is there a problem?"

I told Mitch everything I'd just been thinking.

"Holly, the four o'clock was Kal's baby. Maybe it's still in. Maybe it's out. It's shaky. Your one-year contract is solid. You are coming from a small market, we're taking a chance on you with your limited experience, and, frankly, your limited talent. I'd be grateful that I had this deal."

Well, excuse the hell out of me! Mitch had praised me as much as Kal Jimper had.

"Mitch, I distinctly remember that you said—"

"Kal wanted to hire you. He's the one who promised to give you a sweetheart deal to anchor—not me. I don't believe in sweetheart deals."

"But Kal Jimper promised me—"

Mitch's voice got cold. "And where is he now?"

"In Toledo," I answered, surprised by the question.

"Then that's where your promise is, in Toledo."

I took a deep breath. "Okay, there's no four o'clock but that shouldn't constitute less than half the money we were talking about. I think we should revisit my contract. I do have this letter of intent."

"And that," Mitch said, his voice rising to a nasty pitch, "is nothing but a paper promise. We've got a signed concrete contract for a general assignment slot—there's nothing here about features. We're short GA reporters. It's a shot. And it is sixty-five thousand dollars—much more than you made in Palm Springs. In fact, Holly, I imagine that's probably more money than your parents ever made, humph!"

"Probably not," I snapped. "My father is a plastic surgeon and before my mother died she was an engineer." I sighed and thought, I wish I'd never come here.

"Well, anyway. It's a fair offer. But let me tell you, I'm fucking getting pissed off here. That letter of intent? It's paper. So now what? Do you want to quit because there may or may not be a four P.M. show? C'mon! Do you know how many reporters are dying, freaking dying, to get to this city? Look at all these audition tapes on my desk. On the floor. Waiting in the mail room to be delivered."

"But—"

"But what, Holly? This is Chicago, the third-largest market and one of the best cities in the world! Not to mention it's a springboard to the national spotlight. Do you know how many damn good reporters would knock you out of that chair on your ass to have had an opportunity to scribble their Hancock on this contract?"

"But I . . ."

"If you don't like it, quit, Holly. I'll let you out of the contract. The chips fall where they may in news. We paid for your move here and we're paying for your hotel until you find a place to live. But let me tell you, if you decide to move back, everything will be at your own expense. Look, take a few days and think about what you want to do. Then let me know, but don't take too long."

I was stunned. Now I knew why Mitch's nickname was the God-father. I felt as if someone had shoved his hand down my throat and yanked my stomach inside out. What was I going to do?

Coming Up Next:

Stay or go? Holly struggles with what could be the biggest decision of her young broadcasting career. Find out how Holly first got started in the business.

And:

Beans is confronted with an offensive incident in the WKBA garage. What brings her close to tears? And does she fight back?

Plus:

Who gets promoted and why? A controversial snub ignites the black workers, putting Denise in the middle.

This Just In . . . *continues.*

Alex
Photographer/Technician

"Hey, Alex, wait up," a voice behind me called out. I had just parked my Jeep in the lot and was walking toward the station. The voice behind me belonged to one of my friends, a brother who was also a shooter at WKBA. His name is Rock Mitchell. We call him Rock because his stuff is tight: When my ace boon coon Rock shoots video it could be a windstorm and he don't move. *Solid as a rock. No shaky video ever!*

"Rock! My man!" I greeted him. Rock is small but incredibly strong; his hands are flat and long and quick. He can change camera shots faster than anyone I know. He's got a short, reddish brown 'fro, sharp black eyes, and a right-sided limp from a fall he took while covering a West Side street fight during the Bulls first NBA championship.

"Alex, you know that management position they created in technical?"

I heard. I also heard that Rock had thrown his brim in the ring.

"They hired some guy from Utah with only eight years' experience in the business!"

"What? They hired him fast! Is the memo up?"

"What memo? It's in The Column! Can you believe they hired some youngblood over me? I've got twenty years' experience here at WKBA—and I had one little bullshit interview."

"With Kal Jimper and the Godfather?"

"Yeah and Milt too." Milt ran the technical department—he was a good old boy from way back and racist as hell. He scheduled the black techs on the worst shifts, he never broke us in on the new equipment, and he never sent any of us on the perk trips. He was strictly an overseer.

"Well, what the hell did they say, Rock?"

33

"Nothing really. They said they liked my work and that people respected me. But they said that they wanted someone with more management experience. Can a management mope do what I do? Can he shoot video in a lightning storm without flinching?"

"I hear ya."

"Can a management mope tweak audio so that a shout is just as clear as a whisper?"

Preach, boy. Rock had skills, no lie. I could hear a quiver of pain in Rock's voice and I struggled to soothe him. "Maybe the man has some other credentials—"

"Yeah, bean counting. So what? Alex, you know what bugs me most? We have never had a black manager in technical here—ever. We have no voice. All the black techs are either on nights, overnights, and weekends despite seniority. We don't get to go on any of the plum trips overseas or work for the network sporting events. We just get the basic shit, and regular overtime. I'm tired and I'm ready to fight!"

He was right. This was bullshit. Rock had a good solid career. Why hadn't he been a real consideration?

"Know what else I heard?" Rock hooted angrily. "You are going to trip off of this!"

"You are Rona Barrett today? What now?"

"The new reporter? The sister Holly? I heard she came in without an agent so the Godfather low-balled her into a crappy contract!"

"She should have had an agent!" I shook my head. "Cold, cold!"

"I also heard that when Holly said something about the contract, the Godfather told her to take it or leave it!"

"What did she decide to do?"

"I don't know. Nobody's seen her. The scuttlebutt is that the Godfather low-balled Holly to save some money to beef up the contract for that young redhead he's been trying to bring in. Kal Jimper never would green-light the deal, so Mitch couldn't hire her. Kirstin something. But now that Kal Jimper's gone, she's in."

"Kal Jimper's history," I shrugged. "So the brakes are off."

"Alex, you know what we need?" Rock said, the words alive with their own revolutionary energy. "We need one collective voice to get some changes around here. We need something like a black union."

"Snap, baby!" I howled. "They'd lose their wigs around here if the blacks got down for the cause like that! That's some Huey Newton–Malcolm X kindah thinking!"

"Why not? Alex, we're all fed up around here. Look, my shift just ended and I'm on my way right now to meet with some of the brothers to rap about the situation. I'll let you know what happens."

"Great, Rock. Keep a sister informed, okay?"

"Absolutely!"

I began thinking as Rock walked away. A black employees group? The idea made me proud. Could it help? How would it be perceived by our white coworkers? But what pressed those questions out of my head was how they obviously had played my man Rock. I had to dig on this one.

I decided to go over to the newsroom before I went to the garage to get my car. I wanted to see if I could get a peek at the real deal. Had Rock really been considered for the management position? There was only one person I could ask. I wasn't sure she'd tell me, but I was sure as shit gonna ask. Ask Denise.

DENISE

MANAGING EDITOR/ACTING ASSISTANT NEWS DIRECTOR

How could I answer that question?

I was in the newsroom. I was talking with the executive producer, Garth. We decided to send two reporters out on stories. One: a news conference at a suburban high school. The school got a half-a-million-dollar "mystery" donation to keep its sports program.

Good story.

Two: a million-dollar drug bust on the North Side. Coke. Weed. All confiscated in the back of an RV. The drug ring had ties to three students enrolled in a *swish* prep school.

That's the lead.

Vera walked by Garth and me. She whispered in my ear, "FYI. Alex is waiting outside your office door. She's mad about something."

What now.

I strutted back to where Alex was standing. We had mutual friends at my last job in another city. So we each knew the other was trustworthy. Helpful. But I'm very careful. No blatant favoritism.

Alex pushes the envelope.

Most of the time I don't let her. I check her. We fight. I didn't feel like it today. I just shut the door. Alex asked about Rock.

Be careful, I thought.

How could I tell her the truth? They had already picked the guy for the job before it was even listed. When they created the job, they created it *for* this Utah guy.

Smoke and mirrors.

The only reason they even talked to Rock was because it's required by the Federal Communications Commission—FCC. Diversity in the newsroom. Fairness in hiring.

There's a tracking form.

We have to fill out a form. Include all the candidate's info. Name. Race. Sex. Position they are interviewing for.

License.

It's required that there is equal opportunity in employment otherwise a television station could lose its operator's license. So the forms are filled out, with the codes, then sent to the FCC. That's proof. Proof that you interviewed a diverse group of people for a job. Being fair.

Good idea. Sometimes abused.

The requirement helps minorities and women compete. But what happens sometimes, as with Rock, white managers already have a candidate they want.

Smoke and mirrors.

They call in minorities just to fill out the tracking form. They have no intention of giving the minority or the woman the job. Rock got caught between a hard place and a harder place. I can't tell Alex that.

Can I?

"Alex, Rock is good. Why take the best shooter in the shop off the street?"

"That's bull, Denise. Why not reward him for his hard work. That would give the blacks here something they've never had—a face and voice in management."

"What am I? A cartoon?"

"Sometimes you're flat, girlfriend," Alex said. She sat down and propped her arm up along the ridge of the couch.

"Flat?"

I pushed her. I started getting angry. I'm in a spot that she and my other sisters and brothers in the newsroom can't even imagine. I'm living in two worlds.

"Denise, I know you care but you can do more. You need to be more of a Rambo, girl."

What made Alex think I had the power?

"Did you speak up for Rock?"

That pissed me off.

It wasn't my department. I can't cross over into the technical side. I can't step on toes.

Basic office politics.

Alex had to know that. Plus I did things behind the scenes. I try to be fair to the black people in the newsroom. The things I can do, I do. Quietly. Effectively.

But the incident.

Alex didn't know about it. I wasn't going to tell her. I have to be careful. I'm a black woman in management. I do things to help. I just can't broadcast them. Alex wants to push me.

I won't let her.

"Alex, I wish Rock had gotten the job. They liked this guy from Utah better. What can I say?"

"Is it true that your boy the Godfather low-balled the new black reporter so he can sign that redheaded reporter he's so crazy about?"

Kirstin Quarterly.

I said, "Mitch wanted to hire her last year. She's been by twice. Yes, Kirstin Quarterly is in. Is it at Holly's expense? Off the record? I think you know."

Alex stood up.

She said, "Okay. But I'm telling you, just so a sister like you won't be blindsided, if this kind of stuff keeps happening some shit is going to jump off and it isn't going to be pretty, al'right?"

"I understand, Alex."

KENYA
Writer/Producer

I've only been at WKBA a few days, but I'm here to tell you this broadcast news is more than a notion! In print you get to the scene, get your facts, interview your sources, and write. Television news writin' is far-fetched from that! I'm learnin' so much.

I've got a heck of a lot to remember. First, each show has what's called a "rundown." The rundown is like a big list. On the rundown all the stories are "blocked." It's like a big outline. Its got the story's page number, the writer's initials, the slug (story title), the anchor's initials, then how the page is set up, how long it's supposed to be, and the hit time—the exact time to the second when it airs in the show.

Writers get the "rundown" and look for their initials and those are your stories. Then you go to the producer of that show and he or she tells you what the story is about, what the angle is, where the video-tape is comin' from, and so on.

It's a lot to take in at once. Like a "vo" is the anchor voicin' over the tape. A "sot" is *sound on tape*, a sound bite, which means a quick quote from a witness or official or expert to go along with the voice-over.

A fire is the most common example. You'd have a vo/sot/tag: voice-over of the fire scene video then a bite from a witness or a fireman at the scene then dump the tape and come out to the anchor on camera with a final point. That final point is called the "tag." Vo/sot/tag.

A reporter's story is called a "package." Reporters go out and do the interviews, bring the tape back, and then work on it with a writer assigned to help if needed.

I've come to one real conclusion. *These folk around here are somethin' else.* It's excitin', wild, and these are the *cussin'est and eatin'est* folk I've ever seen in my life. Yesterday when I came in there was a big ole spread of Italian food laid out on the counter by the assignment desk. I asked one of the stagehands, "Where's the food from?"

He said, "Who knows? Somebody's always sending the station free food. We never know, we just eat."

Today there was a sheet cake folk was nibblin' on but mainly every-body was hoverin' near Rod and the fax machine. Rod is one of the assignment editors who works the desk. He's a fun-lovin' guy, tall and skinny like Abe Lincoln, but put a baby face with a big smile on top of that lanky body. Everybody in the newsroom loves Rod. He has a brilliant sense of humor. Rod made the place fun.

"What's going on?"

Rod cocked his head to the side and started just ah laughin'. "Well, Kenya," he said, "this is a little game I made up. Whenever we get another news director around here—everybody runs around trying to call somebody at the guy's old job to find out what he's like. Then we'd tell each other what we found out."

"Boring!" a writer shouted from a nearby desk.

"Right! So I thought why not make it really fun? I came up with this little sheet. I call the assignment desk of the station where the new guy is coming from. I brief them on what it is. Then we fax my little questionnaire over for them to fill out and fax back."

Rod began quotin' out loud from memory.

"Question one: "If the new boss were in a movie what would it be?" Question two: "What character would he play?" Question three: "Best line?"

Someone from the back shouted out, "Rod is a fucking genius. You should be on Letterman, man."

Rod grinned at me. "It is fun. Everybody always plays along. We just heard that the new GM is coming from the network-owned station in Detroit. It's been boring around here today so even though we don't normally do it for the GM we decided to go ahead and have a little fun. So, I faxed their newsroom. They just called and said they're faxing me back now."

A producer spoke up. "The game is more fun when it's the news director. They've been rolling in and out of here ever since ratings started to slide."

"Yeah," someone else explained, "when we were number one, we'd have fabulous victory parties! Champagne at the Ritz!"

"Now we just keep getting new boss after new boss and no victory parties!!!"

"Hey," a cameraman standin' by the fax machine said, "remember when Mitch's fax came back?"

"Yeah! How about an instant replay for Kenya?!"

"What movie?" Rod shouted, happy to oblige.

"The Godfather!" the crowd answered.

"What character?"

"Michael!"

"Best line?"

"It's not personal . . . It's strictly business."

The fax machine started gurglin' and we all hushed. Detroit was faxin' back the game sheet about the new boss.

Rod started readin' the fax as it came out, "What movie: *The Wizard of Oz!*"

"Oh no!" the crowd shouted.

Then folk just started yellin' out crazy stuff.

"It's the Tin Man—some heartless motherfucker."

"No, the Scarecrow—another guy with straw for brains!"

Some people shouted: "Toto! Toto! Toto!"

"Shshsshh!" the majority hissed.

Rod read, "What character: the Wizard."

The crowd rocked back on its heels like a horse bein' yanked by the reins. I thought, The Wizard?

"Best line: "Don't pay any attention to the man behind the curtain!"

"Oh no!" we all moaned.

Holly
Reporter/Anchor

Stay or go?

Over the weekend, I packed and unpacked my bags three times! Stay or go?

I'd left Palm Springs after a big going-away party. If I went back now what would people say? Kal Jimper's dismissal wouldn't be enough to excuse my stumbling so quickly. Plus, they had already promoted another reporter to my anchor spot. Without work you look like damaged goods to some employers.

I was unsure of what path to take. So I decided to try to digest everything that had happened. I thought about what led me to WKBA in the first place.

I'm a television reporter/anchor and, in the business, we're called "talent." In television news, women who are "talent" have to always look good. For women, our television careers are "looks"-driven whether we like it or not. When we have a *cosmetically challenged* day like other women, it's not personal—it's public. You are on display.

The day your hair is out of place or your makeup isn't just so, the viewers call up with quips and tips. Even your seasoned coworkers, who really do understand the story chase that reporters go through, will sit around and comment on who looks good and who does not.

But as society deems with so many other things, the script is invariably altered when it comes to men in television news. The men can mount that anchor desk and look distinguished with their gray, prosperously plump, or powerfully plain.

And older men are really allowed to get away with capital cosmetic crimes. They can wear polyester and checks, even wrinkled shirts or ties on-air. For them, it's called "character." For a woman, it's called "bad taste." Women in television news are not afforded the right to be judged purely on skills and black women certainly aren't.

I look in the mirror often because looking good is my business.

When I was a child, my three older sisters would envy me because people constantly referred to me as "the pretty one." Some mean kids gave us a nickname. It spread like a chain letter throughout school: Beauty and the beasts.

My sisters were not, are not, ugly. They are simply plain in comparison with me. Just as I seem dumb in comparison with them. They are brilliant. All three are doctors like my dad. They graduated from Yale, Howard, and Meharry medical schools. I'm very proud of them.

My father is a man who believes in building up one's strengths and overlooking one's weaknesses. He gloats over how pretty I am. He gloats over how smart my sisters are. When we were growing up, Daddy tried to balance his praise, but I always felt outnumbered and never quite equal. My family reveres the power of success and academic credentials. I'm competitive. I want to succeed too.

I graduated from Cal State. I was headed to graduate school in journalism three years ago when I withdrew because I received a job offer to be on-air in Palm Springs.

The news director saw me at a charity fashion show where I was a model and the MC. I told him I was a journalism major and he asked me to FedEx him my audition tape. He said I had talent and could anchor weekends.

My father said, "No graduate school? Over my dead black body!"

But I wasn't dropping out; I was dropping in on my career. Palm Springs is a small market but to get a job as a TV news anchor was a plus.

I went into my father's study armed with a *Broadcast* yearbook. The yearbook contains a list of all the television and radio stations in the country. It gives details about the number of viewers, the call letters and addresses of the stations, and the names of the people who run those stations. Job contacts. Market size.

"What's a market?" Daddy asked.

"Market is what the broadcast viewing area is called. Each market encompasses the cities and towns in a particular state. Each market is ranked."

"Ranked how?"

"By number according to how many viewers the market has. Palm Springs, where I want to go, is number one sixty-four. At the top, New York is the number-one market. Los Angeles, number two. Chicago, number three."

"Fine, go to L.A. That's closer to home and it's tops."

"Daddy, you can't start in those big markets. That's like performing surgery without going to med school."

"Okay," Daddy said, looking at the *Broadcast* yearbook. "Madison, Wisconsin. We've got family there."

"But, Daddy, Madison is eighty-five, bigger than Palm Springs but not better. Who will see me in Madison? Farmers. Factory workers. Students. Palm Springs is a vacation spot, Daddy. Hollywood people have homes there. Famous politicians. Wealthy businessmen. I've got a chance to be seen by someone with the power to get me to that next job."

Daddy took off his glasses. When he did, I smiled at his cleft chin, strong nose, and deep sandy brown eyes. My three sisters bore a remarkable resemblance to him. "DeDe, Crystal, and Ronnie look more like you every day!"

Daddy rubbed his eyes and said, "And you look more and more like your beautiful mother every day. She'd turn over in her grave with the notion that you passed up an opportunity to go to graduate school."

"Daddy, Mama would turn over in her grave if she knew that I had a great opportunity and you stopped me. This opportunity is now." Finally Daddy gave me his blessing.

The pay in Palm Springs was pitiful. So what? Daddy sent me money. Glamour? Please. I served it to them every time I anchored on the weekend—my makeup was flawless and my clothes were designer bests in vibrant colors. I anchored every weekend. During the week, I did soft features, stories that were positive about events, people, concerts, and charity foundations. That's a tremendous amount of face time. Face time is to talent what playing time is to a pro athlete. I'd found something I was *good at*, not just something I looked *good doing*.

Being on-air in Palm Springs gave me fabulous exposure. Someone would see me, as I had explained to my father. Someone would notice my style, my flair with words, as I had told my sisters. That someone turned out to be the GM at WKBA in Chicago—Kal Jimper.

Chicago is the third-largest market in America. WKBA is a network-owned-and-operated station. It's not an affiliate, like Palm Springs and other places where the station is just *affiliated* with a big network and carries its programming. I was headed to an O&O: a station *owned* and *operated* by the network itself.

My news director in Palm Springs warned me. "WKBA is cutthroat. And, Holly, your reporting skills aren't quite there yet. But anchoring, you are one of the great ones. Wait for another chance."

A friend warned me too. She'd heard that WKBA was so racist that the black employees used to joke that the call letters stood for, "*W*hites *K*icking *B*lacks' *A*ss."

But why listen to that? I was promised I was going to be groomed, brought along slowly. So I came. And now I'm staying. I have something to prove to everyone, including myself.

Mitch was neither happy nor sad with my decision. I decided to ignore his indifference. It's spring, time for new beginnings and renewed determination. I came into the WKBA newsroom ready to go.

I spotted the new writer, Kenya. Being the two new kids on the block, we had eagerly exchanged our phone numbers.

"Hi, Kenya," I said, trying to be cheery.

"Hey, Holly," she twanged, and gave me a big smile. "Everyone's buzzin' 'bout the new general manager."

"Really?" I said. I want Kal Jimper's replacement to push New York to go ahead with the new show *with me* as the principal anchor. I've got to shine.

"Hello, Holllleee! What's on your mind?" Kenya joked.

"Nothing. What's the new guy's name? Where's he from?"

"Name's Vin Hardy and he's from Dee-troit. Already got a nick-name too—newsroom's callin' him the Wizard! But I don't have time to worry about him. Shoot, I'm still tryin' to get a handle on this com-puter system."

"Oh, I'm a whiz," I said, pulling up a chair.

Kenya and I huddled over her computer screen and couldn't help overhearing the telephone conversation Dragon Diva was having at her desk.

"Oh, Bette, they're hiring nothing but cub reporters here. It's get-ting embarrassing too! These rookie reporters are *green and cheap!* The latest one is some redhead from Phoenix. Kirstin Quarterly. I hope management doesn't think I'm going to carry her!"

I whispered to Kenya, "What an evil witch."

"Hazel probably can't help it. She's a pampered one. I heard her fa-ther was an ambassador in the Kennedy administration and her mom was the daughter of some rich European landlord. They say she lived in a castle when she was a kid, until the family lost all their money and had to come back to America."

"She didn't lose that princess air unfortunately."

"Don't mind her, Holly. She's hangin' on to evil 'cause she thinks that will keep her on top here. I don't know why she's worryin'. She can't possibly go down."

"Why?"

" 'Cause shit always floats, don't it?"

I looked at Kenya and she looked at me. We laughed until we coughed and had to pat each other on the back.

Beans

Photographer/Technician

Aww c'mon, I never thought that Alex wouldn't back me up on this, and why not? It was supposed to be a party just for the guys, but Alex and I stumbled on to it in the garage. I couldn't believe it, but I heard the raunchy yelling and the loud laughing and, of course, we were curious. We opened the door to the lunchroom area in the garage; there were about six of the guys—one of them, Benny, is engaged to be married. There was some funny business going on, some funny bachelor business.

There was this woman who was half naked and belly dancing around. Some of the guys were yelling nasty stuff at her and one of them palmed her butt. I shut the door, looked around, and Alex was gone!

Those guys were wrong to have that bachelor party in the garage, and yeah, I know we've had birthday parties and going-away parties, and rowdy "Thank-God-the-boss-is-gone" parties. But c'mon, geez, a stripper is way different. I don't need that in my workplace. It's sexist, and it's disgraceful and I was offended. But Alex wasn't backing me up, so, of course, hey, I called her on it.

"Beans, it's not worth the hassle. You know how long it's taken for us to make those guys treat us decent? If we tell on them, there's gonna be hell to pay."

"Alex, think a sec, how can we as women just let something like that go? That was *not borderline*, not even close, that was *across the line*. I know they saw us, and that sends a bad message if we don't do anything."

"Check it out, Beans. If those guys wanna stand around and hoot and grab crotch over some bimbo in an *I Dream of Jeannie* outfit, let them."

What was with Alex, making this so simple, she knew it wasn't? I felt myself getting angrier and angrier. My throat got tight, then I chose my words carefully, I didn't want to stutter. "If it was another issue, a black issue, you'd take the risk in a heartbeat."

"Oh, so now you're fronting, Beans."

"Alex, c'mon, if that was a black girl jumping out of that cake, showing tits and ass, and those *white* cameramen were doing the same thing, you'd ah lost your mind."

"Beans, you are tripping. Why are you making it a race thing?"

"Because *if* this was a *race* thing, you'd go all out to make a stand for what's right. That's what you do, stand up for what's fair. But you're not doing it now and I've got a problem with that, Alex."

I felt sweat beading across the back of my neck, I'd broken our promise.

Alex
Photographer/Technician

Man, Beans went and did it! Beans broke our promise!

Several years ago we promised each other that we wouldn't discuss racial issues. The last time a racial issue was flush up in our mugs was when we were covering the 1983 political campaign of the late Mayor Harold Washington.

I don't even know if the rest of America knows it, but back in '83 when brother Harold was going for the big gig, this city showed its natural behind, okay?

I was new at the WKBA shop. Beans just had a few years in on the job. She'd started out as a secretary scheduling the other techs. Beans ended up getting tight with the boss. He gave her a shot at running camera when they said they wanted to hire a handful of minorities.

So Beans was out shooting on the street, just starting to learn, and I was inside running taped commercials. I was dying to get on the street. I had experience and talent, but the technical boss wouldn't give me a chance. It was a race thang at WKBA just like the political race thang going on in the election.

Chicago was divided in *rank* fashion along racial lines. Brother Harold was running on the Democratic ticket. Everybody and they great-granny knows that Chicago is the home of the Democratic machine. Old man Daley damn near elected JFK himself rigging those extra votes or so the story goes. But when Brother-man Harold won the party ticket, some people started to jump square and run over to the Republican side to vote for the white candidate.

Damn, it got so bad that some of the police officers, firemen, and other city workers started wearing political buttons big and bold as you please. There were racist buttons too—watermelons with red lines through them and others said crap like "No Sambo's in City Hall." The *Chicago Tribune* endorsed Harold and got a bunch of "nigger lover" mail. Someone put up flyers around town that said if Harold won, the city would have to rename the El line, "Soul Train." *It was foul!*

There was this black woman who worked at a school in Bridgeport as a cook. Now Bridgeport is a neighborhood on the South Side of Chicago and it's racist as hell. Girlfriend had put Harold bumper stickers on her ride. When she got off work, some white kids were in the parking lot trashing her car. Then they started harassing the mess out of her. When the black newspaper, *The Chicago Defender*, picked up the story people were pissed off.

So one of the black sororities, Delta Sigma Theta, decided to support the sister by having a march through the neighborhood. Harold Washington said he was going to attend.

Say what? All of a sudden, all the TV stations got Black Power religion. They wanted to send black employees to shoot and cover the big story. It just so happened that at WKBA that day some of the New York brass were in town. That meant the managers got tight butts. The managers here do that, they get tight butts when the big boys ride the wind into Chi-town.

So the head of technical wanted to make himself look good by sending a black woman photog to shoot the story. He thought that would make WKBA look all progressive. True it was a scam but it was a scam that brought me an opportunity to shine. I was down for it— but he had promised the assignment to Beans. She got bumped.

"I can cover this story, pull yourself off of it, tell them you can't go," Beans had said to me.

I looked at the chick like she was modeling a straitjacket! "No way, Beans!"

"I'm a woman, I'm more than capable of bringing something extra to this story," Beans had yelled.

"I know the victim is a woman and the rally is organized by a sorority. That's incidental. They didn't trash her car because she was a woman, they trashed her shit because she was black supporting a black candidate. Racism is at the heart of this story not sexism."

"Well, since you brought up race, I didn't want to say but since *you* brought it up, let's put it out there," Beans said angrily. "If you weren't black they wouldn't have switched us. How would you feel if you were me?"

Shitty, *but* I told Beans I was due. I could put a fucking camera together from scratch. And I'd been shooting for a year at the public television station before I got to WKBA, so they weren't giving me jack but my propers!

After that throw-down we didn't speak to each other for two months and we were the only women photogs in the shop—*and still are!* We were going through hell too. We had guys saying foul stuff to us. We got the worst assignments. They wanted us to quit. Instead we got hip and bonded.

That's when we promised right then and there that no matter what racial conflict jumped off in the world at large, or at the station, we were not going to talk about it with each other. "What happened to our promise, Beans?"

She just huffed and got in on the passenger's side. I got in on the driver's side. After traveling a few miles in silence, I said, "Beans, please don't ever break the promise again because it helps hold us together. Now the other thing that holds us together is backing each other up. So I've got your back on this stripper thing. It'll be hell for a while, but hey so what? It's been kindah boring lately anyway."

Beans wiped her eyes and reached down to squeeze my hand. I could feel her warm tears on my skin.

Beans

Photographer/Technician

We complained to management, both the head of technical and to the news director. Both men told us that we were making something out of nothing, that we were trying to create controversy where there wasn't any. I didn't let it go at that, I told Millie, the personnel director, who reminded the *two good old boys* about sexual harassment, which I wasn't thinking about per se. To me it was just the fact that it was rude, and not to mention tacky, and just out of place for a T&A bachelor party to be held at work.

Then a memo went up in the garage, reprimanding the "unknown" parties who had been involved, and warning that action would be taken *next time* if a similar incident took place. Someone leaked the incident to The Column; they ran two lines about a "seedy incident" and a "stern memo."

All that grief, for a one-graph memo with no teeth, and a blurb in The Column. All the guys knew we told, and Alex and I didn't try to hide it, and neither did they try to hide their anger.

Mysteriously our unit got a flat tire every other day for a week, and an important videotape I shot "accidentally" got erased. When either Alex or I walked up to a group of the guys in the garage they would stop talking, change their regular speech, and say, "Watch what you say. We have ladies present. We don't want to get into trouble, do we, fellas?"

It was regular prank stuff, until one day, I came into the garage and they made me so mad that I was just struck silent. I went into our raggedy bathroom, hitting the door so hard that the MEN sign nearly fell off. Then I came out, sat back down, and sulked. That's when Alex came in.

Alex
Photographer/Technician

As soon as I walked into the sitting room of the garage, my *central warning system* started doing the herky jerky. I knew something was seriously wrong.

Beans was sitting by herself, and I could tell she was pissed off. The guys had been riding us like crazy ever since we went to management about that bachelor party. Beans had tears in her eyes. I looked from her to the group of guys, about five, sitting in the corner. Three were old heads; techs who had been brilliant in their day, but were now on the easy road to retirement. Two were young guys who were the main ones giving us shit. They were snickering.

I looked down at Beans' feet; next to her lay our tripod. That's the long stand with three legs that you can put the camera on and clamp it down. It's money for a steady shot, guaranteed. In the business we call it a "stick." I picked it up. Someone, guess the fuck who, had glued the legs of the tripod—one leg shorter than the other. I tried to sit it up. When it fell over, all the guys laughed. Will, one of the young shooters, he walked over and said, "Got a problem?"

I looked around the room. "Yeah. I'm looking at my damn problem."

Will winked at the fellas. "We're not your problem. It's the equipment. Looks like your stick is short."

They laughed again.

"Well, at least I'm in good company. Your wife says your stick is short too!"

Will sneered at me, "Bitch!"

I reached down and grabbed a beta tape. I wound up like Nolan Ryan or somebody and threw it at him. He ducked. Beans grabbed *two* tapes and hurled them. The other guys started scrambling for cover. I threw another tape at Will and nailed his butt.

"Awww! Are you nuts?!"

Then Rock came in and grabbed me. "Alex! Cool down."

"Cool down?" I shouted. "He called me out my name. I don't play that. And Will broke our stick!"

Beans stood next to me. "Tell Will, tell him, he's the one who needs to cool down!"

All the damn commotion drew a small crowd into the room. Rock asked, "What happened?"

"He called me . . ." I was so mad I couldn't repeat it.

"It rhymes with snitch!" one of the old heads shouted from the corner.

Rock shook his head. "Okay. Hey, everybody, look, this has gotten out of hand. Enough already. Let it go."

"Let it go?" Will laughed sarcastically. "Rock, you were here when we broke the stick."

"I know. I didn't say anything *then*. I'm saying something *now*. Leave the ladies alone."

Perkins, a white technician who usually edited videotape, was standing next to Rock. His cigar was hanging out of his mouth. "Rock's right. This stuff has got to stop. Now it's our business."

I was stunned. The quiet ones who didn't want to tip the boat or piss off the old heads and the troublemakers were now grumbling in our favor. Beans squeezed my shoulder.

Will looked around the room, shrugged, then glanced at us in a tough fashion before leaving. Then we knew. Our hazing days were finally over.

Beans

Photographer/Technician

It took, oh about say, three weeks before everyone got comfortable again. Both Alex and I were glad, but it just made me angry, angry that I had to take all that because I was in a male-dominated arena. I knew a lot of people in broadcast news thought that shooting video was a man's job, done best by men, and no women were needed. Alex and I were accepted, sure, but really not welcomed yet.

I was stewing about it a bit, riding with Alex one day, and I said, "I'm tired of climbing in and out of this truck chasing fires, crooked politicians, and WKBA is enough of a nuthouse without the guys screwing us over!"

Alex laughed. "Beans, it was a bitch. But it's over now. It was just a handful of the old photogs urging on a couple of young bucks. It wasn't all the guys—not Rock, Perkins, Todd, or Abraham . . ."

"But hey, those guys, they should have stopped it sooner!"

"They wanted to be considered one of the boys. Even though they don't agree, they went along."

"You know, Alex, I was on the phone last night, talking to Boardwalk about everything that happened."

"That's your friend in New York—stockbroker, right?"

"Yeah, Alex, we grew up together; remember, I told you about her."

"Right. Right."

"Well, she and I got to talking, and I've decided. I'm going to play the market. I'm going to try to get enough money to buy myself a camera and an edit console, you know, the works, so I can start a small production company."

"Wow, they pissed you all the way off this time, huh?"

"Alex, I'm tired of the grind, of chasing fires and doing silly animal stories, of standing out in flood waters up to my knees for hours. I want to be able to pick and choose the work I do, and who I work with. Plus I came to this job with both my youth and my health, now I've got headaches, irregular periods, gray hair, and love handles with no love life!"

Alex laughed and held out her hand. "Give me some, girlfriend!"

I slapped her five, then offered her part of my dream. I said, "Alex, you want in?"

"Naw, Beans. I like having the security that this j-o-b gives. We've got seniority and that's hard to let go. And venturing out with a start-up company too? No. If I ever go after my dream, it would be to make a film. I'd love to make a film. Beans, shit, girl, that would be fantastic for me!"

"Well, I'm giving Boardwalk about fifty thousand dollars I've got saved and I'm going to let her gamble it on the market and hopefully, it'll grow like Jack's beanstalk. I figure I'll need about a hundred and seventy-five thousand dollars, maybe a little more, to get all the equipment that I need and enough extra money to hold me over."

"Beans, why not take out a second mortgage on the building you live in? That would really jump-start your dream."

"You know how I feel about borrowing money; ever since my mother almost lost our home I-I-I . . ."

"Right, I forgot. But Boardwalk thinks she can run your fifty grand up to one hundred seventy-five thou?"

"She says the market is on a tear; it's possible that I could do it, taking a lot of risks. Alex, I could hit and get a big payoff, if I'm lucky, and, God, do I hope I'm lucky."

"Me too," Alex said. "Here's hoping for you, girl."

Coming Up Next:

The new GM puts on the pressure: ratings must come up. Dramatic changes are demanded—changes Denise doesn't agree with. Does she go along or fight?

Then:

Rookie writer Kenya Adams learns firsthand about the tensions of "Hit Time."

Plus:

Holly struggles to prove her journalism skills to the newsroom. Meanwhile her competition comes in—Kirstin Quarterly.

Those stories and more, straight ahead.

Holly
Reporter/Anchor

In television news, many are hired but few are chosen.

Kirstin Quarterly is the new reporter on the block. She started right at the beginning of ratings, the May Sweeps to be exact. Kirstin is a pretty girl with stunning red hair, high cheekbones, and luminous, chestnut eyes. The camera loves her, just as it caresses me. Kirstin's desk is one row over and three desks away from mine.

"Hi, Kirstin."

"Hi," she said warmly. I needed to feel Kirstin out. She'd come in on my heels. I wondered about Kirstin. I'm no fool and I've got ears. WKBA insiders, plus two reporters at the other shops, all hipped me to street rumors that this woman is the Godfather's chosen one. He'd stolen Kirstin from the Phoenix station where she did features—which is my forte. I also noticed how he buzzed around Kirstin's desk as if it were a hive. Kirstin never lifted a buffed nail to shoo him away either.

"So how do you like it here so far, Kirstin?"

"Great."

Caution is the stage mother of truthfulness, my father says. Kirstin has a pleasant manner and even though I want to instantly dislike her because of the privilege she obviously has at her fingertips, I don't.

Kirstin said with no malice or rancor, "Mitch has been trying to get me here for over a year now. Finally we were able to make it happen. WKBA needed a feature reporter."

My ears burned. *Features.* That's the job Kal Jimper promised me before he got fired. Mitch took Kal's promise and gift-wrapped it for Kirstin. What's a Godfather to do? I was going to be chasing fires, going to murder scenes, political rallies, and that's it. No features. No anchoring. I caught myself giving her the evil eye. Then I switched to a sweet smile. "Kirstin, you seem very happy here."

"Aren't you?"

"Of course. I'm sure you'll love the party scene here and all the excitement Chicago has to offer."

"Well, Holly," Kirstin said, stretching. "I'm low key. I just want to turn in my feature stories and go home. I've got a boyfriend in Milwaukee. I wanted to get closer to him."

Just as she finished speaking, Mitch came over and sunned in Kirstin's face. I was invisible. Kirstin giggled and cooed him, warmed his ego. There was no Godfather mode when Mitch was around Kirstin. After he left, Kirstin winked . . . *"I let him smell it but he can't get a taste."*

I just nodded and walked away.

When I joined WKBA, I was low reporter on the seniority totem pole. Consequently I was given Tuesdays and Wednesdays off. Kirstin now had the least seniority, but she had Fridays and Saturdays off. My complaints went unheard. Seniority mattered when I was at the bottom of the ladder, but not when anyone else was.

Another reporter came in behind *both* Kirstin and me—white, male, middle-aged, wife and three kids—he got Monday through Friday 10 A.M. to 6 P.M. This time *both* Kirstin and I complained, this time it was explained to us that he had a family, and a father needs to be home with his children in the evening. *Unbelievable.*

I was irritated and I was angry. It wasn't so much the days and the long hours because I was eager to prove myself; it was the disdain at not being treated equally or being measured by the same yardstick. I wanted fairness in the media. Was that too much to ask?

I kept telling myself, keep going and keep working because hard work and prayer pay off. That's what Daddy always said. He said, "Baby, God doesn't give us more than we can bear." Sometimes, I wonder. Maybe God is overestimating me? TV news requires the strength of

Moses—I'm somewhere along there with Aaron. I keep working and praying, hoping that my hard work will pay off soon.

DENISE

Managing Editor/Acting Assistant News Director

We're off to see the Wizard!

Everyone is calling the new GM *the Wizard*. His real name is Vin Hardy. It doesn't matter. He's the Wizard.

The Wizard wants changes.

He called a managers meeting. Me. Mitch. The technical operations manager. The VP of finance. I was the *only* black. I was the *only* woman. I *was* Diana Ross.

We're off to see the Wizard.

The Wizard called the meeting for 8 A.M. Studio B. That's the main set for our 10 P.M. broadcast. He wasted no time. The Wizard wanted to redecorate Oz.

"It's the set."

That's what the Wizard said. What? I thought. The Wizard said WKBA's ratings were dropping because of the set. Redesign the set. Redesign the graphics.

I wanted to laugh.

"Our audience," the Wizard whizzed, "needs something brighter and more inviting. This set is blue and cream, almost like a hospital! I want a design that takes us into the next century! Bright colors. Computer-age design. Corporate is giving us five hundred thousand in capital to redo the set."

I thought, That's wasted money.

"Also," the Wizard whizzed, "I want robotic cameras for the set." I said, "That's three studio jobs lost. The union isn't . . ."

The Wizard snapped.

"We need increased productivity. Robotic cameras are never late, they don't call in sick, they don't go on strike, and we don't have to pay them benefits or a pension."

Money man not a people man.

"And finally, I also want us to lease our own chopper," the Wizard went on to say. "WGN has *Skycam 9*. WBBM has *Chopper 2*. WMAQ has *Jet Copter 5*."

The Wizard wanted flash.

"We," he said, "need more presence. We need a chopper. Top of the line. Aero Special. We'll use it for traffic. We'll use it for breaking stories. That's the answer."

A chopper?

Viewers don't tune in because you have a chopper. Viewers don't tune in for the set. Viewers tune in for news. They tune in for talent. His wish list. Lease a new chopper and pilot. All this would cost big money.

How much?

"About thirty-eight thousand dollars a month," the Wizard announced. "Maybe more depending on how much we use it. But let's be a little frugal and say about four hundred fifty thousand for the year."

Big money.

We all cut our eyes at one another. WKBA would have to pay for that. Not Corporate. Who was going to ask? Mitch was the one. He had the guts. Mitch finally asked.

"What about our budget?"

"Find it," the Wizard said. "Just find it."

Mitch and I stayed up with the VP of finance until 1 A.M. both Friday and Saturday. You can't find what you don't have. There was no fat in the budget. No extra cash. What could we cut?

The muscle.

"Let's just lay off some people," Mitch said. "The phone receptionist. A couple of secretaries. What about security? Some of them could go."

I bargained.

"Just cut overtime," I said. "Then at least everyone keeps working." He agreed. The good thing? It was a bad thing. There was going to be hell to pay. The overtime we paid out was tasty gravy. But it was also needed to help cover overlapping shifts.

We had no choice.

But the rank-and-file wouldn't see it that way. They'd see money missed. Feel misused. After the budget trimming that was coming, there wouldn't be a person in that building who would buy us a cup of coffee.

And not spit in it.

Holly
Reporter/Anchor

It was a constant stream of criticism:

"You didn't have enough facts in that story!"

"The sound bites were too long!"

"Your copy was written too cutesy!"

"Why do you take so long to conduct an interview? You're always late getting back to the station."

Mitch was badgering me. And because he had the power of the Godfather just like his nickname, Garth started badgering me too. The Godfather thought I was weak, therefore, the executive producer thought I was weak too.

I struggled to stop my waning confidence. I felt as if I had the story when I was out there in the field. I felt good about what I was getting.

But if Mitch didn't like how the story was shot? He would be on me. If he didn't like how the story was edited? Mitch? The Godfather. He was on me!

When you're on-air, all the good and bad falls on you—not the behind the scenes people who help make it happen. My success or failure was affected by committee—did the assignment desk give me a good story? Did my cameraman shoot me enough video? Did my executive producer add copy to my written script that didn't really work?

I know about dues and how they must be paid. But I know I'm good. I'm a damn good anchor. And I'm a damn good reporter in my area of expertise. I'm a feature reporter. I'm not a run and gun reporter. Each requires a specific talent and each should be respected. But my dilemma is genuine. I feel that WKBA isn't giving me an opportunity to shine in my area of expertise. I get the tough stories. Kirstin gets the easy ones.

I tried to get a read on where all this was coming from by asking Denise. Could she help me with Mitch? She seemed sympathetic. Denise said she felt for me but there was nothing she could do. Mitch was Mitch, she said. But I felt like since she was a sister *in there, in there,* that she could do more. Why couldn't Denise do more? What's the use of having someone black in management if they can't help?

I got called in on my off day to help cover for another reporter, who phoned in sick. I dragged myself out of bed for my thirteenth straight day of work. My legs hurt. My head hurt. My back hurt. I struggled to put on my face and I wanted to cry because I was so beat up both emotionally and physically. I pulled it together somehow and made it down to the station.

Garth, the executive producer, met me at my desk. He said, "Holly, there was a food poisoning scare at a South Side meat house. A fight broke out. You've gotta break ASAP to make a live shot for the noon. Everyone else has got a jump on this thing and we'll have our asses hanging out in the lake breeze if we don't get there. And you know how ballistic the Godfather can get."

My shoulders sank but I made a crisp about-face. Then I walked over to the assignment desk and asked Stat, "Who will be my crew?"

"A courier car will take you to hook up with Unit Sixteen. That's Alex. She's rolling in from another location. Hey, watch Alex."

What did Stat mean, *watch her?*

Stat explained, "I told Alex we were sending you and she said she didn't think you could handle it. Another thing. The techs are bitching because their OT's been cut. They've got a work slowdown going on. So they're dragging ass. You have to ride with Alex. She's got an attitude problem anyway. Now add this too? Watch out for her, let me tell you. Alex is on her way to the scene. Let's hope she's set up by the time you get there."

I was tired and I was irritated. I flipped open my reporter notebook in the courier car and called back to the station. Kenya was my writer; she helped by telling me what the police had told WKBA researchers.

The details were sketchy. It happened at a store called Miss Porky's wholesale meats. The store was having a ten-year anniversary sale. But apparently two people had complained that they had gotten bad meat from the store. When they tried to return the food, a fight broke out between the manager and the customers. Seven people were hurt and ten more people were arrested for disorderly conduct when the fight spread out of control.

I got to the store and it was a big gray building with a mural on the side of the building. The mural showed a cow, a pig, and a turkey wearing overalls, smiling, with the caption, "Fine enough to eat, and cheap too!"

There was a crowd milling around outside anxiously awaiting the next incident. Three people recognized me and ran over begging, "Can I be on TV? I wanna talk!"

I needed to get some interviews to use during my live shot. But where was Alex? I checked my watch. We had thirty minutes to air.

That was it. I'd get the blame if we didn't have any video for my live shot or if it looked sloppy in any way. That Alex! Stat told me to watch out for her. Where was she?

Alex
Photographer/Technician

Where the hell was I? I was busting my ass from south suburban Calumet City, with construction on the Bishop Ford Expressway, to get to the location at Forty-ninth and State. I wasn't supposed to be busting my ass, because management mopes cut our overtime. I was supposed to be on a work slowdown. Don't mess with my money! For real, don't mess with my monah-nay.

The only reason I was hustling? It was because it was Holly. The whole newsroom was talking about how they were running her black butt ragged. People were D-O-G-ing the sister big time. They were talking about how the Godfather said her stuff was weak on air. He was bitching at her all the time.

Me myself, I hadn't really had a chance to talk to the sister. But Kenya and I are cool. We've gone to lunch together a couple of times and she and Holly are tight. They've been helping each other. Holly knows TV and Kenya is a good writer. Damn right, black folks have got to help one another. We better stick together. So, I'm hustling up for Holly. I got there about twenty minutes before air, which was a miracle the way traffic was backed up.

Now I'm happy as hell when I pull up. I see Holly in a crowd of *Negroes* looking around like she wants to take off running. I mean she's got that Cal-ah-forn-I-ay Mo' Money look. And let's face it. This was a rib tip crowd. I couldn't help but laugh. I was not laughing *at her*, but *at the way* the situation appeared. Holly looked over and saw me laughing, I guess, and just started fronting on my ghetto style in front of all these people.

"Where've you been, Alex? I've been waiting ten minutes! Don't you know we have to go live? I don't have time to do any interviews now. I'm not playing with you on this one, Alex! If it gets screwed up, you're just going to have to take the blame this time, not me!"

Why was she tripping out like that? "Hold it, Holly—"

Miss Thang waved me off. I heard someone in the crowd say, "Da-ah-agggg!"

"Just set up, okay, Alex?"

Fine, she wanted to call all the shots? Miss Thang was on. "You want to call all the shots, Holly?"

"Obviously that's the only way I'm going to be able to pull this off. Alex, just set me up over here. Get the building in the shot and the crowd behind me. Stay wide because I look tired. I haven't had any rest. I think my makeup is okay but I'm still not comfortable with how I'll look on camera today."

"But . . ."

"Just stay wide, Alex."

Stay wide the entire live shot? I knew she was tired, I knew they were running her ragged. She even had pissed me off but I tried again, damn, I said, "Holly . . ."

"Please, Alex! Stat told me about you! Just do as I ask. I'm tired and I'm angry. Just get behind the camera and stay there so we can get this live shot over with, please?"

Stat told her some lie about me and her stupid butt believed it? Now I surely don't give a good goddamn.

I set up the shot and stood my happy ass right behind the camera. I knew what was coming next. But Holly didn't.

K E N Y A
Writer/Producer

I heard Garth growl, "What's that on our air?"

I looked up, y'all, at the monitor in the newsroom and there was Holly standin' outside live somewhere's with a whole bunch of black folk behind her.

There were streamers flyin' in the wind and some R&B music playin'. There was a mascot or somebody dressed in a pink pig suit with a shirt on that said, "Pork: the best white meat!"

I hit the volume up higher. I saw Holly tryin' to talk but the music in the background got to playin' louder and louder. Holly was darn near shoutin':

"Just a short time ago a fight broke out here at Miss Porky's wholesale meats . . ."

When she called out the pig's name? Not a real pig but the person in the pig suit? Miss Porky just hip checked Holly out of the picture and started dancin' for the camera. She was doin' a hip movement like with that old sixties dance the Swim. The crowd was eggin' on, just chantin', "Go, Porky! Go, Porky!"

Holly tried to get back in the picture and the crowd froze her out. Meanwhile the newsroom was howlin'.

Why didn't the camera push in and go tight on Holly? That would take the crowd out of the shot. Why didn't the camera pan away? Do somethin'!

Miss Porky was doin' the Michael Jackson moonwalk in a circle. Now the crowd was chantin', "Go, Porky, it's your birthday! It's your birthday!"

Finally the director in the control room killed the live shot and came back to the anchors on set. Lordy, the anchors had commenced to laughin' and could not stop. I ain't seen nothin' like it in television ever. It was material for one of those Blooper shows. The anchors couldn't stop laughin'. Shoot, they had to go to a commercial break.

"What a disaster!" one of the white writers said sorrowfully. "She's just too green."

"Management is doing it more and more—going for 'a look' rather than experience. But to Chicago from *Palm Springs*!" A white editor shook his head.

A black stage manager walkin' through the newsroom jumped in on the fly. "Well, they let these young white reporters come in here and they train them. Kirstin's here. Then let the sister get her kinks out too. Why not?"

"Black, white, or purple—it doesn't matter!" a veteran Hispanic reporter snapped. "Back in the old days, you had to be seasoned and top shelf to get to a top-three market. The standard is being watered down by the 'pretty' factor. These kids are coming up too fast."

All debate got thrown from the mule when the Godfather burst into the newsroom. He was cussin' like the devil was gonna get him and sweatin' too.

The Godfather yelled, "What the fuck are we running here? A clown show? And we're in May Sweeps too! Does anybody here care about our ratings besides me? I'm up in the GM's office watching the show and I'm totally embarrassed. Holly is an idiot. I knew when Jimper wanted to hire her she was a lightweight. But Jesus H. Christ! And who the fuck was on camera? Get them on the phone now!"

I sunk down mo' low in my seat and said a prayer for my sisters. I heard later that Holly and Alex both got hauled into the office, and the Godfather balled them out.

Holly and I were supposed to have dinner at 6:30 P.M. and she said she was still on because she needed a drink. I called Alex over in the garage. I told her to meet me at the same little bar around the corner from the station. I was gamblin' after that big ole mess they had today. But I couldn't let my two new friends become enemies, could I?

I didn't tell either that I was invitin' the other. My aunt Rae used to say that you never fire off a shot to warn the rabbits that you're 'bout to come huntin'. So Holly and I were sittin' there—then Alex walked in.

If looks could kill? There'd be a wake right now.

Alex
Photographer/Technician

I stopped. Holly got her skinny behind up and put her hands on her hips. We both looked at Kenya and she said, "Y'all grown tail women will not clown on me in public. I'll treat y'all just like my two-year-old son Jeffie and get them legs!"

I sat next to Kenya. The table was a triangle with a safe amount of distance between Holly and me. *I wanted to jack her.*

"Y'all need to talk things out," Kenya said in that honey accent of hers. "What happened?"

Holly blurted out, "Alex left me hanging."

"Oh, pah-lease! You started it."

"No I did not!" Holly said, tapping her glass with her lime green stirrer. "You could have cleaned up that shot and you didn't! You made me look bad."

"Holly, I didn't *make* you look bad. I *let* you look bad."

"What the heck is the difference, Alex?" Kenya asked, picking at the frost saturating her beer mug.

"Really," Holly sneered.

"I didn't catch for you—catch your mistake because you wouldn't let me. I could have tightened that shot. But you, Miss Smarty, wouldn't let me do my job. Holly, I had to hustle to get to that live location—

and I got there with twenty minutes to spare. You started tripping out on me. You ordered me to get behind the camera and shut up."

"I never said that, Alex. I don't talk to people like the rest of you WKBA old-timers do! I'm not evil."

The waitress came by and I said, "Appetizers—your favorite, bring them, please." Then I turned back to Holly. "You snapped because Stat lied on me and you believed it."

"Sure, Stat warned me. He told me that you had a bad attitude, Alex. He also said that the techs are on a work slowdown," Holly growled. "Why not warn me?"

"Whoooo wee," Kenya said, "that work slowdown is for real. All my tape was late today. It really worked my nerves somethin' fierce."

"But I hustled for you, Holly, because I know you're trying to make it. Stat says I have a bad attitude because I call him out when he starts playing tricks. Stat lets his boy Will slack off at my expense. That's why my attitude *with him* is bad. Besides, how are you going to let some white boy tell you something about a sister? You let Stat play us off one another. I'm supposed to get the benefit of the doubt just on GP."

"She's right too, Holly," Kenya said, taking the basket of nachos and buffalo wings being set down on the table.

"I'm on my umpteenth day straight, tired, abused by Mitch," Holly explained. "Alex, why didn't you just say to me, Holly, you're going to blow it! You should have tried harder to help another sister, *just on GP.*"

"She's right too, Alex," Kenya said, piling hot peppers on her nachos.

I decided to break it down for them. I'm a vet, paid up in dues and then some, and I'm a sister in the know. Both of them are coming in right out of the box—neither one of them was thirty years old yet and both of them were from small markets. I said to them, "Do you guys know where you are?"

"WKBA Chicago!" they answered in unison.

"Right. Network O&O. The third-largest market, not some little affiliate station owned by some golf bag manufacturer in Palm Springs . . . or a small-town newspaper owned by some Southern land baron. This is WKBA. Big time. Big pay. Big bullshit."

They both stared at me because I was preaching.

"What your mamas told you about being good girls—throw that out the window."

"Hey listen—"

Holly had the nerve to try to interrupt. I wasn't going to let her.

"No, you listen, Holly. Kenya, you too. What you learned in kindergarten about playing fair—that goes out the window too. But do keep believing in God because you will have to call on him often. Kenya and I are already friends. But I want us all to be friends and help each other. We all have to stick together because there are so few of us in this business."

"Alex," Kenya asked me, "what about this rumor I've been hearin' about the black employees gettin' together to form some kindah group or somethin'?"

"You know how it goes; something happens and people get pissed. Then everybody talks about doing something but it takes a while before anything truly gets organized."

Holly grumped, "All talk and no action, huh?"

"Naw, it's not like that. It's just that you get used to a lot of drama in this business. It starts to become the norm rather than what's out of the ordinary. You get comfy with the money, the benefits, and the perks. Think about it. The jobs that we have now, black people couldn't even dare dream about. The only time blacks were on TV back in the day was when they were getting chased by dogs and sprayed with water hoses. Quiet as it's kept, the reason we broke the barrier in numbers was because the white media was afraid to cover the riots in the sixties— Had to hire some Negroes to go in and get the news. Isn't that deep? White journalists could go overseas and cover Vietnam with bombs going off all around them but they were too scared to go into Watts and the West Side of Chicago to rap with some angry brothers and sisters."

We all got quiet behind my little observation.

"Let's make a pact," Kenya said cheerily. "Let's stick together through thick and thin—no matter what."

"A secret sister-girl network," I laughed.

"Yeah, Alex," Holly said, smiling at me for the first time today. "We back each other up to the hilt, *just on GP!*"

"Surely," Kenya added, then she planned, "let's meet regularly for dinner or lunch. We can share stuff, how we feel . . . what's goin' on . . . everythin'."

"Let's ask Denise too?" Holly suggested.

I shook my head no, "She won't come. Denise is management. Don't get me wrong. Denise is cool but she can get funky about stuff like that. I wouldn't even ask her. Let's keep it small with just us."

"Okay, just us then," Kenya said. "Y'all agree?"

I held out my hand. Kenya grabbed it. Holly grabbed her hand, then mine. And damn if it wasn't done.

DENISE

MANAGING EDITOR/ACTING ASSISTANT NEWS DIRECTOR

I work hard. I start at 7 A.M. Go until 7:30 P.M. Weekends I'm on call. Holidays too. I've got my pager. My cell phone.

My Sony handheld TV.

This week I had to cover for our executive producer, Garth. He's on vacation. Garth has tons of vacation time. Cut a sweetheart deal with Kal Jimper before he was canned. Garth has ink black hair. Long body. Not very talkative. Fidgety but still a solid newsman.

Garth picked a good day to be off.

I had to break up a fight. One fight between a reporter and Stat. Staff problems. I had two sick calls. One person AWOL. A truck broke down on the way to a story. It boiled down to one thing. One.

Perceptions.

At work: I'm a journalist, a manager, a referee, a psychiatrist, a mother hen, a disciplinarian, and a credit to my race.

At home: I'm a black woman in need of love.

My *baby, baby* is Perry. I heard the cork pop out of the champagne downstairs. I heard Perry's sensuous laugh. My steps creaked. I slipped off my robe.

"Ooooh we-weee, baby, baby . . . "

I closed my eyes. Raised my arms. Hugged myself. I get so tired sometimes. From the work bull. The tension. The stress. The pressure. Raise ratings. Be fair. No favoritism. Fight the power. *I'm every woman.*

"Oooh we-weeeee, baby, baby."

Born and raised on the Penn/Jersey border. Daddy a math teacher. Mom a real estate agent. Little brother and me. Big house. Big yard. College funds for us. Retirement funds for them. For my parents: middle class accomplished. For me: Upper-class dreams.

"Ooooh we-weee, baby, baby."

Achieving workplace success is a burden. I need relief from that burden. Enter Perry. Perry had been in the army. He developed computer systems. Now he worked for a company that customized computers for big corporate businesses. Perry has traveled a lot. He wants to settle down. Now. Right here.

So do I.

Perry is my rock. He tells me I'm sexy. Perry tells me nobody does it better. Work can piss me off. Perry takes my mind away. What would I do without Perry?

We're good for each other.

I felt Perry's presence behind me. I could smell him. Then I could taste him when I kissed his fingertips after he touched my face. I reached back. Low. I pulled Perry's thighs tight against my naked hips. *I was melting.*

Then: My pager went off.

My eyes popped open. Perry whispered, "Don't you dare. . . ." I relaxed again. Like synchronized swimmers we raised our legs; arched our backs; stepped into the bubbly, scented water of the tub.

"Oooh, we-weeee, baby, baby . . ."

Coming Up Next:

Why aren't more black professionals used as experts on

television news? Hear the debate and can Alex and company

come up with a solution to fix the problem at WKBA?

Then:

We shall overcome—or will they? A painful incident puts

Beans at odds with some of the black women in the

newsroom.

Plus:

Kenya gets a taste of office politics during the infamous

"Post."

This Just In . . . *continues.*

Alex
Photographer/Technician

Man, news can be boring sometimes! Holly and I have been waiting all day long in the lobby of police headquarters. This is the part of the job I can't even stand. *Wait, wait, and more wait!* We're waiting for the cops to walk a man they say is a serial killer.

The last murder happened in a loft building being gentrified in the Bucktown neighborhood. It's the fifth crime in a series of murders there. Each time, a witness saw a dude running away. He was wearing a hooded jacket. Never could get a decent description of the man. The media dubbed him, "the Bucktown Slayer."

Now the cops are charging a suspect. They say their case is wrapped up sweet. They say they found a knife in his locker at work. They say he confessed during questioning. Dude is more than likely headed straight for Death Row.

This is a big-ass deal. So naturally every shop in Chi-town has a crew waiting to get a picture of this guy! We're hoping to get an interview too—a cop, a lawyer, a prosecutor—it's called a "gang bang." Everybody bum-rushing and interviewing someone at the exact same time.

The murders were ugly even when measured by a big-city yardstick. All the victims were stabbed. Their heads were shaved. Their fingers were cut off. Everybody wants to get a shot of this psycho. And Skippy peanut butter with nuts you better believe if every shop is there—your station better have the shot too. Don't let another station get something you don't have. When it runs in somebody else's newscast? Your ass is broken glass.

Sometimes news is nothing but hurry up and wait. Holly went and got us something to eat from a vending machine. In a case like this, do you know we can't even make a run to Micky D's? I popped the top on a Coke Holly bought me and grabbed a bag of chips. "Holly, watch. As soon as I start to chow, all hell will break loose." Ten seconds later, I heard one of the other crews yell, "Here they come!"

"See!" I said, dropping the chips and Coke, grabbing my camera. "What I say? Huh, what I say?"

All the reporters and crews were anchored together at the bottom of the stairs, waiting. I threw my weight back, and I heard heavy breathing. White overhead lights came on as all the shooters aimed their cameras at the top of the stairs. I pulled out my shot and I saw the cop walking the suspect down the stairs, his hands cuffed behind his back, head down, trying to hide. *Please.* A blond mop of hair flopped up and down as he was dragged down the steps.

Holly and I were anchored in the front. When the murder suspect hit that last step, the cop on his left jerked his arm up. This squared him for our cameras; he blinked at the bright lights then scanned the mob of reporters with his eyes. He stared at Holly before whispering to her, "Hello."

I got the shot, his face and all, as they led him away to another holding area out of sight. A three-hour wait for a thirty-second shot. That's news.

Holly and I looked at each other with relief on our faces. We got in the unit with our tape and headed back to the station. Holly would write a story for the ten o'clock. I was getting off. Kenya was working 2 to 10 P.M.

"Hey, Holly," I said, "let's get Kenya and go out for a quick bite. We haven't had one of our outings in a while."

We got back to the station and walked into the newsroom. They were just starting the Post—as in postmortem—as in dissect the body and find out what killed it.

The Post is what the meeting *after* the newscasts is called. To break it down, it's a bitch session. Usually the Post is in the news director's office but today everybody was gathered in the newsroom for it. What's up with that? It must have been some kind of screwed-up show. And a public Post all out in the open and jive, with everybody front and center? I told Holly, "This is going to be some foul stuff."

Holly
Reporter/Anchor

It reminded me of a funeral gathering. The anchors, writers, reporters, researchers, editors, directors, everyone was in the newsroom for the Post. That's where you stand up and either praise or curse the dead. And like at any real passing where the family comes together, it is sometimes angry, sometimes thoughtful, sometimes petty, but it's always an emotional experience.

Mitch was standing in the center of the room, his voice chilled to the bone. "The six o'clock stunk. But the five o'clock show? That show really looked like shit!"

As if that wasn't bad enough, Dragon Diva spoke up. "All my scripts were late. They were just being shoved in my face like a *streetwise newspaper!*"

The floor director growled, "The scripts were given to me out of order."

A desk assistant, who is responsible for taking scripts to the set, said, "How can I get the scripts off the printer, put the pages in order, then run them into the studio thirty seconds before it's supposed to air live?"

The five o'clock producer yelled, "I printed the scripts as soon as they were filed in the computer."

A writer spoke up. "You can't finish writing a story without cutting the videotape that goes with it. Two videotape editors were out sick today."

"And they weren't replaced on the schedule either," a videotape editor chimed in. "There's no overtime. We had to do twice the normal workload in the same amount of time."

I thought, Here we go around the blame bush, the blame bush, the blame bush.

"Cut the bullshit!" Mitch shouted; he was in Godfather mode. "This is news. We have to rise to the occasion. The tape for the lead story was not there! The reporter babbled like an idiot trying to stretch. Why was the lead story so damn late in the first place. Kenya?"

Everyone turned to my girlfriend. She said, "Mitch, we made the decision to finish the story completely instead of stoppin' and airin' part of it. That made us late."

"We who?" the Godfather snorted. "Who is we?"

Kenya looked over at Garth. He said, "Next time, ask me, Kenya, and I'll make the call."

Kenya's eyes bucked and she looked totally confused.

The Godfather kicked a chair. Then he knocked a stack of newspapers onto the floor. The Godfather ended by shaking his fist, raging, "We have a mandate, ladies and gentlemen. Bring up the ratings and quickly. There's no room to screw around either. I mean these ratings are going to come up if it's the last thing I do, dammit! And believe me, before I get fired, I swear by God some of you will hit the door on your ass first."

KENYA
Writer/Producer

Well, sir, I felt as big as a squashed black-eye pea. The Godfather singled me out. We had hustled as best we could. And still the Godfather threw a cussin' fit. And Garth ordered me to finish my story, then lied about the decision in the Post.

Holly and Alex suggested grabbin' a bite to eat. Fine with me, I needed to talk. I told them on the walk over about how Garth lied to protect himself. Alex threw a fit!

"Kenya, it's like I've been trying to tell you, girl. There is a shit load of covering your ass going on in these newsrooms." We sat down in the taco joint. Holly said, "The buck should stop with managers, not you!"

Holly and Alex ordered. I'd lost my appetite.

"Cheer up!" Holly said, huggin' me. "You're learning fast and you're doing well!"

I managed a smile but I was still stingin' inside. I changed the subject. "How was y'all day?"

"Cool but boring," Alex answered. "We waited forever until the cops finally walked the Bucktown Slayer. All the while though I was thinking just one thing."

"Just like me, Alex," Holly laughed. "You were thinking, *Please, God, don't let him be a black man!*"

"Girl, you know it. I've never been so happy to see a white man in my entire life."

We all laughed, then Holly spoke next.

"Doesn't that make you feel funny though, Alex?"

"Truth be told? Shit, yeah, because I shouldn't care what color the guy is as long as he's arrested and off the street. But it's just that we are always putting black men on TV news as criminals."

And wasn't Alex right for sure?! I told my friends, "I'm really careful about images now, shoot, especially since I got little Jeffie to raise. Showin' black men as criminals all of the time is hurtful and misleadin'."

Alex played with the salt. "As many experts as our industry uses on television how many are black?"

I snorted. Alex bucked her eyes in agreement.

"Zip plus one, maybe!" Holly answered. "And what really gets me,

ladies? There are plenty of black doctors, lawyers, FBI agents, psychia-
trists, and sociologists but you just don't see them in news coverage."

I offered hope. "There are more black lawyers on TV."

"True, Kenya," Alex pointed out, "but that was mostly during the
OJ trial. Face it, it's screwed up. I'm tired of only seeing black people
on television as criminals or victims. Shit, we are more than that, we are
better than that."

Holly lit up and crackled like a fresh log tossed on a smokehouse
fire. "I've got a fabulous idea. Now we all agree that it is our responsibility to do what we can to change what's going on. I mean we're insiders
and if we don't make a special effort to change TV news, who will?"

"Right," Alex and I agreed.

"Excellent. Let's put together a file of black experts in various
fields—surgeons, criminologists, political consultants, and lawyers. Then
let's pass that list on to all the producers, the planning department, and
the assignment desk. It will have a bio and contact numbers."

"Outstandin' idea, girl," I cheered. "Let's call that bad boy the Du
Bois list!"

"Shiiit!" Alex hooted. "And we stay dead on 'em to use the people
on that list too. No excuses."

"Say, Alex," Holly said, raisin' her taco in salute, "what's the latest on
the black employees' group?" Suddenly her eyes got big and she
stopped chewin' as she looked up.

Beans
Photographer/Technician

What's going on, why didn't they invite me to sit down with them
to eat?

I was on my six-thirty break too. I'd run out to get *Money* magazine, and then grab a couple of tacos. I needed to squash the hunger pains that were shredding my stomach, pains that were getting help from the stress I was feeling from working a double shift.

I walked into the taco joint, in the rear I saw Holly, Kenya, and Alex laughing and talking at a side table. So, of course, I went back there to say hi but the response was so rude!

They all looked at me in a quiet, but stunned, sortah quasi-strange manner. I didn't know but it made me uncomfortable; usually I'm always comfortable around them, so what gives? I got nervous and stuttered a little. "Is som-something wrong?"

"No," Holly said. Alex and Kenya shook their heads, agreeing the same.

I swallowed and chose my words carefully, to steady my voice, and I said, "How about that Post, boy oh boy, that was out of control, huh?"

"Yeah," Alex said, sipping her pop.

"It was a caution," Kenya tossed in.

I fingered the brittle edge of a white plastic lawn chair; their coats rested there, and I looked from one person to the other and waited for the invite that never came.

"So you're putting a bit of grease on top of all that stress too, just like us, huh, Beans?" Kenya said with a smile.

"Yep," was my answer, as I thought, Should I just sit down and invite myself? Why were they acting funny toward me, what was wrong, had I done something?

Kenya reached for the coats, then hesitated and drew her hand back. Holly and Alex shot her a quick look, and it wasn't nasty but it was more along the lines of surprise, and I was hurt so I said, "No, I'll stick to take-out. Bye."

I never looked back at that table; I was busy nursing my insides from the anger and hurt I felt. I realized that they had excluded me, not 'cause I'd *done something* but because I *wasn't something, and that something was black.*

K E N Y A
Writer/Producer

How did I get into this mess? How did I end up gettin' stuck doin' the apologizin' to Beans? All of us were upset somethin' fierce. Alex said what we felt: *We couldn't ask Beans to sit down because, cool as she is, Beans understands the struggle but she's not in the struggle.*

So we voted. Alex said leave it alone and let it blow over. Holly said apologize. Not only did I end up breakin' the tie, I also ended up gettin' chosen to talk to Beans. Alex refused. Holly said she was too embarrassed. So that left little ole me.

I waited till the next day for two reasons. One, I had to think about what I was goin' to say. And two, 'cause Beans was goin' to be my shooter for an interview I had to do at Cook County Hospital. The interview was for our medical reporter, who was busy interviewin' burn victims at another location for a story on a new procedure to do skin grafts. I was gonna spend half the mornin' with Beans. The ride over would be the perfect time to talk. It would be just the two of us.

When I got home I told Jarrett about my nerve bustin' day and the incident with Beans in the taco joint as we looked in on Jeffie and got ready for bed.

Jarrett listened and said, "You are sorry, right?"

"Yeah."

"Well, that ought to be good enough."

"But, Jarrett," I said, snugglin' up under his arms as our conversation continued beneath the covers. "Suppose she asks me what we were talkin' 'bout? I can't tell her 'bout the black employees tryin' to get a group together. It's hush-hush."

"Well, whatever you do, Kenya, don't lie. What was that your aunt Rae used to say all the time?"

"Truth may break the skin but a lie cuts to the bone."

That phrase was ringin' in my ears when I saw Beans the next day. She was getting her unit ready for our trip over to Cook County Hospital. "Beans, I want to talk to you about yesterday evenin'—"

"Forget it, I'm over it, and it's no problem," Beans said as she continued to check out the truck, addin' tapes and checkin' the camera. She said fine but didn't look fine.

"No, it's not fine, Beans. We know you were hurt when we didn't offer you a seat with us. We were talkin' about some things that were botherin' us. We were so into our conversation that we forgot our home trainin'."

Beans squinted.

"That means manners. Please accept our apology."

Beans looked at me, shrugged, and gave a half smile. "I accept the apology, but I don't like what happened there. You guys expect me to understand things, to treat you fair, then you turn around and treat me different."

"It wasn't in that spirit. That's what we want you to know, Beans. There are a bunch of unfair things that go on here at WKBA. I'm learnin' the history of blacks being paid less than their white counterparts, the lack of promotions, the unfair schedulin', so we have a lot to think about sometimes. When your back is bent carryin' a burden, sometimes you forget to look up and bump into somebody accidentally. That's what happened yesterday."

"I know what you mean, but I still didn't like what happened," Beans said. "Let's just move on."

"Okay," I said as we got in the truck and started headin' over to the near West Side. Ridin' over to Cook County Hospital, it dawned on me that I didn't know that much about Beans really except that she was from here. So I asked her about herself, about growin' up in Chicago.

Beans

Photographer/Technician

I grew up in Chicago, on the southwest side, in a loud neighborhood crowded with cookie-cutter brick bungalows. I viewed the world through the rectangular windows, spotted with factory grit and half-moon glass, from the door that helped me spot the insurance man making his monthly rounds.

I was a change-of-life baby, which means, I think, that I changed my mother's life because I came so late. She said that I restored her youth and stole away her menopause because after she had me, Ma never had another period, hot flash, or irritable moment. Ma believed that was why I stuttered, because I took away her discomfort.

I was a quiet child I think because of the stuttering, and as a change-of-life baby I was *really* an only child even though I have two brothers. Mike and Donald, my big brothers, are eight and ten years older than I am.

My brothers were my father figures because my papa was a traveling salesman who went on long road trips to make his money, even though it wasn't much.

Our money was scarce and once my mother borrowed against the house we lived in, which she inherited from her parents, and we almost lost it. We, my mother and I, got dressed and went to church. We stood, heads down, before the congregation to ask for help, something that I'll never forget, and to this day I will not borrow money. But the church members gave, happily, especially after I begged in my nervous stuttering voice.

My life was hand-me-down, from my mother's affection that passed from Papa to my brothers to me, to my clothes and toys.

The only new toys I got to play with belonged to my friend; she lived down near the end of the block. Her name was Carolann and she had lots of new toys but, most of all, she loved to play Monopoly. We'd play all the time and her favorite property was Boardwalk, a nickname I gave her and she still loves that nickname to this day.

Boardwalk is now a stockbroker in New York, and we're still best friends, even today. She is fun, real, and was one of the few neighborhood kids who didn't tease me about being poorer than the rest, or a stutterer.

Poverty did not break me but it clings to me still, like mist, and the discomfort of not having enough bugs me. I always felt that my brothers, who worked with their hands and never could get ahead, would have been great men of the world had they had the money for higher education.

I learned to stop my stutter by talking in phrases, with little breaths, and although it's not perfect, it works.

But before I mastered my voice, I learned to communicate with pictures because, obviously, I didn't like to talk much. In sixth grade the teacher said, after spring break, we would have to come back and tell the class what we did over the holiday. I did not want to stand up in front of the class, and who would, if they stuttered.

My father was in town, a rare event, and he asked me why I was so down in the dumps. I told him and he said that he would fix it, and at first I was angry because I thought, you mean all this time he could have stopped my stuttering, and hadn't?

But Papa didn't fix my voice, but he went out and came back with a little camera, in a new box, a camera that turned out to be the first new thing that I ever owned.

And after spring break, I went to class and showed pictures of where I played, and of my grandma who came to visit us that spring, and it was there that my love of using pictures to tell a story started and has not stopped.

I asked Kenya about her family, about how she came to be a journalist.

KENYA
Writer/Producer

I grew up in a town hard and sweet as sugarcane; a town called Honesty, Texas. It has the prettiest flowers in the county, three roads leadin' in and out, all of which were paved back in 1974, the year my parents were killed.

I was born two years before in the livin' quarters of a four-room whitewash buildin', built with the help of a government grant for social equality. My parents had written the grant proposal and used the two back rooms and bath as their livin' quarters. They called the buildin' "Honesty's Center for Political and Social Change."

Daddy and Mama had grown up two lots apart, he in a brick house and she in a warpin' wood frame because Honesty only had one colored section of town and despite your circumstances that's where you lived.

My father's people had money they got from being iron masons for rich folk across Texas. My granddaddy Jefferson, who my father and now my son are named after, could fashion anythang 'maginable out of iron.

Granddaddy Jefferson was well paid and was able to build for his family the first brick house in the colored section with a front porch and swing.

My aunt Rae reports that it was sittin' on that swing that my father first kissed my mother in front of everybody in an act of love and defiance. Ma's daddy, a horseman who bought and sold stock for rich white men, had demanded that the two stop courtin'. Grandpa Jimmy didn't think that my daddy was gonna do right by Mama because in his words—"The rich will reach down and pet the po', but they sho' won't make no effort to raise 'em up."

But Daddy had gotten his political science degree from Fisk, decided against teachin' in Atlanta, and made his mind up to marry Mama and stay in Honesty. It was a decision that cost them both their lives.

My father was always complainin' about the inequality of the schools, the jobs, and livin' areas in Honesty. Most of the folk, colored and white, didn't listen to Daddy much until he wrote and received the government money to open up his office—"Honesty's Center for Political and Social Change." Black folk noticed but so did the Klan.

One night, after leaving me in the country to visit with my aunt Rae, my parents' car went off the road and crashed into a ditch. My mother and father were killed. The sheriff said it was an accident, that my daddy lost control of the car on the road slick from a late evenin' rain. But black folk said there was another set of tire tracks. My parents' car had been run off the road.

My grandparents decided that it was best to leave me in the country with my aunt Rae for a while. But we ended up never wantin' to leave each other. That's where I was loved most, that's who I loved most, that's where I stayed.

I was fifteen when I ran across an old trunk in the back of the barn of Aunt Rae's farm. In that trunk was a brown torn clippin' from Honesty's newspaper, *The Bugle.* It was an article about the crash that killed my mother and father back in 1974. The newspaper said that it was an "accident."

The article upset me somethin' fierce 'cause I knew it wasn't true. In 1982, the man who had driven the other car confessed to rammin' my parents' car off the road. It was a death bed account overheard by the housekeeper who happened to be an usher at our church.

Everyone accepted confirmation of what they already knew but no one made it official. Now I was fifteen and it was 1987. I took the clip in my hand, clutchin' it, in a rage. I decided then and there to write the true story myself. I got the facts from the old *Bugle* article because the circumstances leadin' up to the crash were correct—just the "accident" part was wrong.

It was at the foot of Aunt Rae's bed, with my spiral notebook in hand, that I begged her to tell me what she knew. Aunt Rae spoke her heart's deepest sorrows to me and look like I felt relieved myself.

My grandparents had died by then but I talked to their neighbors. I even tried to talk to the dead man's wife, who cussed me each of the four days I stepped onto her porch. The fifth day she threatened to call the police on me.

The fifth day was key.

Another relative, who also lived in that house, became my first source. She followed me part of the way home that fifth time and swore me to secrecy after confirmin' everythin' I'd heard. I promised to keep her identity secret and never come back to their house again.

Then I wrote my story. The editor of the black paper, Honesty's *Journal*, refused to print it. He said, "Let the past be."

That Sunday in Bible study we came up to the point where the minister asks if anyone has a question or a particular passage they want to study or discuss. My aunt Rae gave me permission to speak. I stood up, said I had somethin' to share, and then I read my story.

The entire room was silent, then everyone burst out with clappin' and shouts of "Praise God!" Our minister grabbed my hand and said to everyone, "Ain't it blessed that we have children now who are not afraid to tell our story?"

"Amen!"

The editor of Honesty's *Journal* was there. He came up to me after class and said he was moved by my words. He printed my story the next week. That was my first clip.

DENISE

MANAGING EDITOR/ACTING ASSISTANT NEWS DIRECTOR

"Watch your back."

A mole called to warn me. I was in my office. It was after the five o'clock news. After the six. After the Postmortem. I was dead on my feet.

It was a warning.

The mole said, "The Godfather is in hot water about the ratings. New York is pressuring him. Watch it."

Watch my back.

A week after my phone tip it happened. Friday morning. Dragon Diva got a copy of the overnight ratings. Dragon Diva loved conflict.

I saw her.

I was at Vera's desk. She was showing me pictures of her twin boys, who were in college at De Paul. Dragon Diva walked right by us. Her meeting with Mitch was short. She came out. Dragon Diva leered at us, "Shake-up time!"

Turmoil.

Vera said, "If she had a shovel in her hand, she'd be a grave digger." Then Mitch buzzed Vera's line. She answered. Vera listened, head down. She looked up.

At me.

Vera said, "Okay," before hanging up. "Managers and producers meeting. Monday. Before the morning meeting."

"For what?"

Vera shrugged. Vera typed the memo and e-mailed it to the appropriate people. I saw Mitch later that day. He hardly spoke. Mitch said, "Monday morning."

All day.

All day the producers were nervous. On edge. They second-guessed themselves. The executive producer, Garth, and the assignment desk manager, Stat, argued. A report of gunshots fired crossed the police scanners.

"Check it out," Garth said.

Stat said, "It's nothing."

Any other day? Minor exchange. But today, add tension. Add Mitch's looming threat. It was a power struggle. Stat called Garth an asshole. Garth called Stat a jerk.

Fight.

They lunged for each other. I stepped back. They pushed. They grabbed. Garth knocked off Stat's glasses. Stat tried to stick his thumb in Garth's eye. Two cameramen separated them. The newsroom was buzzing.

Mitch came out of his office.

He smiled. Mitch knew. He'd caused this tension. He looked around at everyone. "What's going on?" Mitch asked.

Silence.

Mitch looked at Stat. Stat smiled and sucked up. "Just too much creative energy, Mitch. I'm always scrapping to do the best job, you know that."

Suck up.

Garth dropped his eyes. Mitch looked at him long and hard. Garth rustled the papers on his desk. Mitch looked over at me and said, "If my managers can't control this newsroom, I'll find people who can."

Mitch walked away.

"Let's get back to work," I said. I was hell to deal with the rest of the day. I barked orders. I gave short answers. Garth was bitchy.

All the shows were clean.

Still I left the office angry. Mitch challenged me. I got in my car. I started driving. I was on Lake Shore Drive Expressway. Southbound. I was thinking.

About the meeting.

Shake-up, Dragon Diva said. Was Mitch going to take some of my responsibility away? Was he going to fire any of the producers? Was he going to berate us like in the past?

I looked up.

The light was red. Red!! I was going sixty-five miles an hour on the drive. I ran the red light at full speed. I had a thought.

I'm dead.

Coming Up Next:

Long hours. Sagging ratings. How much stress can an overworked sister take? A grueling seesaw schedule begins to take a toll on Kenya—at the office and at home.

Then:

The story chase heats up. Holly works to land an exclusive with the main suspect in the Bucktown slayings. Does she succeed or does she fail?

Plus:

Alex gets an SOS call. Who is in trouble? And how can Alex help?

There's more . . . **This Just In** *. . . straight ahead.*

Alex
Photographer/Technician

Man oh man, traffic is muffed up! I'm running late, shit. I've got to drop off these tapes at the studio and break over to Rock's place. Rock and his brothers opened a restaurant on Wabash around Cermak. He'd reserved the back room for us.

"Us" being the black employees interested in getting together some kind of a group to deal with the serious racial problems at the station. Rock and I decided that we shouldn't meet on company property yet. We didn't want to tip our hand and have management trip out before we were ready. We wanted to steal on those suckers.

I finally beat the traffic and dumped off my tapes in the newsroom. Holly saw me. "Alex ! Get over here!"

I walked over. "Holly, you know the meeting is tonight! I've got to stop by the bank first. Talk to me there I—"

"Guess who I spoke with this morning?"

"Denzel."

"Get real. I talked to Donovan Bailey, the Bucktown Slayer."

"No shit! What'd he want with you?"

"Bailey says he hasn't been given a fair shake in the media. Alex, remember the day when he was arrested and the cops walked him for us?"

"Uh-huh."

"Bailey says that I was the only one who didn't look at him like he was an animal. That's why he called me. I'm getting an exclusive sit-down with him. Bailey told me to set it up through his attorney."

"Holly, I know you're happy. And this could be great—"

"Absolutely! I'll show everybody! Dragon Diva. Denise. The Godfather. I'll show them all. Stu isn't the only person around here who can get an exclusive!"

"I hear you, but, ahhh, wait a minute. This Bucktown Slayer is a sicko psycho."

"I'll interview him at the jail."

"Holly, this man didn't just put people in their coffins like an average murderer, remember? He put them in there *in parts and pieces*. You know, a finger over here . . . a leg over there. That's some *Silence of the Lambs* bullshit."

"I'll make sure we have extra guards in the room then."

"We who?" I said, and bucked my neck.

"Something wrong with your neck?"

"I don't want any part of a creature feature flick!"

"Alex, please," Holly said softly, "I need someone I can trust on camera. And I need that person to be ready to go at a moment's notice when I finally get this exclusive set."

Then I had a thought. "Ask Beans. She'll have your back. Besides, Beans worked the story before. Matter of fact, Beans was first on the scene when the bodies were initially found—maybe she'll do it. Ask Beans."

DENISE
MANAGING EDITOR/ACTING ASSISTANT NEWS DIRECTOR

"Lady! Lady! Are you okay?"

I was shaking. My fingers locked into the grooves of my steering wheel. Why did I leave work so angry? Why did I get behind the wheel driving like a mad woman? Why did I let the foolishness of the job get to me so deeply?

Carelessness.

I ran the light. I hit the brakes. The paper truck swerved. I ran up on the curb. My rear left tire popped.

Carelessness.

"You blew my after-vacation glow!" the truck driver said. He was twentyish, lanky, wearing a blue jean shirt and pants. His blond hair was apparently bleached white by tropical sun. His skin was too tanned. A fat wallet weighed down his front breast pocket.

"What the hell were you thinking?"

That's what the truck driver said. I laughed. Hard. Gut nervousness. What were the odds that only one vehicle would be coming my way? We missed each other. What were the odds?

God's grace.

All the stuff in my purse was scattered on the car floor. Lipstick. Pens. Cable bill. Wallet. Cell phone. I grabbed the phone. I needed my flat changed. The motor club would take too long.

Perry.

I called him. He dropped everything and came. The cab pulled up behind me. Perry got out. I hugged him. He gave me a reassuring smile. Then Perry popped the trunk of my Mercedes and pulled out the spare.

"What happened?"

I shook my head. I didn't feel like talking about it. Not yet. I wanted to tell Perry everything. I couldn't there. He changed the tire in twenty minutes. Perry drove us to my place. "What about work?" I asked him.

"It'll wait."

And Perry said it with such ease. He waved his hand. He poured our wine. He handed me my glass. He sipped from his. Perry said, "Work will get done when it gets done."

Awe.

I felt awe. I couldn't let my ambition go like that. I felt stupid. Why couldn't I let go of work like Perry? Why was I so driven?

"How do you do it, Perry?"

He laughed. Perry has a beautiful, gurgling, boyish laugh for a big man. It's adorable. So adorable that I didn't even get angry that he was laughing. At me.

"In the army."

Perry said that life was even keel but harsh. He said that work was life or death in the army. The Gulf War. Now work was work. A living. Not life.

"I know."

I said that. I didn't always practice it. It irked me that a surly son of a dog like Mitch could get the big job. One hundred ninety thousand dollars a year plus perks. But yet Mitch can't run a newsroom. It irked me that the Wizard could whiz. Two hundred fifty thousand dollars a year. Company-leased Jeep. Expense account. Season access to Bears skybox. Free courtside seats behind Spike when the Knicks played the Bulls.

I'm slaving.

I was slaving to get to the top. Working. I told Perry about what happened with Mitch. I told him about the meeting Monday. Who knew what Mitch was going to do?

"Can you change it?"

I knew what he meant. No I couldn't. Not while Mitch was running it. But if I could just run it one day.

"You will."

When? I get tired of the long hours. The stress. I get tired of covering for these white guys who don't give me my due. I'm going to take mine. Perry looked at me.

"Take it. Just don't worry about it."

Beans

`Photographer/Technician`

Would I, after what I saw, go back and shoot a sit-down interview with the man known as the Bucktown Slayer?

Didn't Holly know that hard news, that murders, were hard to deal with when you first start out in this business? I knew why Holly was excited; this was a hard news story that could help boost her rep. Don't we all, people on jobs everywhere, want the best reps possible? But I'd been there the first time, yeah, I had.

The bodies were partially buried, they were in a hole, the hole was in the garage behind a run-down building. Someone heard a strange noise in the garage, they called police, but not soon enough. The Bucktown Slayer was lucky, *then*; somehow he escaped before police arrived.

I wasn't so lucky that day, I was the closest to the location. The assignment desk got a tip, a friend at police headquarters said, Hurry, we'd better get there. The source said it was big, a real big story, just developing.

The source didn't say, at least no one told me, that it was not only a big story but gruesome too. I've been to crime scenes before, drive-by's and domestic shootings, deadly hit-and-run accidents.

I remember the first murder victim I videotaped; how could I forget, some things in this business stay with you. It's the little things, well, at least the seemingly little things, that stay with you. In that first case, I had to pysch myself up; being the only woman photog at the time, they didn't want to send me. I could cover anything, I said all sassy, just like anyone else.

It was a man who lived along the wealthy North Shore, big businessman; his brother later confessed. They were feuding over the family business, a business worth millions. To me this man's name is lost, but not what I videotaped that day, not the ring.

The blast had tore at his hand, a reflex he had to protect his face. I remember the jagged prongs of the ring, the hole in the center, then the diamond nestled in a pool of blood. The flashing bulbs from police evidence techs made the diamond sparkle, beautiful, and ugly too. I had nightmares for the next week, about jagged prongs, about a flashy diamond floating in blood.

As the years go by, covering crime scenes gets so routine it's usually no more disturbing or lingering than your leg falling asleep. You shoot it, call into the station, then go grab a burger for lunch. If the killer is caught and tried, you might work the trial, might rack up some overtime covering it.

But the Bucktown Slayings, that crime, it made me question humanity. The cops had the garage door open, it was night, and the only light was coming from an alley street lamp. It was more golden than moonlight, and eerier than a scene in one of those cheap summer horror flicks. I was the first camera there, I didn't hesitate, I started rolling despite a cop's warning—"You don't wanna . . ."

I panned my shot down, I videotaped the hole where the bodies were partially buried. This is when I heard myself wheezing, not breathing. It wasn't especially chilly, and I had on plenty of clothes, I layer for work because there's no telling where you'll end up. I was wheezing, and my eyes, they started tearing up. I had a nervous twitch in my stomach and a flat taste in my mouth, couldn't swallow, just wheezed.

Only two series of the video that I shot could be used, the rest was too graphic, too ugly. One series was standard and safe, an exterior of the garage with police activity. The other series showed the bodies being brought out in little bags, like sacks of heavy groceries. I panned from the cops' shoes as they walked, up to the bags, swinging freely, near their knees.

I'd have to think, very long and very hard, about Holly's request. Would I, after what I saw, go back and shoot a sit-down interview with the man known as the Bucktown Slayer?

Holly
Reporter/Anchor

I made three more calls. I still wasn't able to get through to Donovan Bailey's attorney. Give up?—no way! I would start working the story again, bright and early in the morning. I got in my car and headed over to Rock's place for the black employees' meeting.

I had already missed 90 percent of it.

I came in on the tail end. Erika, the only black person on the assignment desk, was complaining. "I work from six A.M. till two P.M. Afterward I have to work another two hours setting up special stories for the weekend before I go home. Now, I've got to pick up one of the weekend shifts that starts at ten A.M. but doesn't end until after the ten P.M. show!"

"You're not union either," someone shouted. "So you don't get paid overtime."

"Right," Rock said. "Are they working Stat and Rod like that?"

"No!" Erika said. "And I know everyone loves Rod. Rod is my guy but still the fact remains that it's not fair. He's got a forty-five-hour work week. I'm pulling sixty hours!"

"Okay," Alex said, writing down notes. "This complaint list is getting long. We've got three incidents where seniority was ignored in scheduling. We've got two people, well qualified, passed over for promotions, including Rock. Three positions came open in the last year and not one was filled with a minority candidate. Denise has been subbing in the assistant news director slot but it doesn't seem like they're going to give it to her—"

"She's management" a voice called out from the back. There were about fifteen people in the room.

Alex said, "She's a sister. And Denise is cool."

"I don't see her here, do you?" one of the black secretaries said.

I spoke up. "She can't be an active part of this and keep her job. We all know that. I haven't known Denise as long as the rest of you but I really don't think she would sell us out. Do any of you?"

A strong "no" rose up from the ranks.

"Good," Rock said. "We're all in this together."

"Okay," Alex said. "Now I don't need to go through the rest of these gripes we have listed. What's up, y'all? Are we going to get an official group started or not?"

"Let's go!" people shouted. "I'm ready! Vote! Vote!"

"Take a vote," Rock said, struggling to restore order. "All in favor?"

Every hand went up to a chorus of, "Aye!"

Then everyone started clapping and making Arsenio Hall dog-pound noises.

"Hold it down! Hold it down! What about a name?" a sales assistant asked.

A graphic artist joked, "Let's get real evil. How about, WKBA Cotton Pickers?"

Everyone laughed, booed, and hissed. Then a woman who worked as a phone receptionist started singing a spiritual, "I been 'buke and I been scorned!"

All the voices joined in for the next line, "I been talked 'bout sure as ya born!!!"

More laughter, then Alex jumped up: "That's it! That's it! Been 'buked. Been scorned. Been. But it's B-E-N . . . Black Employees Network!"

It was so right. It felt so good. The name passed unanimously. We set a date and time for the next meeting to talk about bylaws, officers, and strategy. Our small group had the energy of an army, our expectations filled the room with joy. We had a group! We had a movement! We were on our way!

KENYA
Writer/Producer

Workin', workin', workin'! Is that all I do?

I was feelin' it fiercely in my legs, back, and neck. Hours and hours I spent hangin' my head over that computer bangin' out copy, squintin' my eyes screenin' videotape. I was spendin' less and less time with Jarrett and Jeffie. Both my men were gettin' salty about it too.

"Why do you have to work every weekend?" Jarrett asked me, sittin' in the kitchen ignorin' a plate of ham and grits I fixed for him.

Did I need this extra stress? Wasn't work stress enough? But I looked at him and my heart melted like butter on hot toast. My Jarrett is a handsome joker. The first time I laid eyes on him, he was comin' across Vanderbilt's campus in cutoffs burstin' at the seams with thighs the color of bread puddin'. He had on a red fishnet shirt that did little tah nothin' to hide a rail-hard stomach. Jarrett's left arm was cocked around a bunch of science textbooks.

"I have to work when they schedule me, baby, you know that," I explained. "And when people turn on their TV's on weekends, late night, and holidays there's news on. Did y'all believe it was magic? Naw, baby, there are folk workin', that's why. I'm just stuck bein' one of 'em."

"Kenya, we hardly have any time to ourselves. I have never pressured you about sex, but damn, girl, this brother is due! I need to hit it!"

"Answer me this, who fell asleep last Friday night?"

Jarrett ignored that little point.

I said with ah cotton touch, "Jarrett, the first year is probationary. You have to play ball with these folk. They are short writers, and even though they were cuttin' back on overtime, they still have to fill the shifts. There are more than enough techs, they're missin' the OT. There aren't enough writers so we're gettin' whupped."

I didn't admit to Jarrett that they were only doggin' me. I checked the schedule pretty regular. I was pullin' all the weekends like no one else. But what could I say? I was in my probationary period. If I didn't work, I know sure as shootin' they'd find someone else who would. Then what?

The doorbell rang, and it sounded like the recess bell, because our Hyde Park apartment is so small. For our little money we could only afford a one bedroom with an alcove that was supposed to be big enough for a full-sized washer and dryer. We had to turn that into little Jeffie's room. We got a baby bed and a dresser in there. I headed for the door to let in our sitter, Miss Billie.

"Hello, dear," Miss Billie smiled. She's a retired teacher and the grandmother of one of Jarrett's med school friends. She slipped her speckled blue and green cape over her head and off her shoulders, handin' it to me with her beret. Then she meandered toward the back with a hippity-hop callin', "Jeffie? Jeffie?"

When I returned to the kitchen Miss Billie was feedin' Jeffie his grits—he wouldn't eat for me. Miss Billie laughed. "Jeffie just wants to make an old lady happy." She peered at Jarrett over her spectacles. "Young man, you're looking a bit down in the dumps today."

"Kenya can't go to the potluck and I won't have a dish!" Jarrett pouted.

"Awwww poor thing!" Miss Billie said, lookin' over at me. "Kenya's working terribly long hours. Well, Miss Billie will have to whip up a black-eye-pea casserole so Jeffie's daddy won't go empty-handed. How's that sound, Jeffie?"

My son gurgled his grits, then swallowed them. His black moon-shaped eyes were wide with happiness.

Miss Billie looked over her shoulder at me, winked, then looked back over the top of her glasses at Jarrett. "Eat up. Or do I have to spoon-feed you like little Jeffie here?"

Jarrett cracked a smile at her and said, "For you, Miss Billie—the world!"

DENISE
MANAGING EDITOR/ACTING ASSISTANT NEWS DIRECTOR

Monday morning.

Perry spent the night with me. He served me breakfast in bed. Eggs. Sausage. Grits. And on a napkin he wrote, "Don't worry." I ate well then headed to work.

Determined.

I cruised down the highway. I was determined. But relaxed. It was sunny. Almost balmy. I sped along. The seashell blue speckles of Lake Michigan flickered.

Conflict coming.

I entered the meeting. Usually I'm a half an hour early for work. Today I was on time. Everyone else was early.

So what?

Mitch wasn't there. Vera smiled at me. She put out doughnuts. Coffee. Juice. Bagels. Cream cheese. Assorted fruit. No one was eating. It looked and felt like the Last Supper.

Where was Mitch?

Speak of the devil. Mitch walked through the door. There was a sense of power about his walk. It was carriage. It was the way he pulled out the chair. He said good morning when there was no good.

Power.

Misuse of power. That describes it. He had our talent, our confidence, and our livelihood held hostage.

Ratings.

We knew they were low. Mitch said, "Our ratings, across the board, are down ten percent from last year. You all are aware of a mandate we have to bring up ratings. Kal Jimper failed to bring up the ratings. That got him canned."

The tension.

Mitch was dead cold. "My job hangs in the balance. Your jobs hang in the balance. I wasn't hired to make friends. I was hired to make money. Ratings equal money. Right now, this team is not doing that, *but* I know we can."

C'mon.

Mitch sipped his orange juice. "We can *with* the edition of a new executive producer. I've hired Abby Halston. She will replace Garth, who is demoted to the ten P.M. producer slot. The ten P.M. producer moves to the five o'clock show. The five o'clock producer goes into the writers' pool. The six o'clock show stays intact. Any questions or comments?"

Garth stood up.

He used a hankie to clean his glasses. Silence. Garth turned to Mitch and barked, "If you think I'm going to take a demotion because you can't fuckin' decide how best to run this shop—you're crazy!" Mitch smirked, "Garth, you can't cut it and everyone here plus Ray Charles can see it."

I cringed.

Garth snapped, "What?! I'll call New York and tell them how you're the problem! I'll tell them that you're the one who needs to be booted out on his ass!"

A calm voice.

Mitch glared at Garth. "Garth, this is my newsroom. Kal Jimper hired you. He's history. Call Corporate. While you're calling New York, why don't you tell them about how Kal Jimper gave you a shot when no one else would? You've been to rehab for drugs twice at two other stations."

What?

Garth's face dropped. He turned placid. His hands shook. Mitch said, "You just can't cut it anymore. We've got a job to do. It's me or you. And I can't have some ex-drug addict in a key position of power. Does anyone here have confidence in Garth?"

Silence.

Garth wet his lips. "I've been clean for a year." Mitch shook his head. "You're not cutting it, Garth. You say you've been clean, but there are some days, Garth, you seem almost unstable. And all that vacation time Kal Jimper cut you was part of your rehab program. What is it? A drug retreat you attend every couple of months?" Mitch was blowing this man up.

Right in front of our eyes.

"Garth, I'm not firing you. I'm keeping you employed. I'm just taking your feet away from the fire. How about it? Stay on in a lesser, noncrucial capacity. Something, Garth buddy, you can handle."

No way.

Garth was a news vet. His ego wouldn't allow him to take that kind of public demotion. Mitch knew it. Garth stuffed his hankie in his back pocket. He cleared his throat.

Then . . .

Garth resigned.

"I wish you all well," he said. "Professionally and personally. Mitch, can you please have Vera clean out my desk? I'll have my brother pick up the boxes from the loading dock tomorrow."

Mitch said, "You're being packed as we speak."

Umphf.

I heard two people sigh. Garth left. Mitch laid out some other small changes. The new EP would start in a couple of weeks. If I hadn't realized it before, I knew it now.

Mitch was dangerous.

The Godfather was the wrong nickname for him. The Godfather had honor. Some values. A code. Vicious, yes. But unnecessarily, no. Mitch wasn't a Godfather.

He was an assassin.

Of course, the morning's events spread through the newsroom. Quickly. Like an arson fire. People were standing around in pockets. Whispering. Talking.

By noon, Perry called.

I briefed him. He said I sounded relieved. I guess I was. I made it through the rest of the day. Perry came over to spend the night. I fell asleep in his arms. It was the doorbell that woke us. Perry was the first to the door. He looked out. "Who is it?" I said sleepily.

Perry frowned.

"Some drunk white man looking for you," Perry said, kind of puzzled. It was Garth. "That's Garth. You met him at the NAACP dinner. WKBA bought a table, remember?"

Perry frowned again.

I opened the door. "Garth?" I said. He smiled weakly. Eyes glassy. Stance unsteady. He was blowed. Garth had on a trench coat. It hung crookedly on his shoulders. He had one hand in his pocket.

What's in his pocket?

Garth said, "It's late." I said, "That's okay. Please come in." Garth said, "No, Denise." He shook his pocket.

"Step back," Perry whispered in my ear. I was cautious. I knew

Garth had been humiliated. I knew he'd left angry. Garth drew his hand out of his pocket.

"This is for you."

He handed me an envelope. I took it. I said, "Garth, come in and sit down." Perry nudged me in the back. "No," Garth said. "I've got a cab waiting. That's a gift for you." Then Garth turned and walked away.

I looked at the envelope.

Perry shut the door. "I didn't know what he had in his pocket. Thought I was going to have to take old Garth out. Damn he's a wreck." I looked at Perry. "Don't you feel sorry for him, Perry? I do."

Perry stared at me.

"I'm sorry for him as a human being," Perry explained. "That's Christian compassion. But let's be real, Denise. Old Garth is still a white man in America. Someone else will give him a chance. Do you think they would send you to drug rehab twice and keep hiring you back in big money, power positions? It would have been over for me and you both long ago. Denise, the fat lady doesn't sing for the white boys. She won't even clear her throat."

The envelope.

I turned it over in my hands and I wondered, What could be inside?

Alex
Photographer/Technician

Damn, I got an SOS call.

"I need your help," that's what Denise said.

I was surprised when she called me in my unit too. That's tripped out because Denise usually never calls me in my unit. Even if the powers that fucking be are mad about something? Denise, she doesn't ring me in my unit. But Denise sounded like it was some serious stuff so I said, "What's the matter?"

"Stop by my office after the Post."

By her office? My homegirl was asking for a powwow in her teepee. It must be something very crucial for this to be going down. I only wished that I could videotape it.

"Shut the door," Denise said.

I did and sat down on the loveseat that was angled opposite her book shelf. I glanced up at copies of *The Wedding, Their Eyes Were Watching God, Family, Love Poems.* "So what's up, Denise?"

She was standing in front of her desk. Without looking, Denise reached behind her and grabbed an envelope. She handed it to me.

Look? I said with my eyes. Denise nodded. Inside the envelope were memos that the Godfather had sent to the Wizard—from the news director to the GM. "Hey!" I joked. "I might turn into a pillar of salt looking at all this top-secret shit."

"Okay," Denise said. "Return it."

"Are you crazy!" I said, snuggling the envelope against my chest. Then I started reading. Mitch wasn't the Godfather for nothing. He was laying out a paper trail to Corporate. He was documenting days when coverage blew up—shedding blame on the managers below him—all Kal Jimper's hires. The memos were directed to the same executive in Corporate. The Godfather also had made a list of all the producers and managers. Garth's name was there. Denise's too. He had written in pencil—*weak*—next to her name.

"Look at the third memo from the rear," Denise said.

It was a memo to the Wizard. It was regarding the problem with minority employees. The memo said that some black employees were unhappy about the lack of minority hires, promotions. He named me, Rock, and Denise as possible troublemakers. The Godfather claimed to have the situation under control and suggested that reprisals be used if a group surfaced. Took the taste right out of my mouth!

Denise said, "Now read the memo right behind that one."

This was a memo from the Wizard back to the Godfather. It said that he wanted the minority issue handled. It also admonished Mitch to temper his tactics because the negative press in the newspapers looked bad for the station. Corporate didn't like it. The Wizard said that he hated negative publicity and wanted it stopped now.

I swallowed hard. "Where'd you cop this?"

"I have sources."

"No shit. Who? James Bond?"

"Alex, this is serious. Mitch needs to be out of here. For the good of the station. For the good of the black employees here."

"Okay, what do we do, Denise?"

"Get him before he gets us."

"Shit yeah, but how?" I asked. Obviously Denise had all this thought out. Girlfriend had her game face on.

"That last memo validates what I've known for a while. The Wizard hates bad pub. He wants it stopped. Period. We've got to make Mitch explode."

"Why not just nuke his ass? We tell both of these lame mothers that we got this memo and sweat them," I said.

But Denise shook her head no. "The Wizard could deny the memo. He could get angry that we have it. He'd be determined to keep Mitch just to show 'us' who's boss. We have to get him to fire Mitch himself."

"How?"

"We make Mitch explode. The Wizard said no bad pub. We bait Mitch. He blows. Mitch makes the papers with a big nasty. The Wizard fires him."

"You've got a plan to take out the Godfather?" I asked her. "Let's hear it and make it good and foolproof, Denise."

Denise's eyebrows raised. "We can do this. Just you and me. But it must be between you and me. Too many mouths can spoil it. Blow it. You're in. I'm in. Simple."

"Show me the bomb, I'll light it! Give me the gun, I'll shoot it!" I said jokingly. Then I whispered, "Just tell me the plan. I'm with it."

"Here's the plan. You are suppose to go shoot an exclusive tomorrow. It's the governor's mansion. Correct?"

"Correct."

"The governor's press secretary is Mitch's pal. This is a give back. Free positive pub. It's down as a one-camera shoot."

"So?"

"So, Alex, you decide that you need another person. You want to do something fancy. Your back is bothering you. You've got to have help. I've checked the schedule. The only other person there will be Will."

"That guy is a screw-up!"

"Exactly. I'm going to tell Rod to get you another camera. Rod won't call in anyone else. He won't sign off on the OT."

"Yeah, but Rod knows that Will is a fuck-up."

"But Rod knows you hustle. You try to do it all yourself. Rod has seen you go the extra mile. This time, you don't. You let Will fuck it up."

"Let him?"

"Let him, Alex. I'm not asking you to throw the shoot. Let news take its course. Let Will screw it up. Mitch will lose his mind. He'll go ballistic. I'll make sure the newsroom is crowded. It'll get leaked."

"To the Wizard?"

"And to The Column. I don't know who the leaks are in the newsroom. But they're out there. What do you think, Alex?"

I looked at girlfriend, long and hard. "Two things. One: I didn't know you had it in you. Two: I hope I don't ever get on your shit list."

Holly
Reporter/Anchor

"*No.*" Beans turned me down flat, refusing to be the photog when I interviewed the Bucktown Slayer. What did I do? I went back to Alex and I begged shamelessly. She finally agreed to work the interview with me when I got it nailed down.

But it really didn't matter. *Everything blew up!* My exclusive with the Bucktown Slayer got killed a week later—and stolen three days after that.

I'd worked the phones constantly talking to Donovan Bailey—he was wavering because his attorney, Ian McNally, wouldn't green-light the interview.

I met with McNally at his office in a loft building in the new and trendy South Loop area. An ex-football player for Ohio State, he had a nose that hooked left after a failed quarterback sneak sophomore year against Michigan.

McNally snarled, "No TV interview. That would compromise all my efforts to keep my client from getting the death penalty. Donovan did not get this advice from me."

I tried to convince him of the merits of an exclusive television interview. But despite my heartiest efforts, I just couldn't convince him. Then Bailey himself called from jail and asked, "Can you get me a radio?"

No! Reporters do not "pay" for stories—that's giving money or buying gifts. It's unethical. The next day they both said, "No interview, period."

Two days of moping came to a head when Stu Ranger walked into the newsroom and said he had something to show me. Stu is a veteran reporter who has worked at two major networks, then was wooed away to WKBA after a big-money bidding war. He's the ace reporter. He's got the prance of a pedigree hound and the snarl of a junkyard dog.

Stu can talk the plug out of a microphone—he is just that long-winded. He's forty-three years old with an odd-shaped body neatly hidden by well-cut suits; short, powerful arms from his wrestling days poked out from a flat, limber torso. His hair and beard are the soft reddish color of fall leaves. Stu has three Emmys and enough confidence to launch a hot-air balloon on a solo mission to fly around the world.

"Holly," he said, "follow me." We went into an edit bay and shut the door. Stu popped a tape into the Sony machine and played it—there was Donovan Bailey sitting down *with him* doing an exclusive interview.

I wanted to wrap my hands around Stu's neck and choke him. I got up from my chair and slammed it to the floor. "You stole my exclusive!"

"I didn't steal it. I saved it for WKBA."

"That's a lie!"

"Holly, I watched you scuffle with this story but you were losing it. I found out that one of the reporters in Channel Five's investigative unit was about to make a move on it. Bottom line it was them or us. And I'm the best of us, so I got it."

"That's a lame excuse not worthy of you, Stu."

"Holly, why lie? Ask one of your friends at Channel Five to verify what I'm saying. They got a tip that Donovan Bailey wanted to talk and that he was haggling with a reporter. I'm trying to teach you something here."

"What's the lesson? How to gut a colleague?"

"Holly," Stu smiled, "an excellent reporter is teacher, therapist, thug, and theologian. I'm teaching you something here."

"If you wanted to teach me so badly, why not jump in and show me how to land the story myself?"

"Because, Holly, the thug side of me couldn't do the work and not reap the reward. TV news is not for reporters who lick a story slow; it's for reporters with teeth who are not afraid to bite down hard into the facts."

I rolled my eyes and looked at the tape playing that showed Stu interviewing Bailey. During a wide shot of the room I saw something sitting on the floor—*a radio.*

"Dammit, you bought this story, Stu!" I shouted, pointing at the radio.

The corners of his mouth turned down slightly. "I didn't buy Donovan Bailey that radio. No money exchanged hands and I didn't give it to him. One of the other prisoners *gave it to him* for some reason. The prisoner happens to be a client of an attorney I golf with."

"You're splitting hairs!"

"So fucking what? The impact of this interview—the coldness of this killer—will help keep him behind bars. It's worth it. Wait until you see this interview—there is no humanity in this man!"

"That's why I wanted this story, Stu! Our eye for what is the best and the worst in humanity is the yardstick by which our audience measures its villains, heroes, and itself."

"Spoken like a true journalist out to change the world. Now, Holly, answer this. 'How does the audience measure us?'"

"I think journalists are beginning to be both envied and despised just like lawyers."

"And why is that?" Stu asked, then answered. "It's because we are exposing what is real and sometimes ugly—facts that need to be known."

"I *still* can't believe you took this story from me, Stu! I can't believe you're that competitive!"

"You weren't *taken*, you were *beaten*. And as for my competitiveness? If people show you who they are, believe them."

Oh yes, I thought, you are certainly showing me.

"Listen, Holly," Stu said, changing his tone. "You're hustling and that's good. You're going to be an outstanding journalist in time."

"I need that story more than I need your faint praise, Stu. I'm fighting to win the respect of the other journalists out there. You just made it harder!"

"If I didn't respect you, Holly, we wouldn't be having this conversation. And you are respected in the newsroom—with your hustle and with your talent. Just keep getting better and don't let this experience make you bitter."

I finally gave up on the conversation and left. My anger swirled around in my body like a tornado. I thought, Okay, I got burned this time. But I'm going to take what I learned from Stu and get better.

Coming Up Next:

Conflict, Lies, and Videotape! The Godfather accuses
Denise of committing a cardinal newsroom sin. Will she lose
her job?

And:

Fed up: Their eyes are on the prize! Members of the
black employees' network try to put the squeeze on The
Wizard.

Plus:

Prejudice percolates at WKBA. Dragon Diva questions the
motives of "BEN." Where does Beans stand?

Stay   tuned.

Beans

Photographer/Technician

"Hey, Beans, did you read The Column today?"

I must have heard that, oh, from about three or four different people today. I was leaving the parking lot, walking over to the station. I needed to check my schedule. I was hoping the OT dry spell was over, I needed to save more money to give to Boardwalk for my investments.

While bumming around in the newsroom, I looked to hunt up a copy of The Column. I wanted to see what the latest buzz was about. A group of visitors was being given a tour of the newsroom, which is a common although sometimes annoying thing. Who wants people staring at you, looking over your shoulder while you work? Touring groups ranged from school children to the sales people bringing in clients to meet their favorite news personality.

One writer, a veteran in his twentieth year at WKBA, didn't take kindly to the fish bowl feeling he was getting as the crowd opening gawked and oohhh and ahhed. He jumped up out of his chair as they approached him, pulled out a roll of yellow and black police crime tape, draped it across the back of his chair, and tossed it across the aisle like a roadblock. Then he barked in a cop-sounding voice, "Move along. Move along. There's nothing to see here! Move along!"

We all laughed, at his quirky wit, and at the look on the faces of our guests, who made a quick exit. I went toward Denise's office, stuck my head in. She gave me a forced smile, a smile that hardly turned up the corners of her mouth and I asked her, "What's the buzz, Denise?"

She pushed the newspaper across the desk, it teetered on the edge, and that was the bait. I was lured inside her office. I shut the door. Then I sat down. The paper seemed to open itself in my hands, just fall open, where it had been bent back and creased by concerned hands and the weight of the impact.

The headline read: "WKBA NEWS DIRECTOR GOES BERSERK!"

Denise said to me, "It's all there, Beans. Mitch's ranting. His raving. The Springfield shoot with the governor? Disaster. They had to buy extra satellite time. Pay double because the crew didn't have the package ready. When it was ready, the video was blue."

"So as The Column says, it was ugly, the Godfather went crazy, huh?"

"Beans, Mitch exploded. He cursed. He threatened everyone. The Column has it all. It quotes one source as saying that newsroom staffers want the GM to fire Mitch. They hate Mitch's mean antics."

Oh boy, I thought, as I read along with Denise's comments about The Column. Right there, in the middle of the article, I spotted her name. I hoped, and prayed, that Denise didn't get slammed and I read on.

The Column said, "WKBA's ratings continue to slide under management's heavy-handed approach. The only top management figure who seems to be holding her own is managing editor Denise Mitzler. She is a candidate for assistant news director, a spot which has remained unfilled for several months. Insiders say Mitzler is hardworking and has a cool head amid the chaos."

"Hooray for you!" I said. "Whoa, way to dodge a bullet."

Denise smiled. "Yeah. The Column is right about the ratings though. They're falling. If only I could get a shot at the top spot. I could fix this place. I could win the ratings war."

There hadn't been a female, or black for that matter, news director or assistant news director in WKBA's history. The odds for Denise, at least according to the buzz, were slim even though she was well respected. "Maybe they'll ax Mitch, huh, Denise? I could get an office pool started."

That made us both laugh because there was always a pool going on for something, whether for the Super Bowl, or for the time and birth date of the latest forthcoming newsroom baby.

The phone buzzed on Denise's desk, she listened, then she frowned and said, "Sure." Denise hung up the phone, looking concerned, and I asked her if everything was okay. She said, "Yes, I've got to run. I'll talk to you later. Thanks for the laugh."

There was a puzzled look on her face; she tried not to show it, but Denise seemed tense. I trailed Denise out of the office, but I didn't follow. I went my way, and Denise went her way, straight toward Mitch's office.

DENISE

MANAGING EDITOR/ACTING ASSISTANT NEWS DIRECTOR

I'm the leak.

That's what Mitch thinks. I walked into his office. He was pacing. Sweating. He looked at me with angry eyes.

Tension.

"Did you read it?" Mitch asked. Of course. He *knows* I read it. "I'm sick and tired of everything in this newsroom landing in the newspaper! I'm fighting to save a sinking ship. But the captain gets no respect. I want this back-stabbing to fucking stop, Denise."

Why tell me? My job is to get news on the air. Help pick stories. PR? That's the communications officer's job. I set Mitch up. But I wasn't the leak.

"Denise, you never get slammed."

My eyebrows curled upward. A vile sensation erupted inside my chest. It scalded my throat. My left ear twitched. "Mitch," I said, "when the station looks bad, we all look bad. We all have to work together. That's the only way WKBA will be number one."

That's how I felt.

"Don't give me that bullshit, Denise. My head gets lopped off first. The buck stops here. You never get slammed. Now you're even getting kudos!"

"Make it plain, Mitch."

"You're no idiot."

"Spit it out, Mitch."

"You're the leak," he said. "I feel it in my gut and I'm going to make it my business to see you canned."

I held my breath, my gaze.

"That would be fine if your gut was enough proof," I said coldly. "But it's not. The fact is I'm not the leak. I resent you accusing me of it. I'm a team player. I'm not stupid enough to jeopardize my career to drop my pet peeves into a daily column."

I waited, he blinked.

"What the hell, Denise? Does the FBI work for The Column? One of your friends may be leaking shit, I don't know . . . but there's an *inside inside* leak and if I *ever* find out who it is, they are out of here on their ass and I mean spinning like a top!" Mitch scrunched a script in his hand.

I played the game.

"And that's what should happen to the leak," I said. "*Whoever* it is. They're disloyal. Destructive. Those are two things I have never been. Never will be."

Mitch swallowed.

"What time are we going tonight?" he finally asked me. Tonight? It didn't register with me. I'd forgotten. "Excuse me?" I said.

"Tonight!" Mitch growled.

Then I realized. He, I, and the Wizard had to go to the monthly meeting of the Chicago Association of Black Journalists. They were having a speakers' series on how news decisions are made. We were the panel.

High profile.

"It's at seven P.M., Mitch. I'll meet you there." Then I left. A new opportunity presented itself. We had a weekend producer slot open. Last month I asked Mitch about putting it in the black journalists' newsletter. He had said, "Go ahead and put it in, but I'm looking for a qualified candidate."

Excuse me?

I didn't say a word at the time. But I'd wanted to smack Mitch. Insulting. Irritating. Of course, what else would a black candidate be? We're always qualified. Sometimes overqualified.

Okay.

I went back out in the newsroom. The day flew by. Then I went to the NBC Tower on Columbus Drive. It was ten minutes before the meeting started. I didn't want to see Mitch any longer than required. Or the Wizard either.

Mitch spotted me.

He hitched himself to my side. Was this the man who had insulted me earlier? What was his problem? Discomfort. "There are a lot of people here," Mitch said.

Yeah, *black* people.

Now he, Mitch, was the minority. I turned left. He went left. I turned right. Mitch went right. I said over my shoulder, "I'm going to mingle."

He said, "I'm with you."

Oh, I see. Suddenly, I'm okay again. This was silly. How often am I the only black person at a management meeting? How often was I the only black person in my college classes? I don't shrink. I don't cling. I cope.

Panel time.

It was held in the studio where the *Jenny Jones* show is taped. The Wizard arrived. We sat behind a long table on stage. There were two hundred people in the audience. Journalists. Students. Public relations executives. The CABJ president introduced us. We talked a couple of minutes about ourselves. Education. Career.

We took questions.

Then I set the trap. I mentioned the weekend producer job. I noted that it was in the newsletter. I turned to Mitch, smiled. On cue. He bit. Mitch said into the mike, "Yes, I'm looking for a qualified candidate and . . ."

Hiss–sssss!

Qualified candidate. Yes, Mitch was naive enough to say it again. The audience gurgled like a volcano. A man stood and said, "Qualified?" If you challenge him . . .

He will blow.

Mitch said, "Yes, a qualified candidate we—" Someone else shouted, "What else would you be looking for *but* a qualified candidate?" Mitch's brow twitched. "Excuse me?"

Dense.

They *made* Mitch get it. "You," a young woman who looked like a student said, "are assuming we are not qualified. To preference it with 'qualified' assumes that we are not." Someone shouted, "You wouldn't tell a group of white journalists that you were looking for a qualified candidate."

Mitch got angry.

The Wizard was quiet, watching. Mitch looked at me for help. I offered none. It got worse. Mitch said, "*You people* are making something out of nothing." *How insulting!* The audience went wild. And in that audience were journalists from every major media outlet in town. Before the meeting, members ate pizza. Mitch was dessert. Then.

And later. In the press.

The Column was on it. The *Chicago Sun-Times*. The *Chicago Tribune*. The *Chicago Defender*. The *Southtown Economist*. The black radio stations—V-103, GCI, VON—they railed against WKBA. Then BEN went into action. They demanded a meeting. A meeting with the Wizard.

KENYA
Writer/Producer

"Do you want this to be another Texaco?" Rock shouted at the Wizard.

We were all smashed up together in the GM's office. I had never been in here before. It had a breathtakin' view of Lake Michigan and there was a conference room off to the side. Through the door, I could see a big-screen television and a bar with tall bottles of liquor lined across the top.

The Wizard had offered to have this meetin' in his office conference room but Rock had said no. He said no because he wanted the group to be uncomfortable just like we were every day at work. The Wizard sho' nuff bucked his eyes then, and after that Texaco comment, he turned white as cotton.

Alex spoke up next. "BEN was formed because we have major problems here at WKBA that must be addressed. We, as black employees, are feeling overworked, mistreated, and passed over despite having seniority, industry accolades, and strong work records. We want changes now."

Rock pulled out a folder that was about a quarter of an inch thick, and tossed it on the Wizard's desk. "That's documentation of racial incidents at this station. There is a history here! Do I look like a jelly bean to you?"

The Wizard never let his eyes drop. He kept lookin' at Rock. "If there are complaints in that file that are valid—"

"They are valid!" a black director shouted.

". . . then they did not happen on my watch."

"Bullshit!" one of the black cameramen yelled out.

The Wizard looked at Alex. "I thought this was a meeting not an ambush."

Alex looked 'round at all of us. Quiet commenced to settle 'round the room. Then she said, "We're here to talk, but we're not here to listen to a bunch of excuses. Mitch has not only run a reign of terror . . ."

Rock said, "And we do mean *terror!*"

Alex kept talkin'. ". . . he has also embarrassed every black person who works here with the racist remarks he made at the Chicago Association of Black Journalists meeting. Mitch—"

"Mitch Saleen no longer works here," the Wizard said. "His office is being cleaned out as we speak."

I gasped. Somebody else gasped. Two or three other folk just flat out cheered.

The Wizard was cool as homemade ice cream. He let the commotion die down then he said, "That was a decision made independent of your group. That's why I fired him before this meeting. I didn't want it misconstrued that I was forced into anything or backed into a corner by one or more employees."

Rock sniffed hard, twice.

"Mitch had to leave WKBA," the Wizard continued, "because he generated too much negative publicity. . . ."

I thought to myself, it's okay to run a station into the ground, but don't embarrass the company or you're out on your tail.

". . . I have a short list of candidates. I plan to fill his job swiftly."

"Hire a black news director!" someone shouted.

"There are black candidates on my short list . . ."

"Who?" Rock asked.

"I'm not going to give you that information," the Wizard snapped then. "But I will consider more than just race as a factor to hire the person for the job. WKBA has to get its ratings up."

"Is it true that the company is shopping the network to sell?" one of the salesmen asked.

"That's possible. The communication industry as a whole is an eight-hundred-sixty-six-billion-dollar-a-year business. You've all seen the sales that have reshaped the broadcast arena: Westinghouse buying CBS, Disney buying Cap Cities/ABC, and so on."

"We don't care who owns this place," Alex said. "We just want to be treated fairly. How would you feel if you were mistreated? Black workers have the same goals, ideas, and intelligence as our white coworkers. We want good shifts, plum assignments, promotions, and a positive work environment, just like everyone else. Treat us like you would want to be treated."

"That's always been my way," the Wizard said.

"Then prove it," Alex said. "Look at the documentation. In that folder that you still haven't picked up, right inside there is proof. There are WKBA employees who have publicly used abusive racial slurs."

"I don't have any knowledge of that," the Wizard said.

"We're providing you with knowledge, but you don't want to get the point!" Rock pleaded.

"I promise that I will look at the information in the folder," the Wizard said, pickin' it up. "But right now my plan is to hire a news director in the next few weeks. Then I'll review the contents of this folder, and schedule a follow-up meeting."

"We are not playing games here," Rock said, levelin' his eyes and turnin' his body squarely toward the Wizard.

"In a few weeks, we'll meet again. That's fair. And isn't that what you have been complaining about today? Fairness? I need some time. I'll meet with the members of BEN soon. Then I will address your problems. Agreed?"

We agreed.

Beans

```
Photographer/Technician
```

"So the Negroes got restless!" Hazel said, stopping me in the news-room. "Beans, I know you heard that the blacks got a group together and had a meeting with the GM. The rumor has it they got Mitch fired. I also heard that they want the next five jobs filled with blacks! Nerve, huh?"

"Hazel, I heard that Mitch was on shaky ground anyway because of the way he flew off the handle, and because of the ratings. So that was why he was fired."

"Are you kidding me, Beans?" Hazel said with a grand gesture of the hands. "The ratings were wrecked when Mitch got here. Mitch was putting the fear of God in some of these *union* veterans around here—present company excluded—who are too lazy or too stubborn to change. The blacks got Mitch fired and every white person in this shop should take note."

I hunched my shoulders, Hazel was pissed.

"Beans, don't you see? Next thing you know this group—BEN—will be deciding what the anchor teams are or what our budget should be. For God's sakes—power doesn't belong in just anyone's hands. It's purely bullshit. Reverse racism bullshit. And Alex is one of the ring leaders, I hear. I've never liked her. And you can bet your sweet ass that Holly was in there angling for my position."

"How do you know who was in the meeting?" I asked Hazel, "and what really went on?"

"They've been walking around talking about it all week. Acting very proud of causing a man to lose his job for no good reason. I mean what was wrong with saying he was looking for a qualified candidate? Mitch didn't mean anything racial by it. And *'you people'*? At what juncture in time did that become derogatory? It's a shame how they made something out of nothing. I haven't seen them this happy since OJ got off."

"Think about it," I said. "Every black person doesn't think OJ is innocent."

"Whose side are you on, Beans?"

"Why are there sides, and who is drawing them up, and why are you trying to get my back up, Hazel?"

"I'm just warning you. I'm going to be careful. I know Holly is sitting her black ass in that meeting scheming to steal my anchor spot. I've worked too hard and too long to give it up without a battle."

"Hazel—"

"Beans, we all work here and want the best. The black employees are no different than anyone else. In fact, they get more leeway if you ask me. I mean what do the blacks around here have to complain about? They've made tremendous strides! What's worse for them than anyone else, huh?"

I let the conversation drop, mostly because Hazel can be very vicious sometimes, and I hated to admit it, but she had made one point. WKBA has big problems, mostly ratings, and it's a problem for everyone and not just the black people. A group like BEN, it will only isolate the employees from one another.

I decided to ask Holly about what was going on, I liked her, and I felt Holly would give me a straight answer. I knew that I couldn't ask Alex, couldn't break our promise again about never discussing race, so I went to Holly.

"I'm curious, Holly. What's the deal with the black employees, you guys have gotten a group together?"

"We decided that there were issues that needed to be addressed," Holly explained. "Instead of going at it one on one, we decided to address the issues as a group."

"Holly, some of the other people in the newsroom, they're getting some wild ideas about the group."

"Are you one of them?"

"No, but don't get pissed off or anything, Holly, I wanna tell you my gut feeling here."

"Beans, this is between you and me. Go ahead."

"Holly, I don't think the group is a good idea; it will cause division among the staff. The black workers here, you guys are in the same boat with the rest of us. The ratings are low, and all our jobs are on the line. We each get the same benefits, and management treats all the workers here like cogs in a money-making machine—we've got to stick together."

Holly looked at me. "I do have more problems than my white counterparts here, Beans. Do I get to cover the stories like a local church group traveling to Paris or the NCAA finals or the President when he's here in Chicago. No, I don't get the big stories or the great free trips. I get what's left."

Holly was wrong, and I told her so, despite the fact that I knew she wasn't going to like it. "Holly, broadcasting is a news business, and a dues business; you've got to pay dues."

"But why are my dues higher, Beans? I don't get the same kinds of contracts or perks or opportunities as my white counterparts. And as a black woman I catch it double—have you ever heard of the black female tax? Do you think this station would pay me the same amount of money as Dragon Diva, Kirstin, or Stu?"

Holly had it rough coming in with Kal Jimper leaving, but it was not racial, it was just broadcasting. "Holly, I'll admit, there are some problems here because of the lame decisions that management makes. But BEN indicts everyone, and what makes you think that's fair?"

"Beans, are you saying you can't see the racism—"

"Wait, Holly, I'm not saying that there isn't racism in the world. Don't get me wrong; as a whole, blacks have made great strides in our country, and in our business. The black workers here, you guys should be real, don't act like no ground has been covered at all. I mean I can understand why someone like Alex, who grew up poor like myself, may be upset, but, Holly, you've—"

"I've what?" she said.

"Your entire family went to college, and are mostly doctors to boot. You've had opportunities I never had—"

"So you're saying, What do I have to complain about?"

"Holly, my brothers and me, we were too poor to go to college. We didn't have the money, or the opportunity you had, despite race, that's all I'm saying."

"Beans, I know that I am upper middle class but it was a struggle for my parents to get there. Both my mother and father are the first in their families to graduate from college. They had to work through school to balance out their scholarships."

"I'm not downing—"

"Wait, Beans, let me finish. My father went to an integrated med school. Do you know what that was like for him way back in the late fifties? He was the only black man in his courses. Daddy had to sit on a separate side of the room. He was called all sorts of racial slurs. And my mother, God bless her soul, it was three years before my mother got her first engineering job despite placing fifth in her master's class. But it was 1962. They both had to scuffle and fight for what others feel entitled to by birthright. But funny how, when it's achieved by us, it all of a sudden becomes a privilege. We have what we have because of our blood, sweat, and tears, and that of our ancestors too. We got what we *strived* for, Beans, and not a gift or stitch more."

Her words hurt me, and I said, "Holly, that's not what I meant and you're taking it way too harshly. I didn't say it was easy, or has ever been easy to be black in America, but don't assume that every white person has a leg up and is eating grapes and caviar at the expense of your race. We are not all ignorant of the past, and most of us want a change, here and now. I still say that great strides have been made, and more needs to be done for minorities including women, but united we stand and divided we will fall. Don't make enemies, or problems for that matter, where there aren't any."

"Beans," Holly said, "this is something that we just aren't going to agree on."

"Right, so can we drop it now, and let's just agree to disagree?"

"Fine with me," Holly said.

I stuck out my hand. "Still friends?"

Then with a wry smile, Holly shook my hand.

DENISE

MANAGING EDITOR/ACTING ASSISTANT NEWS DIRECTOR

I want *the job.*

I'm managing editor now. I'm acting assistant news director. I've been doing two jobs. I deserve the news director job.

I should go for it.

With Mitch fired, I had to run the newsroom. I couldn't go to the GM's meeting with BEN. I heard about what happened. A mole told me. The Wizard said he had black candidates on his short list. I asked him in the hallway.

Am I a candidate?

He said yes. My heart started to beat. I knew better than to tip my hand. So quickly, I nodded assuredly; of course, I thought to myself, I'm a candidate.

The interview.

I set up the interview with the Wizard's secretary for two days later. I wasn't nervous. I was excited. Perry was excited too. "You're going to get it," he said, hugging me. "How can he not give it to you?"

I felt good.

In the interview the Wizard asked me about our news coverage. Specifics. The Wizard smiled. He looked impressed with my assessments. The Wizard asked, "If there was a change you could make to our early coverage, what would it be?"

I told him.

I told the Wizard that we had strong lead-ins from 2 P.M. till 3 P.M. But from 3 P.M. to 4:30 P.M. it's weak. Every day there's a ratings drop. Serious drop-off. That happens *before* our first afternoon newscast at four-thirty.

I told him.

"Sell commercial time to businesses during the weak hour and a half. We'll lose a little revenue. During the boom hour, 2 P.M. to 3 P.M., fill the commercial breaks with nothing but promos. Cut clips from the 10 P.M. newscast the night before. Brag how we brought the big story into their living room."

Build.

I said, "That'll draw more viewers in. That aggressive promotion will work. We haven't been aggressive enough."

Good idea.

That's what the Wizard said. Then I was rolling. I was smoking the interview. Then the Wizard asked me. He said, "Did you know the black employees were starting a group?"

I was ready.

"I knew that some employees were unhappy," I said. "I knew that there were issues. Racial incidents. I did what I could to diffuse some situations. I did not know that an official group was being organized."

He tripped.

The Wizard said, "You didn't tell me the blacks were unhappy." I said, "Mitch was aware." The Wizard said, "But *you* didn't make *me* aware. Didn't you feel that you could come to me with that information?"

What?

"Mitch was aware and he said that he was addressing it," I said. How the hell could I go to him with that? And surely he knew. The Wizard knew. I had the memos—the clandestine ones. The ones that Garth gave me. I asked him as if I didn't know, "Weren't you aware?"

The Wizard didn't bite.

"The point is, Denise, you have to trust me as the leader of this station. As part of the management team, you have to come to me with critical information like that, *even* if you think I already know or someone else is handling it."

Bull.

"Denise, I have to have someone in the news director spot whom I can trust. I have to trust that that person will always put WKBA, the news product, and our management team first."

Oh no.

The Wizard wasn't going to give me the job. I could see it in his eyes. I heard it as he talked more. I'm invaluable in the newsroom. I'm respected by the staff. My news judgment is strong. I'm getting a big Christmas bonus.

I went home.

Perry blew up. "Sue those MF's!" I looked at Perry and shook my head. "How?" I said. "If I sue they'll blackball me. I'll never work in broadcast news again. I won't be able to find a job in television." Perry thought and said . . .

"New gig?"

"Management jobs are scarce. Especially for blacks in broadcasting. It's better than it's been, but it's hit and miss."

Perry said . . . "Lean on them.

"Denise," he explained, "when he hires a white man for that spot you got him and WKBA by the nuts. Go in and work 'em. I'll bet they'll give you the job that you're subbing in *plus* double that bonus. Then you get in writing that the top spot is yours when this latest hire fails."

I hugged Perry.

"The Wizard is about to hire one of his good old buddies, Perry. I'll call him on it. BEN, I'm sure, will call him on it. Right now, I have only one choice."

Wait.

Beans

Photographer/Technician

The techs bought pizza, one of the writers baked a sheet cake, and one of the anchors popped big bucks for a case of champagne, that's how happy everyone was that the Godfather got taken out.

It was 10:30 P.M., Friday night, and the last show had finished, fine, no problems. Word of mouth spread that a little party would be held, be there or be square, at the end of the day. Someone—I don't know who, but it seemed like a Rod idea—someone found Mitch's photo ID, Xeroxed it, and posted it on the door. Beneath Mitch's picture was the handwritten line, UNEMPLOYED—CAPTIONS PLEASE, and people wrote:

*RÉSUMÉ: PENNY PINCHER, NO NEWS JUDGMENT BUT WILL-ING TO KISS NY MANAGEMENT'S ASS.

*NEED A HATCHET MAN? BRINGS OWN AX BUT DOESN'T CLEAN UP OWN MESS.

*BOAT CAPTAIN. CAN'T STEER BUT KNOWS HOW TO BAIL. LAST SHIP SANK: KBA CHICAGO. ANCESTORS AT THE HELM OF THE *TITANIC*.

I saw Denise out of the corner of my eye; she was hanging around the back hallway. She was smiling at the juicy proceeding, but clearly Denise was not going to venture in to take part even though several of us waved for her to come over. But Denise waved good-bye, briefcase in hand, and left through the side door.

Rod screamed, "Where is that fax?"

One of the anchors said that he had been up in the Wizard's office, had actually seen a draft of the letter naming the new boss. His name was Xavier Helston, he was coming from Cincinnati, and he was to start right after New Year's. Rod found out what station he worked at, then he called there. Rod explained the game we played, then he faxed over his infamous sheet—the one about movies—and now we were all waiting.

Suddenly the fax machine gurgled, and I guzzled the last of the champagne in my glass. I crowded around the fax machine with everyone else smelling of bubbly, pepperoni, and strawberry icing.

Rod began reading the fax. "What movie . . . *Glory!*"

"*Glory?*" someone said. "That's that Civil War flick with Matthew Broderick."

"And Denzel," Holly said.

"He won an Oscar for best supporting actor," Alex spoke up—the resident movie historian—"that scene where Denzel cried when he was beaten for going to look for shoes was powerful."

"Matthew Broderick's character was a good guy. Maybe we're going to get a decent boss in here for a change!" one of the production assistants cheered.

"Ssssh!!!!" the crowd quieted, Rod began reading the next line of the game.

"What character? Mr. Rollins."

"Who???" rose a mix of quite tipsy voices.

Alex said, "That's Morgan Freeman's character. He's the brother who was a leader among the men. They made him an uncommissioned officer."

"That explains this next part," Rod laughed. "Best line: 'I ain't sure I'm wantin' this job, Colonel.' "

Alex
Photographer/Technician

Damn, Denise didn't get the job. I thought the sister was going to get it. The Wizard passed right over her. But at least he hired a brother. What can she say? What can BEN say? Not jack. I've been in TV news for damn near twenty years and I've never, ever had a black boss. Never. America the Beautiful, with its spacious skies, has little space in its executive suites for people of color.

Hang on, baby, and pah-lease squeeze me tight and do not get me wrong. I am not an ex-patriot like my grandfather. He fought in World War II, won a bronze star, and returned home to Virginia only to be picked on by redneck stooges who made him the main attraction in a circus of terror for being "uppity." Granddaddy decided after fighting overseas for *liberty* and then at home for *life* that he should retire. Granddaddy proceeded to have a sit-down and, besides odd jobs, never made an effort to fight with anything besides the whiskey still he kept percolating in the backyard.

I love my country but there is a lot of screwed-up stuff going on here. Racism. Sexism. Reckless capitalism. Most of the ideas that get planted in people's heads come from two sources: environment and media—television and movies.

Edison started some shit, didn't he? Images, man, pictures can translate emotion like nothing else. Do you hear me? I mean you can read a book and start to cry at an emotional passage. But if you *see and hear* something on television or in the movies that makes you cry, that image is burned into your memory and can be replayed in flashbacks and dreams.

Human beings have minds that are visually absorbent, soaking up and spilling stuff over. I'm telling you, man, that's why what we do in television news is so damn important. Our images and words shape the thinking of America. And how you think directly affects how you act or act up.

If your managers are WASPS, suburban, and upper class, that could be all they know. If that's all they know, then, hell, that's all they will gravitate toward. Like wants like. Your news coverage will reflect that. What they don't understand is that your stories have to reflect the diversity of the audience. News just like your damn newsroom should have diversity.

But you start getting pigeonholed. They have to put minorities on-air so that there are faces out there front and center—but, shit, there's not enough of us making the call from the coach's seat. Al'right, I'm trying to be understood here. Am I making sense?

Check it out. There has *never* been a black president of a network news division ever. Not at CBS. NBC. ABC. Never in the history of America. There are black White House cabinet members. There are black astronauts. There has even been a black governor of my granddaddy's Virginia.

But TV news? Broadcasting? The barrier is still in good-goddamn shape like some steel ribbon waiting to be broken with a brain thrust and lean; a win that would represent a new standard of mental and visual competition.

I feel like my World War II vet granddaddy, who used to sip whiskey and say, "I'll stop drinkin' hooch when a colored man is sittin' in the governor's mansion in Virginia." Shiiit! When I told him about Doug Wilder, Granddaddy said, "Well, I can't stop drinkin' now. Where's the party? I gotta celebrate, don't I?"

I definitely understand how Granddaddy was drunk with the inability of the world to change; then he was drunk with the realization of change. That's how I feel now, kindah freaked out and giddy, wow, we're going to have a black news director at WKBA! It's not like being head of the entire network news division, *the big gig*, but it's a rung on the ladder. In a newsroom ruled by race, the color of power is about to change.

Maybe that will mean some positive changes? Hey-hey, *maybe*.

Coming Up Next:

Crossroads or Crossfire? Holly is determined to negotiate herself a better contract. But first she needs inside information to do it.

And:

"Won't *Glory* be the Black Messiah?" Who says this to Alex and can they back it up? Let the verbal joust begin!

Plus:

Kenya starts to feel more pressure as work begins to interfere with her family life.

There's more **This Just In . . .**
straight ahead.

Holly
Reporter/Anchor

Why is it every time there is a story in the projects, or a poor black neighborhood, they try to search out and send a black reporter and crew first?

There's a drive-by shooting with several wounded.

Search out and send a black person.

There's a community meeting to protest shoddy maintenance in Chicago Housing Authority high-rises.

Search out and send a black person.

Am I just paranoid because I've been working so hard, trying so desperately to prove myself? But the stories that I keep getting are what we call "cheap." Stories that need to be covered but that would either be low profile in the newscast and in danger of getting killed *or* top stories that are stereotypical crime blotter stuff.

"You're on ghetto patrol," Mack Richardson said, laughing at me while turning to The Column. "Wait, Holly, let me check The Column to make sure I still work here! That's how one reporter found out he was fired—in the paper. This business is so cold they could sell Popsicles!"

Mack Richardson is a black reporter who has been at WKBA for almost fifteen years. He is fifty years old but looks more like he's thirty. Mack is wiry yet Harlem Globetrotter tall. He's as smooth as a ballet dancer. His hair is groomed well enough to be featured in a Soft Sheen hair ad. Mack has lover eyes, brown as oyster gravy, and he has the longest lashes I've ever seen on any man.

Mack is smart too: Phi Beta Kappa from Northwestern. Mack also has a karaoke voice; one that is limber and can be manipulated to imitate almost anyone. When the story calls for a timber of seriousness or a hint of giggle in the voice, Mack can deliver. He's complimented me on my voice because I have a similar gift, though not as rich as his.

Now Mack was comforting me, purring, "Which project is next?

Robert Taylor. Cabrini Green. Harold Ickes. Have I named a housing project you haven't been in yet?"

"Mack, it's frustrating! How can I show the producers, the executive producers, Denise, and this new boss coming in that I have skills if I don't get good stories?"

Mack touched the sterling cuff links that dotted his French vanilla shirt. "I had the same problem when I started here years ago. They wouldn't give me a story with teeth in it. The most disturbing element of that shitty fact is that in TV news you're only as good as the stories that get on air. Your rep in here, and on the street, hangs in that balance."

I shrugged my shoulders in agreement.

"Holly, why don't you go over there and demand that Stat give you a shot at a big story?"

"Do you really think that'll work?"

"Never worked for me, but might work for you," Mack said with a cloaked laugh.

"Mack!"

"Look, Holly, I stopped letting these people worry me a very long time ago. I've got a wife to support and a daughter in college. I've got years of experience. I've nothing to prove and every reason to get paid. I've taken enough shit off management over the years for you, me, and any other black reporter they would have a mind to bring into the fold. TV news is a hard plantation to work. But maybe there's some hope."

"What, Mack?"

"Well, this new brother is coming in. Xavier Helston. Everyone's calling him *Glory*. Maybe he might do something for you. The Wizard might listen to his house Negro and take a little pity on one of his field hands. What's to lose?"

The idea sounded excellent to me. Mitch and his Godfather reign were over. Maybe new blood could mean new life for me.

"Holly!" Rod yelled across the newsroom from the assignment desk. "Got a breaking story at the Crieger Homes. A little kid fell out of a window! Beans will shoot it—she'll be rolling up out front any second."

I looked at Mack, Mack looked at me, and we both looked over at Kirstin. Then we both looked over at Stu Ranger. Kirstin was china and got the easy stories. Stu was top dog and only got the big stories. Neither of them ever got the project stories.

Mack egged me on. "It's now or never!"

I got up and marched to the assignment desk and confronted Rod. "I've been running all day. Stu is sitting over there reading the paper. Send him on the breaker."

Rod's snappy wit vanished as he asked seriously, "If you were poor and black, living in the Crieger Homes, and your kid fell out of a window would you want to talk to Waspy Stu Ranger?"

"Rod, that's not the point! You guys never—"

"Okay! I'll send Mack—"

"No!" I shouted.

"I can't send Kirstin," Rod said, rolling his eyes.

Then I whispered, "Stu. Send Stu."

"I don't want to fight with him—I can't fucking win. *C'mon, Holly.* Don't I look out for you whenever I can?"

He did. So, I yanked up my purse, my pad, got my crew, and hightailed it to the location at the Crieger Homes. Little did I know that details were emerging that would make this *some* story.

Beans

Photographer/Technician

Who in the hell invented the stock market, that's what I want to know. It goes up and down without warning, like a kid with a straw playing with a soda. I bought Technogram at thirty-two dollars a share, it shot up to fifty-two dollars in two weeks, then dropped fifteen dollars two days later.

The stocks go up, and they go down, and you don't know when to sell and buy something else. I watch and Boardwalk, she watches. I'm reading everything I can get my hands on, and each time I get tired of looking, I think. I think about carrying forty pounds worth of equipment, standing for hours in subzero temperatures, the grind of it all. I think about my knees that ache, without warning, because I stood in flooded basements along the Des Plaines River.

Every time I think about chucking my idea of having my own thing, my own place and space, I keep on. I keep on reading, researching, playing the market, but most of all hoping. My two-way radio, I keep it cranked up high, I hear Rod giving me a 9-1-1.

Breaker . . . Unit 2 . . . Breaker . . . Call in for details.

I grabbed my car phone, dialed up Rod, and said, "What's going on?"

He gave me marching orders, pick up Holly, roll to the Crieger Homes, a kid fell out a window.

Holly
Reporter/Anchor

With the small steps of a child I made my way up the dark stairwell where it all happened. Each step I took was slow and the rim of my toes mashed against the minced pieces of concrete that took me one rung higher to the crime scene. I knew that these were the very steps that the little girl had marched up, though her climb had been taken in Minnie Mouse sneakers with more speed and considerable more naiveté. Her name was Ramona.

Ramona had been promised candy by the friends of her older sister.

The same older sister who could not save her. She had not been there to tell Ramona not to be so trusting. After living in this harsh world of public housing, wouldn't Ramona's senses tip her off? Why would I think that? Why would I suspect that a six-year-old girl would think that two ten-year-old neighbors would push her out a third-story window?

This urban wasteland I suddenly found myself in had grown its own wild herbal smell of musk, urine, and stale food. The smell choked me until I reached the third-story landing. Once there I could breathe sufficiently enough to report on this tragic story.

Ramona was playing in the sandlot of the project. She was waiting for her big sister, Joni, age nine, to come home after being bused to a gifted academy. Ramona was slow. Joni was brilliant. Some of the other girls, pals of Joni's who went to school in the neighborhood, thought their smart friend had begun to think *she was something*. Jealousy knows no age, race, or status. This was my thought as I reached the vacant apartment as open as a mouth with a cry left on its lips.

There was a tight ball of crime tape tossed in the corner of the front room. It lay among a dozen or so flattened tin saucers that once held malt liquor. Insiders had already come to look in shame while outsiders, like Beans and me, came to gather the story. I imagine that we could all spend half a lifetime here and truly never make sense of it all.

The window was open. Beans dropped to her knees and crawled her way across the floor, getting a shot that would be similar to Ramona's perspective.

I felt the wind come through the window and it chilled the tears that puddled in the corners of my eyes. I looked down out of the window and saw spots of blood and the indentation left by a crooked leg in the muddy patch where grass would grow later in summer time.

I wrote and I wrote in my notepad, deeply feeling this story. I had already interviewed the police, neighbors of the two juvenile suspects, Ramona's mother, and with the family's permission, her sister Joni. I wrote and I wrote. I felt and I felt. In the whistling wind, I heard this little girl's scream.

The ten-year-olds said that Ramona climbed out onto the windowsill herself, answering a dare that would win her a bag of grape lollipops with pink bubble gum inside. It was when Ramona looked down, got frightened, and grabbed them that she fell. They told the police that Ramona was too far out on the ledge; that she had already lost balance. Ramona, the children said, had grabbed them and was pulling them down too. They swore they had to push Ramona's hands away to save themselves. And that's when she fell.

Nine-year-old Joni saw it. She had just gotten off the bus with the nervous driver who consistently pulled away before Joni reached her doorway. The dust spinning off the rear wheels of the bus got caught in Joni's throat. She coughed, turned her head, and looked up.

It was then that Joni saw the big red "R" and "L" on the bottoms of the dangling feet. She had written the letters to help her little sister learn how to put her shoes on correctly. It was then that Joni ran. She dropped her books and galloped up the stairwell. Joni saw her little sister fall just as she made it to the doorway. She turned and ran back downstairs, leaping at each landing.

I interviewed Joni with her parents' permission. I asked her why she'd run downstairs and not to the window.

Nine-year-old Joni said to me, "I was trying to catch her."

In her child's mind, you see, Joni thought she could run down three flights of stairs fast enough to catch her falling sister.

Joni cried when she said it. I cried when I screened the tape back at the station, and again, later that night at home. I cried for two reasons: one, Ramona's tragic death, and two, because I had assumed Ramona's story was cheap and I had almost fought my way out of telling her story the way it should be reported.

I ended up doing three follow-up reports. The ten-year-old girls had no previous records and showed considerable remorse, so the State's Attorney's Office decided not to prosecute them.

Ramona's family didn't have enough money to pay for her funeral, so Liberty Baptist Church along with St. Sabina Parish both held special fund-raisers for the family.

Beans worked that story with me too. Without saying a word to each other, we both began collecting money from the newsroom. Everyone gave. And everyone gave freely. "Here's something for the kid," they would say or, "Let me know if you need more." Even Dragon Diva dropped twenty dollars on my desk despite not uttering so much as a civil good morning.

We collected $1,300. Of course we couldn't give it to the family outright from the WKBA newsroom. To the other stations it might appear that we were trying to buy special access to the family's story. Denise suggested we give it to one of the pastors as an anonymous donation.

The third and final story I covered was Ramona's funeral. She was buried on a bitterly cold Chicago day. The sobs of her family mixed with the sound of ice breaking beneath the snow as the pallbearers walked through the media circus outside the church. Respectfully, we shot our video but did not badger them with questions or requests for interviews.

Later, back at the scene of the accident, in the little muddy plot where I'd first noticed the indentation of Ramona's leg, a memorial was set up. There were watercolor winter scenes painted on cardboard paper, wilted flowers, a chocolate-colored Teddy bear with Ramona's obituary paper propped up against it. Across the top, scribbled in a child's hand, it said, "Miz you."

Somehow, we all did.

DENISE

MANAGING EDITOR/ACTING ASSISTANT NEWS DIRECTOR

Xavier Helston.

He's the new boss at WKBA. A black man. I heard the news and I cried. I didn't sob. I shed tears. I'm angry.

I'm jealous.

What the heck is going on? If the Wizard wanted a black person for the job, why not me? Haven't I worked? I've done everything I can to show my stuff!

It's not fair.

What do they want? What are they searching for? They want experience. I've got eighteen years. They want a worker bee. I pull twelve- to fifteen-hour days. Most weekends. Some holidays.

It's not fair.

I know news. I'm not afraid to make a decision. I stand by it good or bad. I compliment good work. I chastise bad work. I'm fair. I'm careful. Maybe I'm not good enough? Maybe it is me. *No.*

It's not fair.

Damn this man everyone's calling Glory. He screwed me up. The brother is stepping in where I should be. I'll bet he sucks up to the Wizard. I heard they worked together ten years ago in Seattle. That's it. They're pals. The Wizard just doesn't want a woman in a key position. Period.

Maybe.

Maybe I could convince Glory to help push for me to keep the assistant news director spot. I could push him to officially hire me for the job. I've been doing the work. Give me the title. The pay. What are the odds of having a black news director *and* a black assistant news director?

A hundred to one.

I've been subbing as assistant news director for several months. Kal Jimper said I was a top candidate. Then Kal Jimper said New York froze the position. New York is considering fazing it out. Cost cutting. Then the Wizard said he wanted the job to stay. He's pitching to New York to keep the slot.

I'm waiting.

While I'm waiting, I'm doing two jobs. I've got two headaches. Two responsibilities. Two titles.

One paycheck.

Management jobs for blacks in television news are hard to come by. And in Chicago, any management position is a tough get. The competition is tough. The pay is great. There just aren't enough opportunities here. And I don't want to leave Chicago . . . or Perry.

I'll tough it out.

I met Glory. The Wizard held a party in the executive dining room. I really didn't want to go. I'm bruised. On the inside. But I couldn't *not* go. I had *to go*. Make an appearance. I can't show my anger. I can't show my jealousy. Office politics.

Let it go.

I don't know what I expected. When you feel slighted, expectations are not rational. No they're not. So I was looking to find fault with him. He had the job I'd slaved for. Black or white or blue. I wanted to find him weak. In any and every way.

Wrong.

Glory is smart. He's sexy. He made me feel that he was interested in what I had to say. Glory has eyes that calm. He spoke firmly. Glory listened intently. He had presence. I watched him handle the Wizard. Work the room with the other managers. I could see in their eyes. Comfort. Understanding.

I got it.

That's how Glory had moved up in the ranks. It's tough for blacks to break into upper management. I know. I felt a little jealous. Okay. A lot jealous. I thought I should be where he is, maybe farther. But he had something. Glory had something special.

Brain picking.

Glory pulled me aside. "Can we have a drink together soon? I'd like to talk about the station," he said. Inside info he wanted. Glory said he'd heard good things about me.

Brain picking.

That was okay. I would do the same. Any good manager needs the lay of the land. Any good manager wants to get the inside scoop. Glory needed an initial in. He looked to me.

Okay . . . but.

There are things I've earned. I don't want to leave Chicago. I like it here. I've got Perry. Our relationship is going well. This is the number-three market in the United States, behind NY and L.A. I need to advance here. Not somewhere else. I need to crack the 100 to 1 odds. I need this black man to go out on a limb for a black woman.

I need Glory.

After the party, I went back to my office. There were two things taped to my door. One was a note marked "Urgent" and the other was a clipping of the latest edition of The Column.

Holly
Reporter/Anchor

I left a note on Denise's door. I wanted her to meet me at a little bar I'd discovered on the near West Side. It was on Morgan Street, a little sports bar, owned by a former pro basketball player. It was called, "Nothing but Net!"

My stories on Ramona had garnered raves around the newsroom. Stu told me, quote, "Outstanding!" Dragon Diva even gave me a compliment by making an extra effort to ignore me. But the biggest kudo came in the form of top billing in The Column. It said my stories had a winning combination of emotion and journalistic integrity. The Column said that my coverage of Ramona's story had outshone veterans at the other shops. Denise had a copy of The Column.

"Oh you cut it out," I said as Denise sat down at the table.

"No," she said, "someone else did. Interesting. It was taped to my door. You've got a secret admirer."

We both smiled.

"Now. What's so urgent?"

In my mind I had painfully rehearsed what I was going to say. Denise had helped me quietly before. She had called me in my unit and complimented me on my live shots. Denise had given me tips on my scripts. Never was she rude or mean like the others doing the Godfather's dirty work. Denise had offered her expertise quietly.

I sensed that she was on my side but just didn't want to be public about it. Why? Why was Denise so secretive in her management style? I can only guess that as a black manager she didn't want to appear to be giving too much help to another black person. Denise was working to appear fair to all, but I felt funny about being so uncomfortable with approaching her in the newsroom.

We had a few drinks and to my delight, Denise finally began to relax.

"It's dynamics," Denise said to me. "The dynamics of a newsroom have to stay level. I can't appear to show favoritism. People won't respect me. I can't manage without respect."

I wanted to ask Denise, but it didn't seem like the right time to ask—I needed her help. Unfortunately for me, it was help that was crucial and available only through Denise.

"Did you meet Glory yet?" I asked her.

"Yes, this evening," Denise said. "You guys will meet him tomorrow. There's a luncheon in studio A."

"What's he like, Denise?"

Didn't I see her antenna go up? She gave me a party line answer if ever I heard one. I said, "Denise, I'm here talking to you and only to you. Our conversation is privy only to us. What does your gut say about this guy?"

"He'll be good," Denise gave up with much thought, as if she debated whether or not to trust me with her instincts. "Thank God too. We need someone to turn this station around."

True. The ratings were continuing to slide. Each day the Nielsen Ratings from the night before were posted on the bulletin board. We were still in last place for ten o'clock. The other afternoon shows were weak as well. "I heard good things about Glory from a friend of a friend in Cincinnati."

Denise raised her eyebrows. "Really?"

"Yes," I confirmed, then sipped my drink. "I heard Glory's very fair but that he doesn't like to rock the boat." Sounds like you, I thought.

Denise nodded and her brow furrowed.

What was she thinking, I wondered.

"Another drink for your thoughts?" I smiled, picking up the bottle of wine. Denise quietly declined with a smile. I eased the bottle back down into the ice bucket and the molten silver cubes jangled like loose change. I kept thinking, ask her. Ask her. It's getting late. Ask her.

DENISE

MANAGING EDITOR/ACTING ASSISTANT NEWS DIRECTOR

Holly's on a mission.

She wants to talk contract. Win over Glory. There's only a little time left on her one-year deal. Holly needs inside info.

I have it.

Holly said she heard Glory is fair. Her contract was *unfair.* Holly is coming on the heels of good publicity in The Column.

Worth a try?

I told her of course. Try. But Holly needs info. Inside info about other contracts. Kirstin's in particular. Kirstin's money. Her vacay time. Kirstin was Mitch's hire.

Inside info.

I said no. Holly gulped her wine. Holly's eyebrows nearly met. The makeup above the bridge of her nose creased. A whistled sigh vaulted off her lips.

"No."

"C'mon, Denise. The Godfather took care of his girl, didn't he?" Holly pressed. Did the question need an answer? I sipped. "Get an agent," I said. An agent knows what he gets his client. What other agents get their clients.

"No."

I asked Holly why. She said, "Look, Denise, I'm already here. I got myself here but got screwed in negotiations *only* because Kal Jimper got canned. An agent will come in and get me more money but after their cut I won't see much of the increase. I want to try to fix this myself with Glory. If I can't, then I'll get an agent."

Begging.

Holly's eyes begged me. She wants to know what to ask for. Negotiate. She wants me to tell her how to get over. Kirstin's money. Kirstin's vacay. Perks. Inside information.

Careful.

That's what my mind said. Be careful. Few had the information I had. I don't want it traced back to me. Holly is young. She's talented. She's black. She needs help. I was Holly at one time. I reconsidered.

"Tell no one."

Holly said, "I promise."

Holly
Reporter/Anchor

Kirstin is making $30,000 a year more than I am. I make 65,000. She makes 95,000. She has a two-year no-cut deal. I have a one-year, with an option for a second year. I have two weeks vacation. Kirstin has three weeks vacation. She has a $1,000 a year clothing allowance. I have nothing.

I have a college degree. Kirstin does not. She left in her senior year to take a job as a reporter for a news radio station in Salt Lake, before getting a television job the next year at a public television station in Phoenix. Three years reporting experience. That's what I have, plus anchoring. I was so mad I was sick. I would get sicker.

Dragon Diva is nearing the end of a four-year deal. She makes $850,000 a year anchoring the ten o'clock news. She has a $5,000 a year clothing allowance! She has a $1,000 a year makeup allowance. Dragon Diva has six weeks vacation a year.

Stu just signed a three-year no-cut deal—$250,000 this year with a $15,000 a year increase *each year*. He has five weeks vacation. He has a credit card to use for investigative expenses—wining and dining sources. Stu has a top-tier $200 a month parking space in an enclosed parking garage paid for by the company.

When Denise told me all that, I literally gagged. I knew that both Dragon Diva and Stu had been in the business a long time. They both started out at the bottom fifteen or more years ago. The small markets pay pitifully. Even now in a market size 100 or higher, like say Rockford, the pay for a reporter is dirt low.

Everybody has to pay his dues. Some people never get to the big markets, but when they do, the payoff is huge. So I know that Stu and Dragon Diva, evil as she is, have paid some dues—but please!

Dragon Diva doesn't even have to cover stories anymore. When Sweeps roll around, and ratings are key, WKBA sends a producer out to conduct the interviews and write the story. All Dragon Diva does is track—read what someone else has written into the microphone.

But not every anchor is like that. Most anchors in Chicago and in other top-money markets work hard; they pick a niche and fill it. Not Dragon Diva. She only comes in for a few hours before the newscast to read scripts. She does the show and leaves. Then she returns after a two- or three-hour lunch. Dragon Diva complains constantly. She sucks down morale and pees it away like bad wine.

And Stu is good. But I know that Mack is good too, yet I'm sure he's not making close to Stu's salary. And why was Kirstin getting so much more than I? Was it really what the market will bare or was it just bare skin tone? Were we being subjected to the melanin challenge?

I didn't want to think too much about the details. I simply wanted to figure out how to get my fair share.

Alex
Photographer/Technician

Man! I saw the shit coming but I was too tired to duck. I'd worked a flood story all day with Stu Ranger. After twelve hours of hustle and stories that were kick ass, we were driving back to Chicago after the ten o'clock news. That's when it started.

"So what do you hear about the new guy?" Stu asked me on the ride back.

I shrugged. "Nothing much, just that he's pretty straightforward."

"C'mon," Stu said with a *wink-wink* in his voice. "You've heard more than that, haven't you?"

"No. Why would I know more than that, Stu?"

"I simply thought you might have heard something juicy. Especially since you're one of the leaders of BEN."

What the fuck do I look like here? I sucked my bottom lip and said in a whisper, "Stu. I don't know anymore about this new black boss than I would about a white boss, okay?"

Stu turned to me and touched his fingertips to his chest. "Are you mad at me?"

"I'm not."

"Seems like you are, Alex."

Why get into this shit with him? I didn't answer.

"Don't be so sensitive. *We're cool*, okay, Alex?"

"No okay, Stu. I'm irritated."

"Why? Makes sense to me. You should know more about the new boss because he's black."

"Why, Stu?"

"C'mon, there aren't that many black managers at the network stations around the country. It simply stands to reason that there's got to be more curiosity among the blacks. It only makes sense that you guys are sure to dig deeper than the rest of us, Alex."

"Stu, I don't like the buzz. Some of the white guys in the garage are already saying that Xavier Helston is going to show blatant favoritism to black workers."

"It'll surely be an 'in.' Won't 'Glory' be the black messiah?"

"That's bullshit."

"Alex, don't get angry. Let's talk candidly if we're going to talk at all."

"Okay, fine. Stu, my man, let's break it down. Why do you assume that the black people will have an 'in' because the new boss is black?"

"One: The blacks will feel more comfortable with him because he's black. Therefore, black employees will go in there and ask for things. Two: Because he's black he will be more sensitive to hiring and promoting blacks. Blacks will have more access to him. That's because it's human nature to give benefits to people who are more like yourself."

"Okay, Stu, let me see if I've got this right."

"Proceed."

"Black boss equals more access for blacks. Black boss equals more black hires and promotions."

"You got it, Alex."

"Then that means *you* have an 'in' when the boss is white. He gives you advantages: more opportunity, more access, more hires and promotions because he is white so he caters to white people."

"Well—"

"No, Stu, you said *like helps like*. So, white power favors whites in the workplace."

"So, Alex, you think whites have had the upper hand at WKBA all these years because all the top managers have been white men?"

"I think white men have the upper hand in the world—not just WKBA. I think white men in America innately walk around with a shirt that says on the front: 'White man in America: Gimme and Get back.' And on the rear it says, 'Now Bow Down.' "

Stu jerked his head back. "Bullshit! And you've got big balls saying that to me!"

"What? What'd I say?"

"Don't toy with me, Alex. That analogy sucks and you know it. I couldn't get away with saying something like that about black men. You'd chew my head off and call me a racist."

"But, Stu, it's true! If only you could see and feel it like I'm forced to. My argument has teeth . . . my example just may have too much bite, but it's so *straight up!* As a white man in America you have opportunities and advantages that I'll never get no matter what amount of education or talent I have. And that's whether you really want it or not. You just got it like that. True, everyone doesn't flaunt or misuse it, but you guys just got it like that."

"Okay, just from a historical perspective I'll agree with you on the innate advantages given to white men. Now, however, you have to agree that with Xavier Helston coming in—at least in WKBA's arena for however a limited time—black men and women will have the advantage."

"Maybe. Maybe not."

"Alex! You're twisting things to be what you want them to be. You're not being logical!"

"Man, when race and power move into the neighborhood, logic packs up and moves out."

"Cop out! Cop out!" Stu chanted, his energy soaring. "Why doesn't the argument work when I choose to make it? White boss equals whites with an upper hand then conversely a black boss equals blacks with an upper hand."

"Because it's not a given, Stu," I said, shaking my head fiercely. "There's shit in the game."

"What?"

I rephrased myself. "There's a mitigating factor. It's not a given, Stu, because blacks in power tend to walk with a fairness crutch."

"What?"

"A fairness crutch. Stu, by the time a black person gets power, or maybe I should say limited power—particularly in the workplace— shit, man, they are trying extra hard to be so fair that it's ridiculous! That's because they've had to jump over so many hurdles. So they want to be extra fair to *prove* that fairness can work."

"Huh?" Stu said confused.

"Black bosses don't want to show preference to other black workers because they want to prove that fairness can work. They won't correct past mistakes even though people have been disadvantaged *because of color*. They want to walk the fairness line no matter what."

"That's a crock, Alex."

"Okay, Stu. Whatever. But make no mistake, my man, you better believe I hope that Xavier Helston will get over that feeling. I'd like to have an 'in' just for a little while to see what it's like, you know?"

KENYA
Writer/Producer

I met Glory at the studio party for the employees. He's about five eleven, muscular, fair-skinned with a brilliant smile. He's real charmin'—in fact, he could charm the blossoms right off a tree. Glory made a point of shakin' the hand of each employee. That seems like a little thing? But that's what most of the employees talked 'bout later—how friendly he was. He even got into the habit of droppin' by people's work stations, just to say hi. There's more.

The followin' week, Glory stopped by my desk. He saw my photo of Jeffie and his finger paintin' artistry. "That's Jeffie," I said proudly.

"Cute. How old is he?"

"Turns three last Saturday of this month. You have a child, right? I think I read that in the office memo about you, didn't I?"

"That's right," Glory said, pullin' up an empty chair and takin' a seat next to my desk. "I've got a six-year-old daughter, Brittany. She lives with her mother in Cincinnati. We're divorced."

I nodded.

"Your son's name is Jeff, did you say?"

"Jefferson. Jeffie for short. He's named after my daddy," I said, takin' a sip of my orange drink.

"Jeffie is a big guy for almost three," Glory laughed. From the glint in his eye, I could tell he liked kids. He said, "My daughter is small for her age. She was a preemie."

"You miss her, huh?"

"Yeah." Glory laughed easily. "Brit is a funny kid, her facial expressions are priceless. I miss her a lot."

"I miss spendin' time with Jeffie. I've been workin' like crazy. I haven't had a weekend off since I got here. My husband Jarrett is in med school. It's tough."

"Hmmm," Glory said, "that is tough. This business can be rough on a marriage. I know. But anyway, Kenya, I just wanted to say hi. I've got to run."

Then Glory left. At the end of the month, I was sittin' at my desk workin' when my line rang. "Kenya Adams," I said.

It was Vera, "I'm posting the schedule! Come look."

I saw that I had Jeffie's birthday weekend off! I didn't even put in for it 'cause I knew they were gonna say no. Vera glanced toward Glory's office. I stuck my head in and asked Glory about it. He said, "Kids love parties. You should have one." Then he smiled.

I was so excited. I only had a few days to get somethin' together. But Miss Billie said she'd help me. I invited Holly and Alex, two of my neighbors who had children Jeffie's age, and Jarrett invited three of his med school friends.

My son came paddlin' into the room with his slew-footed self. I put his party hat on just as I heard the doorbell ring. An hour later, everybody had arrived. Alex and Holly both came in hidin' behind the biggest Teddy bear you ever did want to see. Then Alex pulled out a little blue and white drum with wooden sticks! I started raisin' sayin' then, "Alex, do you know how much noise Jeffie's gonna make with that thing?"

Alex laughed. "I don't live here." Then she gave me a big hug.

Our music alternated between the greatest hits of Motown and Sesame Street. The phone rang and I answered it. Maybe it was the clown I'd ordered; he was late.

It was work.

I cursed myself for answerin' the phone. Why did I pick up that phone? There was a breakin' story. A huge gas leak had caused two hundred people in a four-block area to be evacuated. One person was dead, a child, and six firemen were injured. One of the three weekend writers had called in sick. "I'm havin' a birthday party for my son," I said.

It was the new EP on the phone, Abby. She was replacing Garth. She came in big bellyin' folk. Abby has a Brillo-pad voice and a snappy attitude but she sho' nuff knows her stuff. Abby said, "I know you have a party but this story is big. We need all hands on deck. I'm the executive producer rallying the troops. I need you on board now. Kenya, this is breaking news! You're a journalist and you need to get in here *like as in yesterday . . .*"

"I can't. My son's party just started and I haven't—"

"Listen, I'm new. So let me brief you on how I work. I run my shop very tight. You've got a party, I'm sorry. I'll expect you here faster than shortly. See ya."

I found Jarrett, took him into the bathroom, and closed the door. "I've got to go to work."

"What?" Jarrett shouted. "Kenya, we've got a room full of people and this was supposed to be our family weekend. Can't you call the black guy and ask him—"

"No, it's just not done. You can't call him for somethin' like this. I'll look bad."

"Well, right now I feel bad and so will Jeffie. They'll get by without you. Why do you have to go? I don't get it."

I thought long and hard, lookin' into Jarrett's eyes. I said, "Remember junior year when they taped up your bruised ribs right before the homecoming football game and I asked you not to go out there. Jarrett, you said, 'When the coach asks you to go—you go. You can't let the team down.'"

"Yeah I remember."

"Broadcast news isn't just journalism, baby, it's competition just like sports. That's why it's called a news team. It's not just gettin' the story, and gettin' it right, but it's gettin' it first and doin' it better than the other team. So when they ask you can you go, you go."

Jarrett grabbed a fistful of towel, held it, then released it. Then he gave me a hug and opened the door.

I went out to the party and told everyone what had happened. Alex said, "Ain't Abby a trip? Flexing muscle early in the game. I hope she's as bad as she thinks—people at KBA will show her what tough is! Kenya, girl, forget them—they'll be al'right without you."

"No!" Holly said, shakin' her head. "Kenya's hasn't got that kind of leverage yet. If she doesn't go in, Alex, they will have an attitude with her for a long time. Kenya, you're stuck."

When Jeffie saw me get my coat off the rack, he jumped down from the couch and ran toward me. Jeffie wrapped his arms around my legs. "No!" he cried.

Jarrett took Jeffie's hands from around my knees and Jeffie screamed, kicked his feet, and held his hands out to me. Jarrett said, "Go, he'll be all right."

Jeffie was cryin' so loud and hard that his face turned red as Georgia clay. I gave him a kiss and Jeffie mumbled, "Stay." I kissed him again and said, "Mommy be back. Mommy be back. Quick." And my heart broke as I turned and walked out of the door.

Coming Up Next:

"BEN" engineers a top-secret plan to shake up management! Will it stay a secret or will it be spoiled by a leak?

And:

Holly finally gets her face-to-face sit-down with the new boss, Glory. How does she handle it? And what dramatic news story will make or break her case?

Plus:

Beans heats up her stock gambles as she tries to get enough money to break with WKBA.

Stay tuned.

Holly
Reporter/Anchor

"So you want to negotiate your contract?" Glory asked as he sat behind his desk, sleeves rolled up, tie loosened.

"Yes. My first contract was rather unfair. The only reason I took it was to get in. On top of that, there were promises that were made to me but were never kept."

"So why did you want to stay here if you were mistreated?" Glory asked.

I was ready for that one. Now I'm beginning to make headway at WKBA. If I can get in another good stint here, just one more year under my belt, I will be able to write my ticket anywhere. *Glory didn't need to be privy to all that. My answer was strictly a team player line.*

"I like Chicago," I said truthfully. "Chicago is a gutsy news town. Politics. Sports. People here are passionate about news. I want to remain part of that."

"Well, Holly, I want to be honest with you. I haven't had a chance to evaluate your skills."

"I brought along a tape for you to see. It has some of my very best work on it." I pulled the tape out of my bag and slid it across the desk to Glory.

"Thank you. I'll look at this. But I still need to talk to some of the other managers."

"Xavier, let me be frank. I came here with a promise that I would do special features and anchor the new four P.M. show. I was thrown into a general assignment reporter slot. The four P.M. show never materialized. So far I haven't even subbed in an anchor spot. Despite that, I fell right in where asked and I've been a team player ever since. I haven't even complained, until now, about being underpaid."

"How much do you make?"

"Sixty-five thousand dollars a year."

"That doesn't seem like minimum wage to me," Glory laughed.

"Another reporter with less experience and no college education came in after me. That reporter makes ninety-five thousand a year. In addition to that, that reporter also has a one-thousand-dollar-a-year clothing allowance."

"That seems inflated." Glory frowned. "I've heard that in the top-three markets the salaries are inflated but again, I really need to evaluate—"

"Xavier, I got caught in the crossfire when Kal Jimper got fired. All I want is what's fair. You can bring me up to par contractually with the other reporters here and around the city. Surely you must know how I feel as a black woman being lied to and paid less."

"Don't you have an agent?"

"No. I thought I could talk to you one on one about righting the mistake that was made on my initial deal."

"Holly," Glory said, rising out of his chair and walking around to sit in the chair next to me, "let me be frank."

"Absolutely, that's what I want."

"You assume that because I'm black and you're black that you can come in here and I'll cut you a deal."

"I deserve—"

"Wait!" Glory said. "If I were a white manager you would not have come in here and asked me that, would you?"

"If you were white, I'd come in here fighting at this point. Because you are black, I'm coming in here asking."

"Holly, we can't always cut another black person a deal *or* make up for the past wrongs of history. I'm learning very quickly that WKBA has an ugly history. But what I will promise you is this. I'm just getting on board here and must concentrate on February ratings."

"I've got a three-part series that will air."

"Good. I look forward to seeing it. Let me get through the February book and then I'll sit down with you. I'll be up front and I'll be quick about it. If I think you don't fit into my plans, I'll tell you so you can start a hard job hunt. If I want you to stay, I'll personally see to it that you get a fair contract."

I put out my hand. "That's all I'm asking."

DENISE

MANAGING EDITOR/ACTING ASSISTANT NEWS DIRECTOR

Glory asked me out to dinner. I drove. We went to a quiet restaurant in Greek Town. We led off with small talk. His background. My background.

Breaking the ice.

Glory said, "Your boyfriend's name is Perry? My cousin's name is Perry, he's a dentist." I said, "My Perry was in the military. He's a computer expert. He designs programs for businesses. Travels a lot."

Personal stuff.

Glory said he's divorced. His daughter Brittany is six. He misses her. Glory said, "Family is very important. I miss that closeness. Already, I miss it."

Quick smile.

We talked about the station. The low ratings. Expectations. Then Glory asked me about Holly. "She was a little green when she came in in terms of hard news reporting. She's made big strides. Holly has talent."

Glory nodded.

"She came to talk to me about her contract. I told Holly that I couldn't tell her what my plans were until after ratings. I also want to further evaluate her skills."

I waited.

"And?" I said simply. Glory said, "I like the tape she gave me. I also looked at some other newscasts. I see her improvement. The camera loves her. Her delivery and voice are exceptional. But I could get a stronger reporter in here for the big raise I'm sure she's going to want."

True.

"But Holly is already here," I said. "Why not let the investment pay off?" Glory took a sip of his wine. "That's an option too. She does have talent. Apparently Holly got suckered on her initial contract. You know that, right?"

Where's he going?

"I heard her talk about it. Sure," I said. Glory said, "She knew a lot about other people's contracts. . . ."

Oh no!

"Really? Well, people here gossip about what the other person is making all the time. You know, agents tell their clients. Things get around."

Glory said, "Holly doesn't have an agent. For someone with no agent, she was dead on about Kirstin's contract. Wonder where she got the inside info?"

No way.

I didn't blink. I didn't nod. I put an angel's face on. I wasn't going to admit to a thing. Glory shrugged. "Oh well. It doesn't really matter."

Now.

I told him what I knew. Be careful. Nothing inside, inside. I told him about a few racial incidents. All common knowledge. I told Glory about the Wizard's promise to BEN. I said, "They were suppose to meet. He canceled one meeting. They rescheduled. He promised them after filling your post, he'd discuss grievances."

Glory stared.

He told me the Wizard was backing out of the meeting again. I said, "Why?" Glory said, "Corporate is coming. There's going to be a big party for the station's anniversary. He's concentrating on that. He's concentrating on which programs to buy for the afternoon slots—*Sally* or *Montel* or some other new talk show. BEN will have to wait."

That's trouble.

Alex
Photographer/Technician

"The Wizard canceled another meeting?" Rock yelled. This time we weren't at his restaurant. This time the members of BEN were meeting in studio A. It was 6:30 P.M., right on the closing credits of the last afternoon show. We decided to do a little chest beating, show a little dap-dap by letting people walk by and eyeball us gathering in there.

We wanted people to see that we were strong. Shit, we had numbers. The first meeting, man, there were only about fifteen people. Today, there were fifty of us. Some of the workers in news radio and in sales decided to take the *Negro plunge* and join our ranks. We are swelling. It felt good as a mug too. Maybe Gil Scott Heron was wrong. Maybe the revolution *would* be televised. At 7 P.M., I went to shut the door. I saw Bradley walking down the hallway. "Coming in?"

Bradley shook his head. "No thanks."

"Why?" I asked, stepping outside into the hallway for a minute.

Bradley exhaled, deep in thought. He's in his early forties and Michael Jordan bald. He wears khakis, white shirts, and striped ties. He's a hard worker who's been at WKBA for twelve years. "Alex, I just don't think having a black group is necessary."

"But, Bradley, the group will give us leverage with management."

"My power is in my work," Bradley said. "I'm the top salesman in this building. I bring in more money than anyone else, black or white. My skills speak for themselves."

"But suppose you have a slump? Then your boss tries to jerk you around. A group like BEN can go to bat for you."

"Alex, if I have a problem with my boss, I can speak up for myself. And if I'm not pulling my weight down the road, then I should be called in on the carpet. Black people have to stop blaming race for everything."

"Bradley, man, there are things wrong here. Think—together we can change things for all of us who do work hard—but unlike you—haven't been given their do."

"Sorry," Bradley said, smiling gently as he began walking away. "Groups like BEN are just a crutch. You guys do what you want to do. Good luck."

Well, we can't win everybody over, I thought as I shut the door so we could finally get the meeting started.

Rock snarled from the word go. "The Wizard is trying to play us. Because he hired Glory he thinks that's good enough. The Wizard canceled the meeting at the last minute, as if to say *so what.* He needs to know that we mean business."

"Let's all call in sick!" one of my boys who ran the studio camera shouted.

"A blackout," shouted a sales assistant and we all laughed.

"No," Mack said. "That eats into our own pocket. You call in sick and you lose one of your days. They'll be forced to cover with overtime. It'll start some buzz, but it's not necessarily dramatic enough."

One of the secretaries spoke up. "Well, today, I was asked to help organize a station anniversary party. We're booking the Hilton, top caterer, a band—the works."

"What's that about?" someone asked. "We haven't had a decent station party here in years!"

"Apparently," the secretary explained, "the president of the network news division will be in town along with officers from the Federal Communication Commission. Maybe we do something there?"

"Great! That's where we make a play! Boycott that bad boy," someone suggested.

"Naw, man," I said thoughtfully, "maybe they'd miss us, but so what?"

Kenya said, "They act like we're invisible now."

"No we have to show up," Rock agreed, his voice low and menacing. "We just have to do something with punch. We have to be visible."

Everyone was thinking. Come on now, we gotta come up with something slamming. What could we do to get our point across? Then I thought about what Rock said. Visible. *Visible.* "I got it."

"What, Alex?" Rock asked.

"We all go to the party wearing head-to-toe black," I said. "Damn! We'll be visible all around that ballroom. Corporate and the FCC bigwigs are sure to notice."

"*Noooo* wait," Rock said, "I got one better. T-shirts! Black T-shirts with something radical on them!"

"Like what?" Mack said. He was pacing the studio floor. "How about—WKBA Slaves."

Everyone groaned.

"Naw, that's too much," Kenya said. Then she snapped her fingers. "How about Invisible Workers?"

"Weak!" someone yelled out from the back. Kenya cut her eyes in that direction.

"I got it!" Alex said. "Not WKBA Slaves. How about . . . Picking Video Cotton."

Mack laughed. "Picking Video Cotton. I love it!"

"That'll embarrass them for sure," Rock said and high-fived Mack.

Kenya said, "Wait y'all. Maybe we need somethin' a little softer? Why rile them up so much?"

Then the debate started. Finally it went to a vote. The WKBA T-shirts won thirty-five to fifteen.

"Now," Rock said. "Those of you who voted no, respect the vote. We've got to stick together. Everyone has to wear the T-shirts. And it's got to be a secret. We want to spring it on 'em at the party. Now let's all try to get there at the same time."

I said, "Yeah. So let's say seven-thirty so everyone is seated, well into their salads. No *Colored People* time, y'all! Seven-thirty sharp."

"Then bang. We all show up looking like we mean business!" one of the editors said.

"Like we just stepped out of the movie *West Side Story*," I joked. "Straight up, I love that flick!"

"C'mon, y'all," Rock said. "We can do this!"

Everyone agreed. Then we set up a phone tree to pass messages along about meetings and such. After we adjourned I looked at Kenya, who had voted "no" for the shirts. I put my arm around her shoulder and said, "You with us, girlfriend?"

"I think it's a bit over the top but I'm the product of two civil rights activists so I'm down for the cause."

"Cool, that's my girl!"

I looked up and saw Holly rushing out of the studio. "Holly, wait up!"

"Call me later, Alex," she said. "I've got to catch someone. It's important."

DENISE

MANAGING EDITOR/ACTING ASSISTANT NEWS DIRECTOR

I let Holly have it.

"I can't believe you!" Holly sat down in my office. She looked confused. She looked innocent.

Please.

"Holly, I told you not to tell anyone. That contract info I gave you was inside." She said, "I didn't!" I snapped, "You did, Holly. What did you say to Glory?"

Stone-faced.

"What did I say?" Holly stammered. "Nothing. I talked about my own contract." *Everybody plays the fool.* Holly said, "I was trying to negotiate for a fair deal. A deal like Kirstin has, but I didn't say you told me anything. C'mon, Denise, I wouldn't do that."

You come on.

"Glory said that you knew exactly what Kirstin made. To the dime. Salary. Clothing allowance. Did you talk about that?" Holly didn't answer.

"Huh?" I growled.

Holly said, "I mentioned her money but I could have found that out from anyone! Denise, I didn't tell Alex or Kenya or anyone else— what did you think I was going to do with that info? I had to have hard numbers in order to ask for my fair share."

No!

"Holly, that's not how to play it. You should have asked for say a hundred and five thousand. You know she gets ninety-five. Then negotiate down to that ballpark. You shouldn't have quoted her exact deal."

Holly sighed.

"Did he say something? Is Glory mad or what?" she asked me. I said, "No. I played it off. But I'm sure he suspects something." Holly's shoulders slumped. She said, "Are you in trouble with Glory? Is he going to be on your back or something? On my back, you think?"

No.

It wasn't that serious. But I wanted Holly to sweat. She was wrong. She needed to learn how to keep her mouth shut. "Who knows? Holly, you have to be careful," I said. "This is a business where you need to be careful."

Holly pleaded.

"I'm sorry, Denise. I guess I wasn't thinking."

Alex
Photographer/Technician

Rock and I were hanging out at the United Center just handling our business. The Bulls had the first of two charity events there for a group of handicapped kids. It was a fun story. Man, I liked stories like that because the kids were so excited. I loved watching them have a good time. The kids were bouncing off the walls trying to hit baskets and get autographs from the players. Man, it was cool. When we finished covering the story, Rock started shooting some jumpers. He had me dying talking about how he could dunk.

"Rock man," I told him, "you ain't but five eight. What, your mama was a kangaroo?"

"Hey, hey!" Rock joked, giving me the evil eye. "Don't be talking about my mama!" Then he drove to the basket and took off. He got maybe, umh, two inches off the ground.

"Pitiful!" I yelled. Even the kids in the wheelchairs started laughing at him.

"You try," Rock said, bouncing the ball then passing it to me. I caught it. "Do I look like Cheryl Miller to you?"

We packed up our gear and got in our unit. We headed back to the station; it was still early morning and we were in great spirits. Tonight was the night of the station party—and BEN was ready for our unity protest!

"Hey," I told Rock as we walked down the hallway to the newsroom. "I got my T-shirt out this morning and ironed it."

"Ironed it?! Why iron a T-shirt?!"

"So it'll look good, Rock. This is an after-five event I'll have you know!"

We both laughed. As soon as we were about to open the door to the newsroom, Glory walked out. He smiled at us and said, "Just the two people I've been looking for. Where's my T-shirt?"

Our mouths dropped open.

Glory shook his head in a sarcastic manner, then held out his palms in a gesture that suggested, *What's up?*

Rock or me? Neither one of us said a mumbling word. We didn't give up jack.

Glory said, "I heard you radio the assignment desk that you were on the way in. I told Rod not to assign you to any more stories because I want to talk. Is my office okay?"

As soon as he shut the door, we sat on the couch and Glory sat down right across from us in a chair. Glory had a somber look, but an easy manner about him. I was tense, and I could feel the tension coming from Rock. But not from Glory.

"I'm disappointed that you guys didn't tell me—"

"How'd you find out?" I asked Glory.

"There's always someone in the group with loose lips, isn't there?"

"Look, brother," Rock said, cutting him short. "We don't have a problem with you. You just got here."

"Our problem is with WKBA management," I said.

"But that's me too." Glory frowned. "Didn't BEN consider me at all?"

"This isn't about you," I snapped. "We're going through with the protest. This is about the Wizard playing us. It's about unfair schedules. Bad contracts. No promotions. The protest is on."

Glory leaned back in his chair and nodded thoughtfully. "I see."

Beans

Photographer/Technician

A copy of The Column, open as bold as you please, was sitting on the table in the lunchroom area of the garage. The headline, in capital letters, read, "QUINCY METRO BROADCASTING UP FOR SALE."

The network was trying to sell all its stations, radio and television, including WKBA. Oh boy, we had heard the rumors, but it changed so much that we didn't think it would really happen. I mean the network's national programming was down, as well as the ratings at most of the O&O stations, but we thought they'd hang on at least until the ratings came up.

According to The Column, the asking price was $13 billion, and that's no chump change, let me tell you. I don't think we're going to sell fast because there aren't too many companies, or people for that matter, with that kind of dough or stocks.

I called my broker on the phone, because I was worried. What would a sale, a big sale like that, do to the stock that I owned? I hadn't been buying any Quincy Metro stock, not counting, of course, what the company gave me through my investment fund. But I was going to draw down some of that money, sooner than later, to help start my production company. My broker, Boardwalk, came to the phone stirred up by today's stock rally, up a hundred points already, and she said, "I was going to call you, Beans. Quincy Metro is up for sale and I think you should jump on it—buy it outside your investment plan."

"I don't know, this company is not what it used to be, but you'd buy?"

"Absolutely," Boardwalk said. "Look, by just putting it on the block the stock has gone up from twenty-three dollars a share to twenty-eight dollars a share today. Quincy Metro is still a strong name in broadcasting. Also I'm hearing that several companies have interest—there could even be a stock split later on."

"That sounds good, but what about your instinct, what's your gut?"

"I think you should sell a couple of the technology stocks you have. Then dig in with Quincy Metro. Also there's a company called Adall that reportedly is ready to market a drug that's being touted as the new Viagra. Right now the company stock is at forty-eight dollars a share. If we look at past performance, I see it going way up, maybe even doubling. It's risky but I think you should split your entire portfolio between Quincy Metro and Adall."

That was almost all I had outside of my pension fund, IRA, and company investment plan. It was risky to put everything into these two stocks, but I was getting tired of chasing fires and shooting murder scenes. I wanted to have my own production company, to call my own shots. I took a deep breath and I told Boardwalk, "Let's go for it, I'm going to go for it!"

"Now," she laughed, "that's the gutsy friend I used to sit on the front porch and play Monopoly with. Talk to you later."

As I waited to get assigned, one of the cameramen came into the garage and sat down next to me. Then, thoughtfully, he looked down at a copy of The Column on the table. He said, "They want to sell this crappy network for thirteen billion? Never get a bite at that price for this dumpsite. But at least it's driving the stock up. We all made a little extra dough today."

I smiled, feeling more confident about my decision, and hoped.

"Yeah, Beans. Just wait, this news will be the talk of the party tonight!"

But surprisingly, it wasn't, not by a long shot.

KENYA
Writer/Producer

Thank you, Lord, for lettin' the station party fall on my off day! I've been workin' like crazy not to mention dealin' with a bunch of nonsense at home. Little Jeffie was still persnickety with me about workin' so much but I had to keep pluggin' away. We needed the money. Jarrett doesn't like my workin' so much either but I've been ignorin' his cracks. I know it's because he's got exams. Jarrett gets tense. He was like that in college too.

"Kenya!" he called out to me. I was in the kitchen washin' up the dishes after breakfast. "Get Jeffie off that drum, please?"

I lifted Jeffie off the floor away from the drum. He took his little stick and started hittin' me in the head with it. "Boy!" I laughed.

Jeffie giggled and threw his head back and screamed with laughter. "Bang! Bang!"

"Kenya!"

"That man," I said to myself. I carried Jeffie into the living room, where Jarrett was readin'. He had moved from the table to the floor. There he had spread out all of his papers and books.

"Honey, I've got some washin' to do. Can I leave Jeffie?"

"Baby, no!" Jarrett said, grabbin' his head. Then he fell out on the floor and threw his arm across his eyes. "He'll keep up too much racket!"

"Go to the library then!"

"I can't stand that library, Kenya! I've been cooped up there for months. I just need to be in my own comfortable space but with *quiet!*"

The phone rang.

I grabbed it. Someone sellin' something. ". . . Porch improvements? . . . No . . ."

Jarrett reached up and grabbed the phone out of my hand. "We don't own the place and we don't have a porch!" Then he hung up the phone. "I need quiet!"

"Tell you what, Dr. Welby. I'mah go down the backstairs, get in the car, and go to the washeteria with my baby. I'mah have lunch with him at McDonald's, then sneak back up these same rear steps. Then we're going to have a nap. We will not bother you again today, until dinner."

Jarrett smiled and blew me a kiss. "Thank you."

I did all my errands and came back to the house. Jeffie and I took a nap before watchin' Nickelodeon. Not once did Jeffie or I go into the living room. The apartment was stone quiet. When six o'clock rolled 'round, I slipped down the hallway and took a shower. I put my clothes on and came back. Jeffie was still mesmerized by Rappin' Ricky, the animated character who teaches children 'bout black inventors. I went into the kitchen and took out some peas, collards, and smothered steak I made yesterday. I fixed Jarrett a plate and took it in to him.

Jarrett looked up at me and smiled. "God, you look like one of those Black Panthers or something."

I handed him his plate, still hot from the microwave. "I feel like it too. When Miss Billie gets here, I'm off to the Hilton."

I waited and waited for Miss Billie. It was 7:30 P.M. when she finally arrived and not 6:30 like she promised.

"I'm sorry, dear," she said. "I had an appointment with the foot doctor and it took forever!"

I told her not to worry. What else could I say? She hardly charged us a thing. I wouldn't be at the party by seven-thirty, but I wasn't worried about stragglin' in. Maybe that was better for me. I didn't want to be there for the big impact anyways.

I drove downtown to the Hilton. I walked in and headed for the ballroom. I saw two or three coworkers as I headed for the coat check. They smiled and said hi. They were white and they didn't act different or anythin'.

I gave my trench coat to the coat-check girl. Her eyes bucked when she saw my shirt. She said nary a word though and handed me my ticket. I walked to the ballroom door and stopped. Somethin' made the hair on the back of my neck stand up. I shook it off and told myself that our protest was right and sometimes you have to shake things up—just like my mama and daddy did. I stepped forward. As soon as I got past the first few tables I heard—*clank . . . clank . . .* forks droppin'.

"How are you?" I said with a big smile on my face. People were shocked. The more shocked my white coworkers looked, the surer I became. I commenced to walkin' taller and speakin' firmer. But still somethin' wasn't quite right.

Then I saw.

I saw Rock, Holly, and Alex. Rock had on a suit. Holly and Alex wore dresses. Their eyes got big and I felt sick to my stomach. I pinched my T-shirt between my index finger and thumb, because my voice was gone. I saw three more black people—no T-shirts. I was the only one there with the T-shirt on!

I heard people start to mumble and the heads started to turn. Alex and Holly jumped up and stood in front of me. Alex said, "Didn't you get a phone call? No one told you?"

"Told me what?"

"We called it off," Alex said. "Glory met with me and Rock. We cut a deal. He hired a black woman for the planning editor spot—she's a veteran in the business and a CABJ member—and Glory is meeting with the group to address the other issues."

"Just go!" Holly urged. "Get out of here."

I turned on my heels and rushed out the door to the coat check. As soon as I pulled my trench across the counter, and turned around there was the Wizard and his guests. All eyes went right down to my T-shirt. What could I do? I smiled, put my coat on, and walked away.

When I got home I was through! I nearly passed out when I walked in the door. I fell on the couch and groaned. Miss Billie said, "Dear, dear! You're sweating! What's wrong?"

I couldn't say anythin'. I waved my hands in the air, in a circle. I mustah looked like the Robot from *Lost in Space*.

Jarrett came in from the kitchen. "Baby, what's wrong?"

Was I goin' to lose my job? How would we make ends meet? Would any of the other stations hire me after they heard why I got fired?

"Are you sick?" Jarrett said, sittin' down next to me.

Miss Billie picked up the phone. "I'm going to call my grandson Earl, he's working at Mercy Hospital and—"

"I'm not sick," I moaned, sittin' up.

Miss Billie looked at the phone and frowned, "Say, there's no dial tone."

"Oh," Jarrett said, reachin' behind the lamp. He connected the line back into the plug. "I unplugged the phones. It was too noisy in here for me to study."

A rage brewed up in me from overwork, from stress, from Jarrett bein' so into his self. I screamed, "It's your fault!"

"What's my fault?"

"They called it off!" I said, yankin' at my T-shirt. "I was the only person who showed up wearin' this! My boss saw me. Jarrett, if you hadn't unplugged the phone—are you nuts? What a stupid, assbackward thing to do!"

Jeffie was standin' there and I didn't even realize it. He ducked behind Miss Billie's legs.

Jarrett jumped off the couch, walked over to the coat rack, and yanked down his jacket. I shielded my eyes with my hands. I didn't move them away till the door slammed and my eyes found Miss Billie holdin' Jeffie. Her eyes had an odd combination of sympathy and anger. Miss Billie walked to the back with Jeffie. I lay down on the couch and cried.

DENISE

Managing Editor/Acting Assistant News Director

What a mess.

Glory and the Wizard huddled near the bar. I waited. The Wizard left. I went over. "What did he say?" I asked. Glory sipped his champagne. "He's livid. Kenya embarrassed the station. She's got to be dealt with."

"Kenya needs this job."

Glory said, "Then Kenya should have thought about that when she decided to walk in here wearing that shirt." I told him, "It was an accident. Kenya didn't get the phone call saying the protest was off."

Glory squinted.

I said, "This is fact. Information. Xavier, if you fire her the writers' union will fight it. And BEN will fight it. The issue will blow up."

Let it go.

"Overnights," Glory said. "Schedule Kenya two A.M. to ten A.M. That will make an example of her." I said, "That's a killer. And she's got a child."

Glory shrugged.

"Denise, I was told to handle the situation. I bragged that it was handled. I can't let this go."

"Why not?"

"Did BEN say it would let the T-shirt business go when I asked? They told me it wasn't about me. That's what Alex and Rock said. I cut a deal with them because they said they had to do what they had to do. Well, so do I."

I understood.

"Denise, I'm a black man in management and people—black and white—test me all the time. I need to show them I'm not a punk and I can't be screwed."

Glory paused.

"Listen," he said. "I'm not going to let this incident ruin my evening. You shouldn't either. Did I tell you that you look great in that dress?" He said it warmly, affectionately, and tastefully.

I blushed.

"Perry picked it out," I said. "Well," Glory smiled, "Perry has good taste in clothes and in women. And speaking of Perry, here he comes." Perry came over. "I've been looking for you," he said.

Glory smiled.

"I'm sorry, Perry," he said. "We were talking shop and we shouldn't. Excuse me while I go mingle." Glory left. Perry said, "I don't like that Negro."

"What?" I said.

"Denise, I saw how he was looking at you." Perry is the jealous type. "Don't start," I said. "He just complimented me." Perry nodded, "Yeah right. Like I said, keep your eye on that Negro."

Coming Up Next:

Stonewalled. Ignored. Holly gets fed up. In a daring move, she engineers a plan to showcase her talent as an anchor.

Then:

An ugly rumor begins to circle the newsroom. Will it affect Denise and how she does her job?

Plus:

TV news photogs are part Spielberg and part Rambo. Alex and Beans set out to cover a raging Chicago blizzard.

This Just In . . . *continues.*

Weather

Alex
Photographer/Technician

What the hell was Beans shouting down at me?

Was it the snow whipping in my face or the ache in my fingertips as I clutched the railing while dangling four stories in midair? Or was it fear that had me blister and panic inside?

I struggled and kicked my feet. I saw Beans looking down at me. I felt her grabbing my right wrist with both her hands. I craned my head up, looking straight at the sky, man, just a sister trying to hold on. The sky was cussing me out with a wind, whipping tongue.

"Don't let-let go, plah–plah-ase, Alex, hang on . . ."

How the hell did I get in this mess in the first place . . .

The blizzard was on its way this morning when I went to work. I walked into the newsroom. A small crowd was huddled at the Doppler radar screen in the weather center.

Doppler is the bomb! It's the foremost computer system designed to track patterns, particularly large life-threatening storms. Like the bad boy headed to the Chicago area today. Weather is nothing to play with in Chicago. Killer blizzards or rainstorms can hit at anytime. That's what this one smelled like too—a real Killer Joe. That's why I rolled through the newsroom as soon as my shift began. I wanted to see what the deal was.

The newsroom crowd consisted of Stat, Denise, Abby—the new executive producer—and our morning weatherman, Lawrence Hernandez.

There was a splatter of clear scribbles coming our way. On the radar screen it looked like spilled milk running across the floor. Lawrence is heavy! Dude has a master's degree in chemistry and has been a weather expert for thirteen years. He's even written a book on tropical weather patterns in his native Puerto Rico.

Lawrence explained the pattern showing on the radar screen—"By afternoon rush hour we could have at least ten inches of snow on the ground."

Denise said, "We need to get a crew out to the western suburbs. That's going to be the hardest-hit area."

"Yeah," Stat agreed. "We need to be all around the city and suburbs, going from live shot to live shot."

Abby turned to me. "But let's get a crew out there now so we can turn around some tape. Alex, you need to hustle. No lazy stuff. I want spectacular stuff for my shows."

Get this bitch trying to grandstand for everybody. "Everything I do is spectacular!" I said.

"Hook up with Beans then," Stat said, "and start rolling out."

"Where to?"

Lawrence laughed. "Just head west, *chica*—the snow is going to be a monster anywhere in that direction."

Anywhere in that direction had sent us on the hunt, that's what shooters do—we go on the hunt looking for that picture that tells the story better than anything else.

The storm was a mother too. The slick, crystal flakes started pouring from the sky messing up traffic. The wind uprooted trees and knocked down power lines.

Beans and I didn't swap chatter; we were too damn busy stopping and starting to grab video. We shot the abandoned semi on its side as the wind spun the wheels like a kid playing with a Tonka Toy.

We got b-roll of people coming out of the Jewel food store. They were slipping and sliding behind silver-colored carts full of food they hoped would be enough to tide them over the weekend.

We stopped and beamed back pictures for the noon show and Stat radioed us, "Fucking fab, you two. We've got the best video in town! Keep it cranking. I'm calling up the competition now to bust their balls!"

Shit yeah, doctor, we love kudos! Beans and I high-fived each other and we started on the hunt again looking for that special picture. Stat radioed us to beat it to a new location, a building with a tree down. A viewer called in with the tip, said the tree was a hundred years old and all the kids for several generations had carved their sweethearts' names in the trunk. Hit time for the live picture: 4:28:30. That's headlines. Top of the 4:30 show.

We got there and the picture was good. There was a huge oak, its top limbs in a lover's delight embrace around the chimney of this four-flat building being rehabbed . . . the trunk was damn near level with the top-story window while the jagged, moist claws of the roots hovered just inches away from a manhole inches away from the driveway's end.

Beans and I checked it out then we looked up at the building and both said at the same time, "Up there!" That was *the bomb* picture. From the ground panning up was good, but from the top floor panning down was aces high, baby.

If I worked the view from those jagged limbs to the center of the trunk where there was a big old cluster of hearts, now singed white with snow—that shot would be out of sight, man.

Like that. Decision made—let's do it. We headed up the exterior staircase of the building; the new wood railings felt solid beneath my feet as we climbed. I reached the top landing and there must have been five inches of snow up there, untouched. Beans used her hands to help me dig a path that I could kick and step through with my hip wading boots. I grunted as I tried to beat to get to the railing to pan down the tree's top.

When I got to the railing and leaned over; that's when I heard a pop! It was loud as hell, like a gun going off. Is somebody shooting at us? I jerked around and looked back at Beans. In a second. In a frame. In the blink of an eye. That's when the railing just surrendered to the weight of the snow and me (in full gear tipping the scale at 190 pounds!).

I screamed, dropped my camera, and managed to grab the edge of the landing. I grabbed a clean seam of landing that had escaped the snow because it was beneath the railing. That seam was my seam and I was damn sure holding on to it for life.

Beans, girl, whatcha yelling at me?

Finally the fear and the wind began to die down and I heard Beans stutter, "Dah-dah-don't lah-lah-let . . ."

Go? And I did.

I felt myself falling in slow motion. I heard two branches pop when I hit them on the way down. I saw my feet kicking and Beans got farther and farther away. I saw her reaching out her hands to me. The camera that I dropped was teetering on the end of the porch near her feet.

It was so wet and cold; then I hit something firm, not hard but real firm, and I yelled, aahh! I wasn't hurt, I was just, well, scared. Then I wasn't moving anymore. I got the courage to raise my head up. I'd landed on a pile of snow and something else; I used my hands to push away some of the snow by my hip and I saw more and more of some pink jive. I learned later that the workmen had thrown out all the odds and ends of the foam insulation they'd used in the building's attic. That insulation with the snow piled on top had cushioned my fall. By now Beans was next to me and her teeth were chattering as she helped me up. "Are you oh-oh-kay?"

I nodded. I wasn't hurt, just scared shitless was all.

But we'd missed our hit time.

We'd missed the live shot at the top of the four-thirty show. Beans called the assignment desk on the phone to explain and Stat went off. "What's your problem? You missed your hit time. You two just screwed up the top of the show!"

Beans finally got a word in and told Stat what happened. That guy? He asked . . . "Did you get the shot?" Beans and I just looked at each other. All that hustle earlier didn't matter. One mistake instantly wiped out all that good. That's TV news. *What have you done for me lately?* You're only as good as your last live shot.

KENYA
Writer/Producer

It is *some* cold at two o'clock in the mornin'. That Chicago wind gets between the fabric of your coat and just unravels it. It's black as a country road outside too and that makes for some lonesome drivin' to work. And my raggedy old car, a 1990 Buick, takes near about an hour to warm up. Sometimes Jarrett gets up, goes out there, and gets the motor goin' for me.

"Kenya, you've got to get off this shift," he says every time he comes back into the apartment. "It's too got-doggone cold this early in the morning!"

I'm strugglin' to hold up, but my body is so confused. It doesn't know when I'm gonna give it rest so it tries to catch as catch can on its own. Like the other day, I fell asleep in the middle of the washeteria—between rinse and spin! I'm so tired. My legs feel like they've been tied to a harness or somethin'. Sweet Jesus, I'm cranky too.

Today I was watchin' the clock at work, waitin' for 10 A.M. Then I was gonna jet out of that studio like nobody's business, do you hear me? I got more energy as the clock ticked closer to quittin' time. I was goin' to pick up Jarrett and Jeffie, then go have brunch in Hyde Park.

It was ten minutes till time to go, when Abby came and pulled up a chair next to me. Abby is tall, nearly six feet, skinny as a twig with big square-rimmed glasses and long red hair down her back. She is quick-witted with a nasty mouth and aggressive to the point of bein' a pain in the behind. In just a short period of time workin' at WKBA she had managed to rile up nearly everybody in the newsroom to the point of extreme dislike. Abby said to me, "You need to stay until noon. We're short for the noon show."

I looked at her like she'd lost her cotton field ownin' mind. Abby was from Montana and she had a clean, outdoorsy look and dressed to match. Pointy cowboy boots, spurs even some days. But Abby had spent some time in big-city newsrooms like Boston, Philly, and Miami. She was bossy.

"Abby, I've been here since two o'clock this mornin'. Ask someone else. I'm near 'bout out on my feet."

"Kenya," Abby said. "We need a body and you're it."

"I can't."

Abby cracked a smile. "Kenya. We need you."

"And I need to spend time with my family. Another hour in here is liable to put me in the ground."

"Did you read the *Red Book*?"

The *Red Book* was the network's official standards and regulations manual. Folk called it the *Red Book* because it was a beet-red paperback. "Parts of it," I said.

"Well," Abby said smugly, "in the *Red Book* it clearly states that an employee can be fired on the spot for physically fighting on company property, intentionally damaging or being grossly negligent with company property, or refusing to cover a breaking news story."

"Now, Kenya," she chuckled, "I'm not using that as a threat. I'm not saying that I would try to enforce that. I'm just telling you so you will understand the magnitude of how important it is to cover a breaking news story well. Think. How will it look when Xavier and Denise hear that you didn't stay? I know you want to get off these fucking overnights, don't you? *If* I were you, I'd stay."

And I did. I was mad at myself for stayin'. I felt like I knuckled under. I felt like I should have tangled with Abby. But outright she had me. The *Red Book*. Why wasn't there anythin' in there about fairness in the media?

I switched my date with Jarrett and Jeffie to 1 P.M. I picked up Jeffie from Miss Billie's and Jarrett said he would meet us at the pizza place. I decided to park my car in the lot right behind the restaurant. There were a bunch of meters there that you had to plug with quarters. I was backin' into a spot right by the restaurant when some guy cut me off and swung into the space before me.

"Hey!" I said, throwin' my car into park. I jumped out. The man got out too. I yelled, "Get the hell outta my space! Have you lost your mind! You can't push me around! Who the heck do you think you are!"

The man pushed his glasses up on the rim of his nose with his middle finger. "It's only a parking space."

"And it's mine! Move it! Move it!"

The man got wide-eyed and backed away. I saw Jarrett out of the corner of my eye. He must have been standin' outside the restaurant waitin' for me. Now he was takin' Jeffie out of the car seat. The man had commenced to backin' out of my space. Jarrett was holdin' Jeffie. I said, "Did you see that, Jarrett?"

"Yeah, it was terrible."

"He just cut me off!"

"True. But you went ballistic on him just like you did on me. Kenya, baby, that's not like you at all. This job is killin' you. Something's got to change."

I exhaled loudly and rested my head on the hood of our car. I looked up at Jarrett and Jeffie. Jeffie said, "Mommy loud!"

I started to laugh. Mommy loud, I said to myself. I got back in the car and pulled into the parkin' space. Mommy's going to get that résumé back out there and make a change.

Holly
Reporter/Anchor

I want WKBA to fix my deal. I've earned it.

Glory keeps saying we'll sit down soon. Trust him. Don't worry. With grace and wit, this man charms the contract issue right out of the picture. He diverts the topic to the ratings—a paramount concern for all—which continue to fall. I need to do something to dazzle Glory, to make him give me the deal I want.

Television news is a doggish business with politics that can drop the ceiling hazardously low. It's not glass. It's gravel—there's a stinging, cutting feeling when you hit it. I decided not to wait for an opportunity but rather to create an opportunity.

An opening presented itself when I overheard Dragon Diva on the phone. "Oh, I can't possibly make the baby shower Sunday afternoon. I've been asked to anchor the five-thirty show. Well, contractually, I'm only obligated to anchor the Sunday night ten o'clock news. That's because it's one of our biggest audiences. That jump-starts the coverage for the entire week."

So what? I thought. It wasn't like Dragon Diva came in to help. She came in at about 8:45 P.M. She read a news break then she anchored the half-hour show at ten—*as if that were slaving.*

"But the five-thirty show on Sunday is starting to slip in the ratings," Dragon Diva went on to say. "So now they want to beef it up. Naturally, they came to me, begging me to save the day. *There just isn't anyone else.* I told them I'd do it for a month until they get someone who can carry that baby, but I can't possibly tie up my whole fucking day *every week.*"

An idea, evil as it was, hit me as I stood there and overheard Dragon Diva's conversation. *There just isn't anyone else.* Dragon Diva knew I was dying to strut my stuff as an anchor and she knew they weren't letting me sub. The idea began to cultivate in my head. It would be a big gamble. If I lost, I'd probably lose my job—but if I won I'd gain a hell of a lot of leverage.

Sunday afternoon right before the five-thirty show, say about an hour before air, I showed up at the station. It was a treacherous day outside, the roads were slick from the snow earlier in the week. Accidents were everywhere. The bad weather would be my ally. I walked in with summer draped over my shoulder. I had on my baddest anchoring outfit in my power color of purple. My hair and makeup were *laid*.

"Wow!" Rod said, as he sat in the slot with both ears hidden by phone receivers. The police and fire scanners were cranked up. "Look at you! What's the occasion?"

"Church. I'm just stopping in to screen some tape on a story I have to do next week."

My plan hinged on the fact that Dragon Diva was not just a creature, but one of habit. *Bingo,* she came in right on cue, and ignored me. Dragon Diva sat at her desk and looked at a few scripts. It was now about forty minutes to air. She then took her comb and brush kit to the bathroom nearest the makeup area. I waited ten more minutes. It was now thirty minutes to air.

"Rod," I said. "I'm going to find an old script I need out back in the library."

He nodded.

I went out the back way and cut through the loading dock. There's a skeleton crew on the weekends. The few writers working were crashing and burning on their deadlines. The reporters were out live in the field. I left the producer hunched over her screen in the newsroom. The hallway was empty. I crept back to the bathroom nearest the dressing room. I heard Dragon Diva chatting with the makeup artist.

You can't see the bathroom door from the makeup room. I slipped inside and I prayed. I looked on the sink and there they were—Dragon Diva's contacts. She practically needed a cup and cane without them. As usual she'd left her contacts there in a case. Dragon Diva always took her contacts out while she was getting made up, and when she was finished she put them back in.

I grabbed the case and palmed it in my hand. I opened the door and peeped out. Was the coast clear? No one—but no one—could see me. I took my shortcut back to my desk. As I moved in a quick, stealthy manner I passed the garbage dumpster on the way into the newsroom. I dropped the case into the trash and kept walking.

I got to my seat and waited. Dragon Diva came tearing through the door. "I lost my contacts!"

"What?" Rod said.

"Get off the fuckin' phone, you idiot! I've lost my contacts! I can't read the prompter without them!"

People started scurrying around looking for the contacts. I helped. "Where'd you have them last?"

"In the bathroom, but I looked!" Dragon Diva snarled. "I must have dropped them somewhere. But I swore I left them in the bathroom. That's where I always leave them."

Twenty minutes to air.

"I can't go on," she moaned.

The producer asked, "Hazel, can you get a cab home and get another pair?"

"In this weather? I can't get home and back in twenty minutes."

"What are we going to do?" the producer groaned. "Call the manager on duty this weekend. Who can we get? Rod, look in the computer and get some of the other anchors' phone numbers. See if one of them can get here in time. Maybe Lawrence can do the whole show by himself."

"The weatherman?" Dragon Diva said with a slither. "Are you nuts! He can't pull it off."

I went and stood right in Rod's face. He looked at me. "Hey! Let Holly do it. You used to anchor, didn't you?"

"Yes. Back in Palm Springs."

The weekend producer ran over to me and grabbed my arm. "Can you help us out, please?"

"Who me? I don't know . . ."

"Please," the weekend producer said, clutching my arm.

Steam was billowing out of Dragon Diva's ears! She snapped, "Just the five-thirty show. I'll be back for the big broadcast at ten."

Rod waited for Dragon Diva to leave the newsroom and then joked, "Do you think her mother ever loved her at all?"

With five minutes left to air, we laughed before I hurried to the set. This was my shot. This was my time. I stepped on that set and sat in that anchor chair. Immediately I felt a pulse of energy. I hadn't anchored since I'd left Palm Springs. Would I be nervous?

Once I got started, it was as if I had never left the chair. I've always been blessed with a quick memory and very inclusive vision. I can take in three lines at a time so I keep a steady, credible gaze into the camera. I talked to that camera like Kate talked to Leonardo in the *Titanic* death scene.

During the first break, the phone beneath the desk rang. It was Rod. "Smoking!" he said in a Jim Carrey voice.

I smiled and hung up the phone. The director told me, "Holly, you're doing great!" The guys on studio camera were cheering me on.

In the middle of the second block the producer whispered in my ear, "We've got a crew going to a breaking story. A possible hostage situation. Hang on. It could be a rough ride!"

Alex
Photographer/Technician

"Yo, baby! Brief me on the breaker!"

Those were my words to the assignment desk as I made a Knievel "U" turn at top speed.

"There's a possible hostage situation . . . A woman called in. Said she was in a furniture store when a man burst through the door in a rage . . ."

I turned and looked at my partner, Lui Chan. He was sitting back, leg propped up against the dash, looking cool wearing a fifty-dollar pair of shades in winter. The sun was sending down a streak of rays that glared off the mounds of melting snow piled all along the road.

". . . she says she was able to run out but heard a shot fired behind her . . . PD are on the way."

Lui was per diem; when they dropped a dime, that's when home-boy worked. Today he was filling in for Beans, who was burning a vacation day. Lui deserves to be staff, but he wanted a tough-to-get gig in technical maintenance—repairing and revamping equipment. That was a plum for the old heads in the shop but they weren't budging. *The maintenance boys died with their cameras on.*

"You're first camera. Stu and unit twelve are working to get there ASAP too. Get there, then set up and go live. We want the first picture . . ."

I stood up on the accelerator. Lui blew a bubble, popped it. Swerve. Brake. Gas. I was smoking the treads, y'all. The clock was ticking, and in TV, timing is essential to the story. *Get it right and get it first.* We reached the location. Lui popped up his shades, peeped at me, and said, "Way to roll, Ms. Alexandra."

We hit the ground running. We saw the furniture store and headed toward it. There are storefronts on one side of the street and a couple of apartment buildings on the other side. It was quiet as we approached.

Was it a crank call? Maybe the woman overreacted? Did she really hear a shot?

As we got closer to the store, we could see a man sitting in a chair near the window, looking terrified at someone. I had my camera on my shoulder, shooting as I walked around. Then I saw . . . the hand with a gun pointed at the man's chest. I couldn't see who was holding the gun—his body was blocked by a cabinet and the door.

We ducked behind a compact car and I kept rolling. I could feel sweat pouring down my ears. God, I thought, don't let this nut shoot this man. Lui was next to me. I heard him whisper, *sheeet*. I was steady rolling. This man was in a scary spot. He knew it too. His lips were moving, couldn't tell if he was talking or praying.

Then I heard this loud screech! And sirens. Three police cars arrived. The cops jumped out of the cars, their guns drawn. Two of the cops spotted us and began to weave our way.

Suddenly the door of the store opened. I zoomed in, then focused. I had a viewfinder's eyeball trained right down the barrel of a gun. My heart lurched. The gunman started firing in our direction.

I ducked my head down but left the camera on the hood of the car, flipped on its side, still rolling. Two more shots whizzed over my head; I heard them rip into the side of a building directly behind me and Lui. Man, he ain't playing at all! F–ing jerk!

The cop huddled near us growled as he shot back. "What the hell are you doing? You're drawing fire!"

"We're drawing fire?" Lui yelled back.

"Really," I said. "He didn't even see us! You drew the fire!"

"The SWAT team is rolling in," the officer stated. "You have got to get out of this area. *Now.* And that's no bullshit. Just do what we say and we'll get you the hell out of here."

My man wasn't bragging for nothing. He and another set of cops

gave cover. I grabbed my camera off the car hood. We were hustled out
of there like convicts in *The Defiant Ones* trying to catch that train. Lui
was with me step for step. There was a little *pimp limp* in my run from
that fall I took off the porch the other day, but still we were able to
make it quickly to a clearing between two apartment buildings.

Lui stopped me and spun me around; I leaned against the side of
the apartment building. I was on a right angle across the street from the
furniture store where this gunman was holding people hostage. We
braced ourselves against the building and started shooting more video.

"Get the fuck out of here!" I heard someone shout over my shoulder. I turned around and there was nothing but chest and riot gear in
my face. Then a bunch of hands grabbed me and Lui. We were shoved
toward a safe area. From there, you could see a corner of the furniture
store and nothing more really. That's where the cops had set up the media line. There was a bunch of news crews there with their reporters.
Including Stu and our other WKBA crew.

"What'd you guys get?" one of my buddies who worked for the
competition blurted out. All heads turned my way.

I popped the tape and held it up. "*The shit*, ladies and gentlemen.
The shit."

Holly
Reporter/Anchor

In the commercial break, I learned that one of our crews was the
first on the scene and was the only crew to get video of the gunman!

Apparently a man had barricaded himself and three customers inside a furniture store. Witnesses calling in to the station said they could
see a couple of people through the window, but not the gunman. He
was using hostages as a shield, holding a gun on them.

The art department whipped up a map that showed the address of the hostage situation. That was the picture. We aired live witnesses on the phone who told us what was happening while we waited for our exclusive video.

Then we got a live shot up. Our reporter had reached the scene. I had a good Q&A with Stu: The man was in his fifties, had lost his job, been out of work for two years. He had four children. His name was Barron Milligan. He was overdue on his payments and the company had repossessed his furniture. That was the straw that made him snap.

All while we talked, the director rolled tape that showed the gunman holding a pistol on a guy sitting near the shop window. Then we had some shaky video of the guy shooting from the doorway.

We had kick-butt video that no one else had so we slapped a big, old exclusive sign on the pictures. After that, we went to a break. Then after the break, we went back live to Stu—rolled the same exclusive video again—then we did sports.

By that time Glory had arrived at the station. He came into the studio during a break. "Listen, Holly, thanks for stepping in. You're doing a good job. We're going to stay hot with this hostage thing. Our coverage is kick-ass. We're going to go back and forth with cut-ins, okay? The chopper is up and on its way for aerials of the scene. Holly, you have to be sharp. Can you handle it?"

What a ludicrous question! Couldn't Glory see? For so long at WKBA I'd felt trapped in a cocoon, fighting to get out. Now that I was anchoring, I felt fresh and free. I was soaring! This is what I do! This is what I am! Couldn't Glory see that?

"No problem," I told Glory. "Let's do it."

By having a jump on the story, viewers were gravitating to our channel. Some of Milligan's neighbors called in to the station. We sent our desk assistant out to interview them until we could get another reporter in on the story. Then I gave updates at the anchor desk.

Milligan had fired a shot and apparently wounded one of the salesmen in the leg. The police convinced him to let the injured hostage go.
WKBA had it live. A reporter was being dispatched to the hospital where
the injured hostage was headed. We were live from there as well. Of course
the other stations were on the story now too, but we had beaten them.

We interrupted the regularly scheduled programming off and on
until about nine o'clock. That's when the gunman finally surrendered.
We signed off. I threw my head back and threw my copy sheets into
the air! "Weeeee!"

Glory came into the studio clapping. "Nice job!"

Dragon Diva was on his heels. "Not bad," she said to me happily. I
thought, Fake.

"Holly was great, Hazel."

"Yes, wasn't she? So thanks for sitting in, Holly. I'll take over now.
What's the plan for the ten o'clock show, an expanded broadcast?"

Did Dragon Diva think she could just dog me without a fight like
when we first met? Did she think she could just push me without a
shove back?

I turned to Glory. "I'd like to stay with it. I've been hot on this story
since it broke. I want to see it through."

Dragon Diva chuckled. "Holly, my dear, just because you pulled off
a half an hour show and a few cut-ins does not mean you can—"

"I'm not talking to you. I'm talking to the boss."

"Hazel," Glory said. "Why not let Holly anchor the ten tonight?"

"Xavier." Dragon Diva laughed looping her arm around his elbow.
She used her index finger to draw circles on his bicep. "I'm not trying
to be rude or demanding, but I anchor the Sunday show at ten. It's in my
contract. It's the top-rated show. Maybe we should call the GM to get a
second opinion?"

Can you believe Dragon Diva would quote contract and try to haul the Wizard into this?

"Okay," Glory said, patting her arm gently. "Do the ten, Hazel. Holly, you did an excellent job. Thank you."

I turned on my toes and I heard my coworkers saying, "Good job." A few people clapped. I went back into the newsroom. I was showered with applause. I even had a number of warm messages on my answering machine from friends, including Kenya, who along with Jarrett and Jeffie left me a series of loud yeahs!

Their cheers were little solace. Why couldn't I ever seem to win? I grabbed my bag and walked toward the front door. Glory was standing there waiting, alone.

I was silent as I moved toward the exit.

"Cheer up, Holly. You lost the battle. But you won the war. Come to my office tomorrow and let's talk contract."

"Cah-cah—contract?"

Glory began walking back to his office with his hands in his pockets. "A good anchor doesn't flub an easy word."

An insanely brilliant smile erupted across my face. The next day, Glory put a contract offer before me. Eighty thousand a year. One-thousand-dollar clothing allowance. An additional week of vacation.

"The money is too low."

"Holly, I'm giving you more than a fifteen percent increase. I can't make up all the damaged ground."

"What about anchoring?"

"I'm going to put you in the sub rotation. When people are on vacation or out sick, I'll rotate you in with the other subs."

"I was promised the four o'clock anchor spot. . . ."

"There may or may not be a four o'clock show."

"I want in the contract that I get the four o'clock anchor spot *if* the new show goes up. I want that contractually as well as my subbing duties as an anchor."

Glory leaned forward and held out his hand. Our fingertips touched, then I jerked back my hand. "This is not a great contract. The other talent still get more."

Glory's tongue was a hammer that broke his thoughts into stones: "One: Some deserve more. Two: Others are overpaid. Three: Greed doesn't look good on you."

I shook Glory's hand and he said, "Good. I'll have the contract drawn up right away."

Beans

Photographer/Technician

I know that newsrooms thrive on rumors; people don't mean any harm, but I think it's stress that drives the rumors. Alex and I were in the newsroom, waiting to be assigned, and Rod said, "Hey, did you guys hear the latest?"

"Man, y'all are always tripping," Alex said. Then anxiously she grinned, "What? What?"

I joked, "Don't you guys ever get tired, tired of running off at the mouth, huh, do you?"

"Like you do, kiss my butt, Beans!" Rod teased.

"What butt?" Alex frowned, peering around Rod's back.

"Don't be a freak! Just be nosy like me. The latest rumor is that Denise and Glory are having a thing."

"What?! Okay, Rod, where'd that one come from?"

"A bunch of people said they saw them huddled up together at the big party. They said they were whispering and making goo-goo eyes.

Then Will says he saw them at that new restaurant on Rush Street—in a private booth looking romantic. How aw'bout that?"

"Rod, you're not using the Chicken McNugget brain you were born with, pah-lease, listening to crazy Will."

"Rye-ight!" Alex laughed.

"I don't know," Rod said, laughing; then he whispered, "Everybody's wondering about it."

Alex snorted, "Why can't two black people get together and handle their business without some nasty talk starting?"

"What's race got to do with this?" Rod said, raising an eyebrow. "This is TV news, we talk about everybody! They could have a thing. He's divorced. She's single."

"But Denise has a boyfriend," I said, "and I've seen them together. Alex, what's his name?"

"*Fine* Mr. Perry!"

"So?" Rod shrugged. "When did that ever stop two people from doing the nasty if they wanted? If it's true, then her job is secure as long as Glory is here. But that's fine because I like Denise. I'm just—"

"Spreading the rumor, way to back-stab, huh, Rod?"

"Beans, what the fuck is your problem? What's so special about this bit of dirt that may or may not be true?"

"Because it could hurt her reputation, and I don't think I'm off base at all on that, am I, Alex?"

"No ma'am, you are not!"

"All right! Jeez, don't shoot me in the head!" Rod said, plopping down in his desk chair, and a second later a sneaky smile slithered across his face. "Did you hear *the other rumor?*"

Alex laughed. "Damn! What else?"

"A couple of the other owned-and-operated stations called and said that Corporate is about to accept a twelve-billion-dollar offer for the company."

"They were asking for thirteen billion. That's a billion dollars short! Damn, they got low-balled!" Alex observed.

My mind, and my heart, lurched in one massive panic-stricken pain. What would that mean for my stock, and for my dream of owning my own company? Alex, she had no clue what I was thinking, as she cracked on the sorry state of Quincy Metro Broadcasting.

"Baby," Alex said, "the shine has worn off this jewel. They better take that twelve bil, keep their stickup masks on, and run for the border!"

DENISE

MANAGING EDITOR/ACTING ASSISTANT NEWS DIRECTOR

It's urgent.

That's what I told Glory. He said, "Your office after the Post?" I said, "No, not anywhere in here." Oh. Glory said, "Meet me at the little bar inside the Sheraton Hotel on Columbus."

I knew.

A mole let me in on the secret. Was it a vicious lie? Or was it the cold, bitter truth. I felt a pinch in the back of my neck. My nervous system fizzled. I was struggling to be calm. One bit of info had led to another.

First the big sale.

The company was on the block. The rumor was out two weeks ago. All the trade magazines confirmed it publicly this week. The Wizard confirmed it to us.

Sold for $12 billion.

The deal was put together by a group of businessmen based in Washington, D.C. It wouldn't be finalized until federal approval was given. That shouldn't be a problem. The buyers had powerful friends in the government.

Changes?

Of course. There'd be some changes. But not this soon. It's too early. Wasn't it? I asked the Wizard. We were meeting about another issue. I asked him again about the assistant news director job.

The Wizard looked.

Then he said, "I'm about to hire someone." My jaw dropped. Obviously it was not me. What about me? "I deserve that job," I said. The Wizard responded, "I was going to give it to you but Xavier said no. I'm going to make an offer to a man he recommended."

"Excuse me?"

"Xavier thinks you're not quite ready yet. I know you understand. You're a team player. You've shown that. Don't be discouraged."

How could I not be?

"Denise, you need a bit more experience. But I hope I can count on you to help break in our new assistant news director. He's not familiar with our setup here or the Chicago market. I'll need you to show him the ropes."

Train him?

That's exactly what the Wizard was asking. I'm good enough to sub in the job. I'm good enough to help train someone for the job. But I'm not good enough to have the job.

ME.

If I had a gun, I would have shot him. First in the knees. Change shot. Right between the legs. I'd save a bullet. For Glory. The Wizard put the blame squarely on Glory. Setup or straight talk? I had to know.

"Tell me."

Glory's face remained calm. He didn't blink. He didn't get nervous. Glory looked me dead in the eye. And I wanted him to say that the

Wizard lied. Glory looked at me and said, "Yes, it's true. But I did it for you."

For me?

I got a sick feeling in my chest. I shook my head. I moaned, "For me?"

Glory said, "Denise, listen. There's a rumor going around the office that we're sleeping together."

I'd heard a buzz.

"The newsroom is always buzzing with something," I said. "Next week, it'll be something else. It's just talk." Glory shook his head. He said to me . . .

"Don't you see, Denise?

"If I gave you that job," Glory continued, "that would be confirmation. Everyone would then *believe* we were sleeping together. Talk would become reality in their minds. Your reputation would be ruined. They'd think that you slept your way to the top. That would follow you. You know how this business is—especially for black people."

I closed my eyes.

"I don't want your reputation soiled like that. I couldn't help you get the job. As much as I wanted to, I couldn't. Can't you see that?"

I hate this business.

"There's more," Glory said after my long slide into silent thought. He said, "I'm leaving." My head shot forward. Eyes wide.

"You just got here!"

Glory laughed. "These new buyers are bad news." I said, "How do you know?" He said, "I've got sources just like you. I'm staying through the May Book. Then I'm going to New York for a VP spot there. Another network."

Big move. Big dollars.

Glory scowled. "No congratulations?" I told him sarcastically, "Well, excuse me if I'm too damn beat down to feel overjoyed for you."

Glory got up from his side of the table. He slid in next to me. Glory took my hand.

It was limp.

"I have an idea," Glory said. I didn't answer. I simply looked. He said, "Now that we won't be working together, I want you to follow me out East."

Follow him?

"I've got a friend in New Jersey who will have an assistant news director job open soon. At my word, he'll hire you. Then we can see each other."

What?

"What about Perry?" I said simply. Glory said, "He's a military muscle head. You need someone with finesse and polish. I'll make you forget you ever knew Perry. I've always thought you were smart, aggressive, and witty. Don't you feel the attraction between us?"

Some, I thought.

But I wasn't going to go there. I had Perry. "Xavier, I love Perry." He said, "I can love you better than he can, Denise. I can give you more . . ."

Too much.

I waved Glory off. I pushed him away. He slid out of the booth. Glory said, "Wait." I growled the words, "No. No. No!" And I left him standing there. Alone.

I skipped the party.

Glory's going-away party was in studio A after the six o'clock show. We had few words to say to one another after that night. But before he left town, Glory sent me a note.

"Denise, if ever . . ."

I crumpled it up and threw it away.

I didn't tell Perry.

Not all of it. He'd have a fit. As it was, he went ballistic. "What?!!
No promotion? They played you again? No, see. I need to come down
there and kick the Wizard's ass. Say the word, baby, say the word!"

"Uhhh . . ."

"That's the word," Perry said, jumping up. I pulled him back down
next to me. "I love you," I said. Then I kissed him. "But no."

A week later, Perry called. Come to his apartment. He had a surprise. I needed a surprise. Perry said, "Tahdah!" And from behind the
bedroom door jumped Marshall.

Perry's best friend.

I like Marshall. But how was that fun for me? They just bar hop
together whenever Marshall is in town. Play ball and chest-bump. I
said, "Hi, Marshall." He said, "I've gotten better receptions than that
before!"

I know.

The funk was hanging over me. Perry said, "Marshall is going to
solve your work problems." Marshall and Perry are old army buddies.
But now Marshall is an attorney in Washington. The Pentagon.

Inside scoop.

Marshall said, "I've got a friend who's working on a potential class
action lawsuit. There are four women, two in D.C. and two in L.A.,
who are thinking of filing for work discrimination and sexual harassment. It's hush-hush. . . ."

"Then how do you know?"

Marshall laughed, "It's hush-hush to the rest of the world, but
Washington lawyers know everything about what's going on with each
other. Anyway, Denise, the suit may not get filed if enough employees
don't agree to be part of it . . . plus the company is trying to cut a deal
with the four women and squash it right away."

So?

"So," Marshall said, "the potential lawsuit is against your network." My mouth dropped open. Interesting! *Wow.*

"Keep going," I said.

"Perry told me how you've been mistreated. Here's the deal. Quincy Metro is trying to squash this case on the hush because they've got a twelve-billion-dollar deal pending. But if a lawsuit of this magnitude is filed . . ."

"The deal is ruined," I concluded.

"Exactly," Perry said gleefully. How was all this to my advantage? "But you're not sure the suit will be filed?" Marshall said, "No. Two of the four women are wavering. One suddenly got promoted with a big raise. The other woman is now under a microscope at work. She's cracking under the pressure. They're building a case to fire her. Both women might bow out."

"Quincy Metro doesn't play," I said.

"So the case could get dropped," Marshall continued. "But if the lawsuit is filed, it could be in court for years. Or the suit could be settled out of court quickly for millions. Texaco settled in '96 for a hundred seventy-six million in a race discrimination case. It's a crap shoot."

"So what's this mean for me?"

"Man! Explain it to her!" Perry said. "You are a smart motherfucker!" They chest-bumped. Marshall said, "Denise, what you do now, is go to the—the . . ."

"The Wizard."

"Yeah, the Wizard," Marshall continued. "And you tell him that you're going to join the lawsuit *unless* you get the job you want. Quincy Metro isn't going to stand for someone new coming into the litigation game."

"But backlash . . ."

"What backlash?" Perry said. "You only talk to the Wizard. Do you think he wants you to go to Corporate? Do you think he will tell them about your threat? No way. He'll want to kill it in house, here. The Wizard wants to keep his job when the new bosses come in. He'll play the game."

"What if he balks?"

"He won't," Marshall explained. "Why would he allow the potential holdup of a twelve-billion-dollar deal? They'd hang him. The Wizard, if he's been doing the things Perry has told me, is smart. He'll give you the job and hope you hang yourself."

Except I won't.

Perry said, "This is your chance. Nuke 'em, baby."

I did.

The Wizard nearly *whizzed* in his Armani. But it played out just as Perry and Marshall said it would. The Wizard said, "The assistant news director job is yours."

Oh no.

"I want the news director's job. The big job," I said. "The assistant news director guy you wanted, hire him. But he'll be invisible. I want to run the whole shop. My way."

The Wizard said, "Hmmm."

"This is no joke," I said. He asked, "Are you ready for this job?" I told him, "I was born for it. I also want free rein to run the shop as I see fit."

He laughed.

"I don't fucking like this much," the Wizard finally said. "I don't like being manipulated." I said, "Join the club. You feel intimidated, don't you? You never dreamed your big manly feet could fit my pumps, did you?"

No response.

The Wizard was stone cold when he said, "Free rein costs." I would go for broke. Nothing less could serve me. My ambition. My drive. My need to rise above the fence this company had built around my dreams.

I'm going for it.

"I'll give you free rein for the rest of the year. That's what, about eight months? That includes the July and November ratings periods. Show me a marked change. Not dramatic. Just a couple of points. A change in morale even. You then have the job for as long as I'm here. No change, you're out. Deal?"

"Deal."

Alex
Photographer/Technician

Al'right, it was me, Kenya, Holly, and Beans. We just bum-rushed Denise in her office.

"Denise, congrats. We heard you got the news director job!" Beans said. She reached across the desk to give Denise a high-five. Denise hesitated, then smacked Beans' palms.

"Denise," Holly said to her, "the BEN meeting was buzzing too. It's unheard of—two black news directors following each other! It's impressive!"

"What did you do," I said, "pull a gun on the Wizard?"

"Talent wins out," Denise answered.

For the first time, I saw her business-business role take a backseat break and I thought, yeah, girl, cool.

"A request," Beans said, winking at me, then Denise. "Can we now, please, get our bathroom fixed in the garage?"

Denise nodded yes. "It's on my list. I've got other things to do first. *But.* It is on the list."

Beans gave her a thumbs-up. I grabbed Denise by the arm. "C'mon. You have to come out to the newsroom."

Everyone was standing around a big cake at the assignment desk. It read, *You Go, Girl.*

Denise grinned at me. "Thanks everybody. Let me say something. This is as perfect a time as any. I want to see a change in this newsroom. We have exciting jobs that can be great fun. Let dedication and a positive spirit drive you. I'm asking for your best work. Your best attitude. Give me three f's—factual, fast, and fun!"

Everyone cheered. "Cut the cake!"

Then Beans said, "Wait, Denise. Of course you know that there's a WKBA tradition for new bosses, a game we play?!"

"Yes," Denise laughed. "The Godfather. The Wizard. I know. But I'm here already. Luckily, I'm spared."

"Says who?" Kenya catcalled.

"Oh no," Denise said, bringing her hands to her mouth. But her eyes were sparkling.

"We don't play, girlfriend," I laughed. "We faxed ourselves!"

Rod stood up. "We had some extra help from Alex."

I threw my hands in the air. "Roger Ebert ain't the only movie expert in town!"

Rod shouted, "What movie?"

All the staffers shouted back, *"Claudine!"*

"What character?"

"Claudine!"

"Best line?"

Alex stepped up and quoted: "I'm scared but I do my job. If you ain't scared you don't have no need for guts."

Coming Up Next:

Denise reveals "The Incident" that has haunted her throughout her broadcast career.

Then:

Kenya struggles with her role as a producer. What responsibility do black journalists have in deciding what images are broadcast about people of color?

Plus:

Still playing the stock market to cash in on her dream, Beans struggles with the rising and falling market.

Those stories and more, straight ahead.

Sports

Holly
Reporter/Anchor

"Heads up, newsroom!"

That's what Stat shouted when he jumped up out of his seat at the assignment desk. "You guys know that rookie ballplayer the Sox signed?"

"Ernest Slaughter," Mack answered. "Hey, he's got that funny nickname too, huh?"

"Sluggo," one of the sports producers yelled out. "He got a big deal with that shoe company. One of those *might be mike contracts*. Gave me a good interview the other day at the park. What'd the kid do wrong?"

"For a change," Stat said, "this is a good story. He's decided to buy new computers for the community center that services the Robert Taylor Homes."

"Good for him!" I said admiringly.

"There's more. We knew the Vice President was flying in tomorrow from Washington for a fund-raiser. Now get this, the VP wants to tour the Robert Taylor Homes with Sluggo to spotlight a new program. It's called Athletes Giving Back."

"Nice heads up!" Abby said.

Stat grinned. "My source owes me in a major way. He'll get us an exclusive interview with Sluggo and the VP."

"Are you sure?" Abby said, narrowing her eyes in a suspicious manner. "If you don't deliver you'll be eating fuck-up for lunch!"

"He owes me," Stat said with confidence. "We're in."

Mack and I looked at each other. This was a rarity—a big local story with national exposure—and it's positive too. We each thought about our continuous stint on ghetto patrol. This time, however, it would be different.

I stood up and then Mack stood up. Would he get it? He's paid more dues. But lately I've been kicking butt. I've been turning in good stories. I'm thriving under Denise because she has a no-nonsense but nurturing hand. Who would get this plum assignment? Mack or me?

Stat and Abby were now huddled together talking. Mack and I had too much respect for one another to back-stab for this story. Like dueling sharpshooters we decided to face off front and center at the assignment desk.

Abby and Stat looked right past both of us. Abby yelled, "Anybody seen Stu? We need to talk to him about this Sluggo/VP story for tomorrow."

"Stu?" I gasped. How dare they!

"Well," Stat explained. "Stu always covers the Vice President when he comes to town . . ."

"Wait a minute," Mack snorted. "I can report just as well as Stu. This is bullshit!"

"What are you so pissed off about?" Stat asked Mack.

"For the same reason I'm angry!" I shouted. "Practically every week you send Mack or me to some black housing project to cover a story. You never try to send a white reporter unless you absolutely have to. You send us there, however, in a heartbeat. Now there's a top story in those same housing projects, and we don't get to go."

Stat said, "I don't send you guys to the projects any more than I do any of the other reporters."

"Are you kidding?" Mack scoffed. "I was on the elevator at the Robert Taylor Homes last week. An old lady said to me, 'Visiting again? Baby, what floor your mama live on?' "

People began laughing. In the midst of all this, the newsroom door swung open and Will strutted in. He was tipsy and bellowed, "Say, Stat, who's my reporter? I'm waiting."

"Mack, just go ahead and cover your story for today. Will's ready to roll. We'll talk later."

"No, Stat, I want to talk about it now."

"Get going, Mack," Abby snapped. "Jesus, stop pissing and moaning over this."

Mack yanked out a chair and propped his leg up on it. "No sir, ladies and gentlemen! I don't want any funny stuff. Let's hammer this out now."

"Right," I said, backing up Mack. "This needs to be addressed immediately."

Will slurred, "Well, I could cover the story by myself but who'd do the interview? Who'd hold the mike?"

Mack jerked around and snapped, "Maybe you could stick it up your ass and bend over?"

Will's face turned pomegranate red and his lips began to quiver before snapping into a swear-laden scenario that ended with, "Go to hell, Mack!"

"After you!"

Tensely and slowly, silence enveloped the newsroom. The sound of footsteps behind me snipped through the dead air. Out of the corner of my eye, I saw Denise.

She said, "I heard there's trouble out here."

"I'll tell you what's up," Mack yelled. "These two are trying to demean our worth as reporters in this shop!"

"Aww, that's crap, Denise. It's more like Mack doesn't wanna do his goddamn job!" Stat countered. "You're not half as good as your hype, Mack. Why don't you get a grip?"

"Like around your balls maybe?"

"Stop it," Denise snapped. "This is old WKBA BS. I'm not having it. Now let's get to the heart of the problem."

Abby made a false start. "Denise, I'm trying—"

Denise lopped her off at the verb. "Excuse me. I'll handle this. Holly, you tell me. What's going on?"

I explained to Denise carefully and without bias. What was Denise going to do? The entire newsroom was watching.

"Stat," Denise said, "I know for a fact that Holly and Mack are often sent to stories that break in Chicago Housing Authority buildings . . ."

"The Jets," Mack said, smugly referring to the street name for the housing projects. "Fair is fair."

Denise looked at Mack as if he were a little boy acting up in church. Then she continued, "Mack and Holly are good enough to cover a drive-by. They are also good enough to cover the prime story. Divide it. Holly, Mack's the senior reporter here. He should get the tour and the sit-down."

A gulp and sigh left my lips. I wanted it, but I couldn't really argue with the decision. I couldn't—and it did my psyche justice to know that at least Stu wasn't going to get it.

"But I saw on the wires that there's a VIP banquet at the Drake," Denise said. "Holly covers that in the evening. That's for doing the grunt coverage normally."

"But," Abby snapped, "Stu will want to know why he's not covering the big story and . . ."

"Excuse me, Abby," Denise said. "I run this newsroom. Not Stu. This time he won't cover the Vice President. Stu is a team player. He'll get over it. Settled?"

"Settled," Mack and I said, smiling at one another.

Beans

Photographer/Technician

"Hey, Beans, did you read The Column today?"

These people in here live on The Column, which I'm willing to wager they read before the newspaper headlines or the sports section, or for me, the horoscope.

"Take a peek; it's interesting, Beans. Looks like the sale of Quincy Metro isn't going to go through," the guys in the garage explained. A copy of the newspaper was folded back, covered with thumb smudges, the marks of culprits who'd already committed the crime of eating up the copy.

I picked it up and read, to my surprise, that apparently the potential buyers suddenly were upset that our network had no big sports package. Our owner, Jeb Quincy, had held on to the purse strings when the other networks shelled out mega dollars for football in what was the biggest cash payout in NFL history.

ABC paid $550 million a year to keep NBC from swiping *Monday Night Football*, which is a high-profile entity, because it's one of the highest-rated shows in prime time. A thirty-second spot on *Monday Night*, where the car dealers hawk and the Bud Frogs croak, cost $30,000 because the audience is loyal and it's raining big spenders across the board.

Sports is big money, a cash cow, for a powerhouse network. CBS lost football, and they lost prestige. Running scared, CBS got football back, but at a cost of $500 million a year for the AFC.

We had no football but we did have baseball, which turned out to be a dog, when, after the strike, the audience shrank and never really came back. We lost baseball when a new upstart cable sports network outbid us, but there were promises of golf and more tennis, but they couldn't fill the void. Now it seems the buyers are being wary, which they should have been in the first place, but The Column said the deal was sliding down the tubes headfirst into the trash.

"So what do you guys think," I asked. "Does this mean a drop in Quincy Metro stock?"

"Maybe. Maybe not."

"Beans, I think it means no deal and they put this piece of shitty network back on the block. It's not the company it used to be, that's for sure. I think the old guy is trying to bail before those crazy twins of his can get their paws on it outright. Did you see Jeb Junior in *People* magazine with that new Hollywood babe?"

"Yeah," one of the other guys said. "She ain't banging him for his looks. Junior's got a schnozzola on him like Durante, just like the old man!"

They all laughed, elbowed and slid down into this T&A thing about Jeb Junior's movie-star girlfriend; I've learned to just leave—as a woman I become invisible anyway.

I began to worry about my dream of owning my own company, about the value of Quincy Metro stock. I was making steady progress toward my goal, and with a little more luck, I'd soon have enough money to leave WKBA.

I called Boardwalk. "Hey, what do you think about dumping Quincy Metro stock. I'm hearing here that the sale might not go through. Maybe I should take the money and run, then look around, try something else for a big short-term gain."

Boardwalk laughed her reassuring laugh. She said, "Don't worry, the stock is holding around thirty-two. Wait. My gut says the sale will go through and there'll be a stock split soon afterward. If you bail out now, Megan, you'll have to stay in the market two more years at least to reach your goal. I say hang in. But it's your call, my friend."

I crossed my fingers, and my toes, and I hung in for the ride.

DENISE

NEWS DIRECTOR

Corporate panic.

The Wizard called me into his office. The network sale is in jeopardy. The potential buyers may pull out. There's a penalty clause for such a move—$10 million. But that doesn't look like enough of a deterrent.

The accountants.

They saw the falling ratings. No true sports dollars. The dip in revenues. Our owned-and-operated station alone had lost millions in profits. We're in a slump. WKBA needs to make . . .

More money.

It's a money game of hard ball. The Wizard said they green-lighted the extra afternoon show. That's more ad time to book, to sell. It's a half-hour show. But no new staff. Stretch what we have.

How?

It's hell covering the shifts now. The buyers think we're fat. The buyers need to see more revenue because of the absence of strong sports and weakening programming.

Get the show up.

As soon as possible. Like next month. "Next month?" I said. The Wizard said, "You wanted this job. Dirt goes with it. Free rein, remember? I don't care how you do it, just get it done. Corporate says so."

I had a hard time sleeping.

I tossed and I turned. I needed to make that show work. Instant success. I racked my brain. How can it be different? How can it be a draw? What do viewers really want? How can I get it up and running with less people?

I had an idea.

I called Holly into my office. I called Alex into my office. I called Kenya into my office. "There's a new show going up next month. The green light has been given."

Holly said, "The four o'clock?"

"No," I said. "I've gotten the okay to put the show at six-thirty. The game show moves up to four. I think more people are home at six-thirty. That's when we can hit a larger audience. I need you guys to make this show work."

I'm banking on them.

"Holly, I want you to anchor." She beamed. "Kenya, I want you to produce the show. You have integrity. You're off overnights."

She stood up and cheered.

We laughed. "Alex, I want to start something special. Every Friday night. I want a photo essay. Once a week. It can be on anything. But I want you to shoot and edit it. I want it to be creative."

That's one idea.

"You guys are the backbone of this show. I want it to have a local focus. Top local stories. Positive features, all local. We concentrate on specific areas each night. Example, Mondays: North Side. So in that section we have positive features about something on the North Side. Tuesdays: South Side—a Chatham spotlight. Wednesdays: Western Suburbs—Oak Park. And so on. That's the plan. But first, I want to tell you three something."

They hung on my every word.

"I want you to know. I'm out there. I'm going for broke to make this work. To make a name for us. For Holly. For Kenya. For Alex. For me. I want you to know where I'm coming from. I want you to know about an incident."

I began to relive it. . . .

It was another network. Another time. I was at a regional conference for managers. This broadcast company was small but it owned ten television stations.

I was an executive producer at the time. I was the only black manager they had.

Period.

I was always well dressed. I did my homework. I knew the names of the other white male managers.

I knew their work history.

I brought up the ratings of my station's early newscasts. I knew my stuff. Higher ratings mean higher sales rates.

Mo' money.

I was a bad black woman. I thought they knew it too. I thought my record spoke for itself.

I thought wrong.

I went to a meeting one day. At a restaurant. I was the only black manager there. But I wasn't the only black person there.

A joke was made.

The black servers were very late bringing out our food. One of our veteran managers cracked a joke at my expense.

Wasn't funny.

He said, "Dee-nice, you sure can organize a newsroom. Well, then, you oughta be able to organize a kitchen too. Those people better watch out. Any minute, we may send Dee-nice here in there to grab an apron and give those people a hand in serving us!"

Everyone laughed except me.

I popped off. I did my Roots *impression of Kizzy. I said, "Yeah-sar, boss. You'se know all black folks likes to serve."*

Silence.

His face turned brick red. After that, I wasn't a novelty anymore. I'd shattered it. Now there was only my record. My record was good. But now, suddenly, I wasn't invited to any meetings.

No promotions.

A white colleague who had been a supporter pulled me aside. He said that my star was no longer on the rise. I left the company. I'd made a mistake . . .

I told them now as clearly as I could.

"There is no room for error. We are black in broadcasting. It's time to move on. Time to be strategic."

That was my lesson, I thought.

"I know not to bend. Not to accept. But to be careful what battles I choose to fight and how I fight them. This battle I want. I choose not to be careful anymore. I'm going for it all."

From the gut.

Holly
Reporter/Anchor

"There's something wrong," the Wizard said, irritated and perplexed.

He was staring at me.

The Wizard and another middle-aged white man, a consultant, studied me with naked openness. Consultants get paid a tremendous amount of money to evaluate news talent. They determine what's good and what's bad about performance and appearance.

I was sitting at the anchor desk, my hair whipped, and my makeup flawless yet they examined me with open skepticism. I felt uncomfortable, almost maligned.

I know there's nothing wrong with me but they make me feel like there's something wrong! Sometimes work can make you feel like you can't do anything right and there's something wrong with you.

I was sitting on the new set for the six-thirty show. I was finally part of the master plan. I knew to keep my mouth shut, I just didn't know how to shut down my feelings.

The Wizard stared at me. I waited . . . and waited. I hated that I had to wait for his approval, and even worse, I disliked that I desired it. But

I had to play the game, to get what I wanted—a top anchor spot in Chicago.

"Something's wrong," the Wizard said. "It's . . . it's . . . her hair!"

I winced on the inside; not my hair! It had taken years to grow my hair out strong and healthy.

"There are too many dark-haired women anchoring," the Wizard explained. "There's Hazel. Marybeth on the weekend. Long dark hair. Now Holly. She should cut her hair."

"Why not have Hazel cut her hair?" I suggested, speaking with a knot in my throat. "Hazel has had the same dated look for years."

Change her, I thought, and leave me alone!

"No," the consultant said, "we conducted an audience survey last year. The viewers like Hazel's look. You're new. You'll have to change. A short cut would be good, like that singer who lost all her money. The one who was on Oprah. What's her name?"

"Toni Braxton?" I huffed.

The Wizard snapped his fingers, "Yes! Brilliant idea!"

I swallowed, "I don't think that's the way to go—"

"Holly," the Wizard said, "you need to get in gear with what we're trying to achieve here. We want a specific look. We want something different. We want a hit. If you're not ready, if you're not willing to work with us, then maybe . . ."

Would the Wizard just take it all away from me, just like that? As hard as I've worked? I went to plead my case to Denise.

"Holly, think. Don't you see what's at work here?"

"No, what, Denise?"

"You've heard the buzz?"

Sure. Everyone was talking about how well Denise was doing. Morale was up. This show had enormous potential. Buzz was that if it was a success, she'd be golden with Quincy Broadcasting bigwigs.

"The Wizard senses success. I'm the architect. Now he wants in. He wants to make a noticeable change. Get some credit. Therefore, change you."

"Denise, can't you just talk to him?"

I watched her chest heave, a dry sigh dripped from her lips. "Holly. Think. You don't really want me to talk to him about your hair."

I cocked my head to the side. "Why don't I?"

Denise softened her tone and said, "I can't waste ammo on that. You want me to shoot at a rabbit when I've got a lion to kill. It doesn't make sense."

"This is TV," I huffed. "Part of the reason a woman is selected to anchor is because of how she looks. Give him some history, Denise. Explain to him about how sensitive black women are about their hair. Maybe that will milk some sympathy out of the man!"

"Holly. Be realistic. That white man does not want to hear that. And if he heard it, he wouldn't understand."

"Denise!"

She shrugged a sorry and changed the subject.

That evening I went over to Kenya's apartment. Kenya had invited Alex and me over for some of her smoking gumbo. The three of us were in the kitchen when I told them what seemed sure to be my fate. Jarrett piped up from the bathroom where he was giving Jeffie a bath. "You better not! You know brothers love some pretty hair!"

Alex added, "And you're not white! Your hair won't grow back overnight!"

I could feel the blood draining from my face.

"But maybe it'll be cute," Kenya said, trying now to be upbeat. "Who's gonna do it?"

"They want to fly me to New York. The consultant uses a French stylist there. He owns a salon in Manhattan."

"French, my ass!" Alex laughed. "Girl, you better find you some homegirl on the South Side right here in Chicago. She'll know how to lay out some black hair."

"If you go South Side, don't come out of there with one of those mile high do's!" Kenya cut her eyes and teased. "I saw one the other day that looked like a replica of the Sears Tower. The poor child had to turn her head sideways to get on the Jeffrey Express bus."

The more they laughed and joked about assorted scary hairy tales, the more uneasy I became. That's why I ended up the next day at a well-recommended salon in Hyde Park.

"Well," the hair stylist said after I told her what the powers that be wanted, "they aren't in my chair. You are. Do you want me to cut it off?"

"No! But I need something that looks different from the other main anchors at our station. This is my wish list. I want a restyling cut that'll be sharp, complementing my face and head shape. I also want to look chic, African-American, but still professional. By all means, not too short."

"Relax. You're going to love what I do."

When I left the salon, I had a cut that was off the shoulder just below the ear in a sassy bob. The top was cut in two layers, a longer section then a short section in front. I could do a sassy swag or throw down some bangs for a different look. The bottom section of my hair was shorter but still long enough for an after-five hairstyle.

I went to the studio for the final set check with my new hairdo. Everyone stared. The consultants. The Wizard. Denise. Everyone stared for about ten seconds, ten seconds going on eternity.

Then . . . they loved it! Especially when I gave them a demonstration of the three different looks I could get. When they left the studio later, Denise winked at me and whispered, "Player."

KENYA
Writer/Producer

Before I worked in TV news, I wondered how stories were selected. There's a meetin' open to everyone both in the mornin' and in the afternoon. During that meetin', stories are written on a board and people shoot 'em down or build 'em up. It's competitive too because there's limited air time in what we call a "news hole."

I really learned about the "news hole" when I was bein' trained to produce by Abby. She didn't wanna train me bit more than the man in the moon but Denise told her to. It was Denise's idea to give me an opportunity to produce. That woman can put the pressure on you too, boy oh boy. Denise said, "I have the power to make this happen for you. I'm going to. You're smart. You're good. Don't blow it."

Abby sat and gave me a crash course and really explained the "news hole." In a thirty-minute newscast you don't have thirty minutes worth of news. You have to subtract three two-minute commercial breaks. That leaves twenty-four minutes.

You have "headlines" at the beginnin' of the newscast and then "teases" before each of those three commercial breaks. "Headlines" and "teases" tell the audience what's coming up next—and they're fifteen seconds each. That leaves twenty-three minutes. Now you subtract three minutes for sports and two minutes for weather. That leaves eighteen minutes.

Then you subtract time for "chat"; that's when the anchors joke a bit with each other and then there's the "kicker." The "kicker" *is that cute, funny, awwww, or ironic leave 'em with a smile y'all come back now ya hear story.* That leaves seventeen minutes for news. You've got seventeen measly minutes to tell your audience about the most important stories in Chicago, the nation, and the world. That's the *hole* you have to fill with *news—news hole.*

When you select the stories for your news hole it's like shoppin' for groceries. If you've got seventeen dollars, you can't buy everythin' you want. You have to pick what you really need but you can't spend more than what you have. So when you put somethin' extra into the cart, you have to take somethin' else out. Whenever you add, you have to subtract. Otherwise you're liable to get yourself into a whole bunch of trouble.

Like I did.

I was a couple of weeks into producin' the new six-thirty show. I was jammin'. Holly was really jammin' as an anchor. This day I came out of the meetin' with good local stories. One: Surveillance tapes were bein' played in court at the trial of a former judge accused of takin' bribes to fix felony cases.

Two: We had an exclusive with a woman who was robbed in a mall parkin' lot and claimed security was lax.

Three: We had a feature on a black dentist who retired then opened a free clinic for poor children.

I added other stories—one about land mines overseas—and some other stories to fill my news hole. But at 5:45 P.M. my smooth show blew up in my face.

"Heads up!" a researcher on the assignment desk shouted. "Three people have been shot in a gang shoot-out! One of the victims might be an undercover cop!"

I jumped up. Abby jumped up. Denise was in earshot. She stopped her conversation and rushed to the assignment desk. We huddled together. I looked at the clock—5:47 P.M. The researcher pulled down a street map of the city. We huddled. We pinpointed where all our reporters and camera crews were located around the city and the suburbs. When you have a breaker you have to get there quick and in some kindah hurry. Who was the closest to the scene?

Mack was the closest. We phoned him in the truck—tellin' him and his photog to hightail it over to the crime scene and be prepared to go live at the top of the six-thirty show.

I ran back over to my computer. I was addin' two minutes for this new lead story, so I had to subtract two minutes. Otherwise I'd be "heavy"; heavy is when you're goin' over your allotted time—too many groceries in the cart.

When you produce you always have "kill pages." Those are the stories in the show that you think are the first to go to save time. I clicked on those stories and deleted them.

By 6:05 P.M. Mack still hadn't made it to the crime scene. "How far away is he?" I asked the assignment desk, whose job it is to keep track of that.

"Five minutes!" was the answer. "Traffic's a bitch!"

Five minutes later he still wasn't there. The lead has to be there. Mack had to make his hit time at the top of the show. I ran into the control room at 6:25 P.M.

The control room looks like the ones moviegoers saw in *Broadcast News* and *Network*. There are a bunch of monitors—mini TV screens—that show the anchors on set and the producer sits behind the director, who decides what camera shots are shown on air.

"Where's Mack?" I asked in a low voice, tryin' to hide the sense of panic I was feelin'. Abby told me he had finally made it to the scene but I couldn't see a live picture of him on the monitor. "Where's Mack?"

On cue, his picture popped up on the monitor. He smiled into the camera as if he knew I was callin' his name. "Audio check . . . check . . . Great black men in America . . . Douglass, Robeson, Robinson, King . . ."

I breathed a sigh of relief. As soon as the sigh left my lips, we were live on-air. The headlines were great. Then we went live to Mack at the scene of the gang shoot-out. He was flawless. He had good stuff. Stuff about the victims: One really was an undercover cop. Mack was rollin'. But then suddenly I remembered I only gave him two minutes. Mack talked for three minutes. "Wrap him," I shouted to the director. That was a nice TV way of orderin' the director to tell the reporter to hush! I was *heavy* again!

I looked at my computer screen and thought about what stories I wanted to delete. Stu was up next. He was sittin' on set with the anchors—he had inside info about the judge's corruption trial. I hit a button where I sat and spoke to Stu through his earpiece. "Make it short. I'm heavy!"

Stu looked dead into the camera, knowin' everyone in the booth was watchin', and scowled, then shook his head.

"Stu, I'm heavy!"

He looked down and waved me off with two hands. I knew he was gonna be doggish and take all the time he wanted.

The director looked over his shoulder and snorted, "You're absolutely fucked now."

And I was.

Despite the stories I planned to delete, plus trimmin' time away from weather and sports, I still ended up two and a half minutes heavy. I had to get back on time. What to kill? What groceries should I put back?

Abby called me from the newsroom and said, "You're heavy as shit. Kill the feature on the dentist!" Then she hung up.

Now I looked at my computer. The gang shoot-out had already aired: black crime. The corruption case with a judge on trial had already aired—the judge happened to be black: black crime. The mall robbery/security story was about to air. The robber was white but still at large—all we had was the black woman who was attacked: black crime victim. The one positive story about a black person in the show—besides Tiger Woods in sports—was the dentist. I fingered the delete button.

"Kenya! What stories are you going to kill!" the director yelled over his shoulder.

My mind was churnin'. Blacks doin' crime or bein' victims of crime. Superstar athletes. Stereotypes. That's what this show told our viewers.

"Kenya! You wanna make some decisions here, for Christ sake?" the director yelled at me.

Kill the dentist package, Abby had said. The positive story. Shoot! Emotionally I felt my obligation as a black person to do somethin' to unstack the image deck. I gulped and spoke up loud and clear, "Kill page twenty-one. And kill Break Two."

Holly
Reporter/Anchor

"Are you insane killing that commercial break?" Abby screamed.

All I saw was Kenya coming out of the booth at the end of the show with Abby on her heels. Abby was screaming like a mental patient in need of medication. "Are you insane! None of the commercials ran!

"Goddammit. I told you to kill that two-minute feature on the dentist. Kenya, you just fucked up the show. Now the sales guys will be bitching at us because those ads didn't run! That's lost revenue. That's money down the drain."

I watched Kenya pivot on her toes, then drop her torso forward as she looked up into Abby's face. "I got boxed into a corner by Mack and Stu. Why aren't you yellin' at them?"

"I don't care about them. I care that you went and made a bone-headed decision despite the fact that I told you what to do. I'm the executive producer!"

I hate it when Abby acts as if she is God in the newsroom. Kenya and I had talked about it several times. Make your point, Kenya, I thought, but be careful.

Kenya said, "And that means what, Abby? Does that mean you get to yell and scream and be mean and tacky? The newsroom is not exempt from manners, is it?"

"Manners? What do manners have to do with the fact that you can't produce your way out of a paper bag?"

"Abby, I had nowhere to go. I'm the producer, it was my show and my choice. I stand by it—it gave the newscast balance and if you can't see that then shame on you."

"Don't give me that "Scarlet J" crap—walking around here as if you're branded and persecuted for being an ethical journalist!" Abby shouted.

Kenya tried to interject, "You—"

"Furthermore, why'd you kill the story about the cat that did the trick with the bungee cord?" Abby raged on. "It was the cutest story of the day!!!"

Now people were coming through doors, watching as the argument between these two kept escalating. Kenya was holding her own. Her reputation would be enhanced after this public interchange . . . Go, Kenya.

"But, Abby," she argued, "there was no journalistic value to the cat story and you know it. The only reason you had me put it in the show in the first place is 'cause you loved the picture."

"Kenya, you screwed up, just admit it."

Alex was coming through the back way of the newsroom. She asked me, "Who's throwing down? Damn, I heard the fight all the way down the hallway."

Instinctively I raised my hands to my lips and nodded toward the standoff in the middle of the newsroom. Kenya was getting dogged. Out of the corner of my eye, in the rear of the newsroom I saw Vera peeping around the crowd. She eased back and disappeared into the office areas.

"The next time I tell you to do something, Kenya, you do it!" Abby threatened. "This is my newsroom."

"I don't think so," Denise said as she emerged from her office. Vera had tipped her off. "This is my newsroom," she said. "No more newsroom brawls. Not on my watch."

Alex started nudging me with her elbow. "Aww shit, it's on now!"

"For Christ sake, Kenya killed a commercial break."

For much of the melee everyone was quiet; now Dragon Diva decided to side with Abby. What a piece of work!

"Well, after all, Denise," Dragon Diva began, "the executive producer has to keep a tight rein. And that bungee story Kenya killed was so cute it—"

"Hazel," Denise said, "when I want your input, I'll solicit it."

Yes! Yes! I thought.

"Kenya, you were wrong," Denise said, holding court in the newsroom. "The executive producer is the last word."

I held my breath. Alex looked at me and shrugged. But what about Abby? Abby was out of line!

"But, Abby, you're dead wrong. You're a manager. Manage without berating. If not, then let me say from the bottom of my heart we will miss you here at WKBA."

After that, the rest of the show was critiqued in an orderly and constructive manner. Kenya said very little. When it was over, I caught Kenya by the arm and whispered, "Let's grab a bite, huh?"

"Naw, I've got to pick up Jeffie from Miss Billie's house."

"The sister girl network hasn't met in a while. Call and ask her if you can pick up Jeffie in a couple of hours."

Kenya gave me a half smile, picked up the phone, and made the call. Miss Billie said it was okay.

"Great. I've got to make some calls on a story first, but you and Alex head over and grab a table." As Alex and Kenya turned to go, I asked, "The table seats four, doesn't it?"

We all understood. Kenya said, "Sure does."

KENYA
Writer/Producer

Where's my first loyalty? Am I black first? Or a journalist first? In my work. That's what I'm talkin' about. Which do I draw on first? Which do I lean on first? My blackness or my journalism skills? When I decide to play a story in the show, do I run it 'cause it's a positive, black story? Do I *not run* some of the crime stories because they are stereotypical and show black folk in a negative light? Am I incitin' or informin'?

These were the questions I served as appetizers as we sat waitin' to order—me, Alex, and for the first time, Denise. Holly was joinin' us later.

"Kenya, you did right, girl," Alex said. "Absolutely you should send out a positive image. If we don't, who will?"

"But it has to be appropriate," Denise argued. "To run a feature, you killed a commercial break. That's a news sin. The advantage didn't outweigh the cost."

"Well damn, why didn't it, Denise?" Alex said. "I know killing a break is a big no-no. But a positive story about a black professional deserves to be in the newscast."

"I'm inclined to side with Alex," I said. "It shows our white audience that black folk are about more than just sports, crime, and entertainment. It shows our black audience that we are makin' an effort to balance out the images. What's wrong with that, Denise?"

"Nothing, Kenya," she said. "But pull it off. Pull it off with no hassle. Morally, I'm in the boat with you. But you can't pick and choose on that basis. Do we kill the story on the Irish pub outside of Wrigley Field? It may imply that the Irish are alcoholics. Now everyone is choosing stories by personal agendas. That's wrong."

I moaned, "Shoot. TV news caters to the ideas and fears of white, middle-class culture. If I put three positive black stories in a half-hour show, an executive producer will say I've got too many 'black' stories in there. If I put in three crime stories that happen to be in black neighborhoods, I don't have too many 'black' stories then. When race is involved and a story is negative, it's still news. But when race is involved and the story is positive, it's not news."

"That's overboard, Kenya," Denise suggested. "There are mistakes. Society is skewed. So news gets skewed. But we have to believe it's not blatant. I have to. Optimism. It's key. Otherwise I'll go nuts. It's a learning process. All of America needs to be inclusive. To be fair. To be both things to people of color. News is part of that."

"Okay," Alex said, sippin' her diet Dr. Pepper. "But my point *again* is that we have to step up. What we do reflects and affects black people. If we don't, shit, who will, Denise?"

"I know that. My point is simple. Be responsible. Do it right. Pick your battles. That way you can win. You can live to fight on. If there's constant conflict, you'll be out of a job."

"They can keep their trifling job!"

"Okay, Alex. Then who speaks up?" Denise asked, then answered, "No one. Our voices are too few as is."

Holly came floatin' into the restaurant. She plopped down at the table, "What'd I miss? Huh? Huh?"

"Bumper pool!" Alex joked. "The media is the cue stick. The stories are the balls. The black employees are the bumpers. And the viewers are the pockets."

"Y'all know what," I sighed, "I went to my church's Baptist tea last Sunday. Everybody at my table was grillin' me about the news. *Why don't you all do more positive stories? Why is the news so negative?*"

"And," Alex snorted, "some of those same people are watching the *Jerry Springer* show every day!"

"Springer!" we all laughed.

"Hey, let's get disguised and go on the show, huh?" Alex sneered and threw up her hands in a boxin' stance.

"That's the last thing we'd need," Denise smiled. "Our station? It's turning around. The ratings chart doesn't lie. Our ratings are going up!"

Alex
Photographer/Technician

Damn, how could I know that some foul stuff was about to jump off? How could I know that by the end of the week one of the two people sitting in my unit would be in the middle of a stank controversy?

Rock and I had such a great day. We were at the United Center for another charity event by the Bulls for handicapped children.

"Remember last time?" Rock smiled, looking at a basketball on the sidelines. "Y'all laughed at me!"

"Rock, you ain't a baller, man! I've seen midgets jump higher than you."

A couple of the ballplayers heard me and catcalled, "Rock! Stay behind the camera, dog! You ain't got no legs, baby!"

"Hey, I'm ready to help y'all take on the Knicks—you need some muscle."

"Oh!" two of the players crooned. "You got game, baby? Rock says he's got game! Go ahead. It's showtime, baby."

Rock put his camera on a chair beneath the basket. He grabbed the ball and skipped out to half court.

"Man," I said, "c'mon! We have to get back to the station. If we don't get back soon they'll hang us."

"Chill, woman. You just stand there and let me dunk over your fat head," Rock laughed. "Bet twenty?"

"If I keep taking your money, Rock, your wife is going to get suspicious."

"Are you scared because I've been practicing?"

"Bet then."

"That's twenty bucks, Alex! Now, get back everybody. Clear the lane. Rock is driving to the hole!"

Everyone stopped to watch. Rock drove to the basket and took off . . . his body went up and twisted, then he came down the wrong way. Rock went sprawling, his heels kicking, as he landed on top of the camera and chair. He went crashing to the ground, and I heard a pop and I saw the lens slide out of the face of the camera.

We all sprinted over. "Rock! Rock!"

We helped Rock up and he groaned, grabbing his back. "I think I might have hurt my back a little bit."

One of the ball boys said, "Hey, the camera's broke!"

Had we been the only crew there, maybe we would have lied about it. I know damn well we would have lied about it. But there were other crews there from the competition, another WKBA sports crew, plus the ballplayers. It would get around sooner or later.

Rock said, "It was an accident. That camera's been having problems anyway. They'll be pissed but it'll blow over."

Obviously we didn't have a clue.

DENISE
News Director

"We're firing Rock."

That's what the Wizard said. "Denise, the *Red Book* says that you can be fired on the spot for being negligent with equipment. He broke a thirty-thousand-dollar camera."

Can I save him?

"Insurance will cover the camera," I said. "Give Rock a break."

The Wizard scoffed, "No."

I got it. He was sticking to the rules with Rock. We've bent the rules for others. But Rock is the leader of BEN. "This doesn't have anything to do with BEN, does it?"

Rage.

"What's going on here?" the Wizard said. "Favoritism? I've heard that you're showing favoritism to the black workers."

"Says who?"

"It doesn't matter, Denise. I like the things you're doing in the newsroom. There's less tension. So far. Not bad. I'm pleased. That's the only complaint I've heard."

"I'm fair."

The Wizard shrugged. "Then play by the rules. Stay out of this. Rock is being terminated. The head of technical will do the firing. There's nothing you can do about it."

And that was it.

Alex
Photographer/Technician

"What the hell is going on, Denise?" I made damn sure I caught her by surprise. I waited until I saw Vera leave for lunch and I bum-rushed the old girl. "Denise, how can you just let them fire Rock, huh?"

She had to know what the deal was, didn't she? Didn't Denise know the scam, the play they were pulling? They were getting back at Rock for starting BEN—it was more direct than Braille for the blind. "What's up with that?"

"It came from the top."

"Denise, you're the news director. Can't you fight for Rock?"

"I tried."

"Twenty years on this plantation doesn't count for shit?"

"Alex, your anger is misplaced. Get mad at Rock. He should have known better."

"It was an accident, Denise. C'mon. There have been times before when equipment has been broken accidentally and nothing happened to anybody. And what about Will? He broke our tripod that time? Remember? And Will, he comes in drunk practically every day. Stat and everybody else around here look the other way."

"Rock isn't one of *the boys*. I'm not. You're not. We can't do what *the boys* do. I tried to fix things for Rock. I couldn't. Let Rock know I tried."

"Denise, our newsroom is finally turning around. Little by little. People aren't grumping like they used to. We're starting, just a little bit, to feel good about how this station is handling its business. Don't do this, not now!"

"I'm not doing it. I just can't stop it."

"Okay, Denise. But you'd better believe this ain't the end of it! BEN is not having this. The union is grieving it too!"

"Let it go, Alex. It could be worse for Rock. If there's more drama over this issue no other station will hire him."

"Do you think they'll hire Rock anyway after they learn that he started a black employee's network here at WKBA?"

"With Rock's skills, maybe."

"Bullshit, Denise. That's a long shot. But say they do. You know it won't be staff. It'll be part time. TV stations aren't hiring staff like they used to. The companies across the board don't want to pay benefits— no health care, life insurance, or investment funds. Rock needs to be back here, reinstated in full. I'll be damned if this goes down without a fight. Lay low, girlfriend, lay low."

At the BEN meeting we decided on a plan of action. First we demanded a meeting with the Wizard. He acted sympathetic but refused to rehire Rock. He said rules were rules. We wore black arm bands in honor of Rock. The Column picked it up. The Wizard was pissed off, like we gave a good goddamn.

Then we decided to circulate a petition. Kenya helped me write it. Vera typed it up for me. If we got everyone in the newsroom to sign, maybe they would rehire Rock. Shit, maybe.

Beans

Photographer/Technician

Sign the petition, or don't sign the petition; oh boy, I had to think long and hard about it. Things get so crazy here at WKBA, I want to be damn sure where I stand.

On the one hand, it's simple, Rock had been reckless with the equipment. That rule is clear, it's right there in the *Red Book*, but I hate to side with management.

Why would he, a newsroom vet, be dumb enough not to take care of that camera, knowing that management is mad at him anyway for starting BEN? And Alex, she's circulating the petition to have all the techs sign and the union is grieving Rock's firing on his behalf, but she needs to watch it too. Some of the white techs are angry that BEN isn't letting the union handle it alone, and they say had it not been for BEN in the first place, management would have let Rock slide.

Alex, outspoken and fearless, is one of the leaders of BEN too. I knew right from the start that the group was bad news; it wasn't going to do anything but divide us, and see I was right.

And what about the consequences, the consequences of the petition? I heard that even some of the other blacks are hesitant about signing the petition because management can be so vindictive and it's obvious, yes, that Denise can't protect people. She's management, and Denise has to walk the line. And anyway, who knows. If everyone signs the petition the Wizard still might not rehire Rock.

"Beans," Alex said to me in the garage—I was fiddling around with a bad light. "I need you to back me up. There's a bunch of static over this petition thing among the techs. If all the techs sign, I figure the writers and everybody else will too. It's for Rock."

I agreed to help because I had made my mind up to sign anyway, so I approached a group of hard-nosed photogs from the old film days. Half of these guys, veterans, were ready to retire within two years. I told them about the petition. They laughed, and one of them joked that it was *a black thang.* I told myself to make one pitch, and one pitch only, and if it worked, it worked. I told them from the bottom of my heart what made me decide to sign the petition myself.

I explained, "I signed the petition, after much thought, for two reasons. First: Everyone makes mistakes, sometimes the mistake alone makes you suffer enough without other people piling on punishment. A suspension without pay—I know that would have been enough, but firing is too much. Rock is a good shooter, and a good guy, so I don't think your mistakes should ever outweigh your achievements.

The second fact is, that if ever I get in a pinch, and I could get in such a pinch, I'd want people to support me and back me up. You can't ever let the company become more important than an individual, you never know when they'll be coming after you. This is not a black thing, or a white thing, it's just a human thing."

I put the petition on the table, walked away, then I went out and shot my stories. When I got back, walked into the garage, the petition was still on the table, *unsigned*. I left it there, determined not to give up hope. When I came in the next day, it was taped to the wall. When I walked over to it, every guy, every last one of those old heads, had signed. Across the top someone wrote in big, bold letters: **UNION!**

But in the end, it didn't do any good because WKBA refused to hire Rock back; he was through.

Kicker

DENISE

NEWS DIRECTOR

Ratings.

Sweeps. The Book. I've talked the talk. Now I've got to walk the walk. We're just a few days away from the start of the November Book. It's the biggest. The most important.

It's crunch time.

I know news. When a story breaks, like instinct, like allowing air to fill my lungs, I react. Quickly. I know the angle. The news peg. That's the most important part of the story. What will make the viewer think? What will make a viewer feel? But it's always back to the bottom line . . .

Ratings.

They will make or break a station. Raise or ruin a career. I have loved storytelling since I was a child. I'd sit in the corner and listen to adults talk. Not being grown. Just interested. Quietly interested.

I would access what was said. Work it over in my mind. Store it. My little brother was a tattletale. I was inquisitive. I'd ask questions. About why grass grew in blades. The distance to the stars.

Pass along info.

I'd share some of what I learned with my little brother. With my playmates. I'd write historical book reports. I liked facts. I wrote skits. Got others to perform them. I've always been best at arranging. Making things happen.

Now.

I've fought to stay afloat in this business. Done my best. Been passed over. Never gave up. Hated the shadows. Waited for the light.

I've got to deliver.

Each day I've come home. Written down my thoughts. How was

our lead story? What interview did we have that no one else got? I challenged my reporters before sweeps. Find me a hell of a story.

I challenged.

I also stood in the trenches, right with the team. I was pushing everyone. Driving them. When someone said, "That's all I can do." I said . . .

"But how can we do more?"

No office hiding for me. I don't hide behind a desk then bitch later. Moan. Criticize. I'm working with my managers. My writers. My reporters. My researchers. It's a glorious feeling. The boulder . . . *it's moving.*

Alex
Photographer/Technician

Awww. . . . Look out, look out, y'all! We're in the November Book and I have never seen a more nervous bunch of people in my entire life. And damn if I'm not including myself in that, you know what I'm saying?

Denise has been riding all of us and at first people were talking shit, but now that they see the ratings are coming up . . . people are getting with the program. The majority of us love news and hustle anyway, now we're killing ourselves. And the few lazy people we have? Well they're still lazy, but not as lazy as they used to be.

It's something about how sistergirl Denise pushes you—just enough to make you want to do all you can but not quite enough to piss you off. I've been watching Denise and her determination—really our collective determination—to get out of last place. I think it's making a heck of ah difference.

We have been looking cross-eyed at the Nielsen sheets, hoping for the very best. And, man, our six-thirty show has steadily been picking up numbers. The ten o'clock even picked up a point, because we've been concentrating less on the crime stories and more on people stories. That's Denise's baby and it's a mojo working.

Even The Column, which usually D-O-G's our station, did a story about the changes at WKBA. The Column gave Denise and the Wizard big kudos. We had a meeting after the six-thirty show and Denise was bouncing off the walls. She said, "Did you see, we gained three points yesterday!"

"We are rolling!" Holly said, stretching out her legs.

"Yes we are," Denise agreed, and couldn't hold back her smile and why should she? It was catching and to be honest, I was getting happy as hell myself.

"We've been fifth for years now," Denise said thoughtfully. "Now we can actually come in third!"

"How about a jam?" I suggested. "If we do place third, huh? We haven't had a sweeps party here in ages. That would be a great morale booster. Yeah a sweeps jam!"

Holly shouted, "If there is no theme, there is no party! Let's pick a funky theme."

And don't you know the ever conservative Denise said, "Let's not brag too much. Too soon."

"Have faith." Holly smiled at her. "It's in the bag because frankly, we've got momentum . . . not to mention good looks, talent, dynamic leadership . . ."

"Stop sucking up!" I laughed.

Holly closed her eyes and gave me the finger. "The theme is sixties. Motown music and sixties' dress!"

"Hey now," I said with a head shake. "Cooley High music! That's my favorite old school flick!"

"Done," Denise laughed. "We pull this off, a Motown Sweeps party it is."

DENISE
NEWS DIRECTOR

Week #1.

Sweeps. The November Book. The motto: News about you. We had stories on how to invest two grand in Chicago companies. We had safety tips. For women who work at night. For seniors. News about you. We're fifth place yet touching fourth's gown.

Week #2.

I pushed harder. Momentum was building. Heavy promotions. More features. A blunder by the #4 station. A technical problem. The station is knocked off the air. During a train wreck no less. Viewers tune in to us . . . and stay. Now we're #4 . . . and hoping.

Week #3.

I feel anxious. What can I do to give an edge? To win third? The Wizard is excited. He smells success. Right now at fourth, we're better. Not best. We need a big threat. A big story.

An exclusive.

I prayed for it. Hoped for it. An exclusive that would capture the attention of Chicago. Of viewers. An exclusive. I again challenged my reporters. Give me that story. Give us a true shot at winning third. Holly. Stu. Mack. And all the rest.

Who will step up?

KENYA
Writer/Producer

The story was Stu's. He'd been hordin' a tip, workin' it secretly for weeks with one of our researchers and an intern. It broke for us. The story was about how this particular police commander was havin' an affair with a convicted felon.

They'd done some diggin'. They turned up more than one instance of association with a convicted felon, particularly former prostitutes. Once Stu started diggin' 'round, secret sources started tippin' him off like crazy with payoff information on how the commander was lettin' his girlfriend's street buddies do their thing without bein' hassled.

WKBA ran with it. Our video was of the strip where they worked and we covered up all distasteful video—no T&A—and we dealt less with the sex as the issue and more on the corruption angle. We played up the effect the unchecked prostitution had on the neighborhoods around it. It was a people angle, hard news, not sleazy at all.

It was the hottest story in town and we had it by the tail swingin' it overhead to high heaven. Everybody else was scramblin' to catch up but a turtle can't catch a hare, especially if the hare has a good old-fashioned headstart. But was the story and the burst of ratin's enough in that last week and a half to help win a respectable spot?

I had played the story as our lead every night that week and it was hot as an Arkansas spring. I didn't use a sexy caption on the graphics. I kept it newsy and plain—POLICE CORRUPTION. The other stations tryin' to limp along and play catch-up had tabloid graphics that said, SEX SCANDAL—INSIDE FADED BLUE or COMMANDER HOOKER AND THE HOOKER.

We stayed clean and consistent and darn if our audience didn't build. More people tuned in. We aired promotional ads that let folk know we were doin' hard-hittin', clean news. No sleaze. The ratin's went up. The Column gave us kudos for an exemplary job.

But was it enough? We'd been watchin' the ratin's and WLS-ABC was far and away the winner in first place, WMAQ-NBC solid at second, but third place was up for the grabbin'. There were only two points between us and the third-place station.

At the end of the ratin' book, we waited for the results. The newsroom was tense with excitement. It was good clean excitement. We'd become a team now that we'd surveyed our ideas and set our boundaries.

"Damn if I don't think we'll place," my favorite editor Perkins said as he sucked on his unlit cigar.

We found out the next day right at 2 P.M. We did it! The entire newsroom erupted in cheers. The on-air talent chipped in and bought pizza, cola drinks, and cake. Denise was huggin' folk. I was huggin' folk.

"We are going to have our Motown Victory bash?" Holly called out through the melee to Denise.

"It's on!" she said grinnin'.

By the time I went into the booth for my six-thirty show, I was glowin'. I called my husband Jarrett at home and told him the good news. He was really happy for me.

I was in the second block of the show, and everyone was jokin' between the breaks, it was just a good day. Suddenly Abby came tearin' into the booth like a helium balloon with the air let out.

Abby began to screech, "YOUUUU . . ."

"No yellin'! Remember what Denise said."

Abby caught herself and I grinned like a Cheshire cat.

"Sorry, but you have to make some kills. We have to get this story in."

My computer was flashin' an URGENT on the national wires. I clicked on the wire story. It read:

Dateline: (New York) . . . Jeb Quincy, Sr., owner of Quincy Metro Broadcasting, died of a heart attack today while playing golf in Miami, Florida. He was seventy years old. His son, Jeb Quincy, Jr., is expected to immediately succeed him as chairman of Quincy Metro Broadcasting.

Beans

Photographer/Technician

Jeb Quincy died, and the company stock dropped from thirty-two dollars a share to nineteen dollars a share the next day. It seemed that industry watchers thought that Jeb Junior was going to mismanage the company, so people were shedding the stock like dead skin, and I saw my dream of starting my own production company slip farther away. Now I had half of what I'd originally built up, and I couldn't really quit with that devastating a loss.

I felt a tearing against my side, a pain from stress, I think, because I had been saving steadily in hopes of buying a shooting and editing unit at a cost of about a hundred seventy-five thousand dollars. But now, with Jeb Quincy, Sr., dead, the stock drop pushed me down to about ninety-five thousand dollars total, not nearly enough.

I couldn't just dump the stock right now, so I'd have to pray that it came back up to at least the thirty-two dollars a share. It was killing me but I wanted so much to have my own business to run, as I chose, with the stories I wanted to work on, the projects I deemed worthy. And now it had slipped farther away and I could only feel frustrated, but a little hopeful. It went up, then down; it could go back up again.

DENISE

News Director

The Wizard summoned me to his office. Urgent. I got a bad vibe. The first bad vibe I got was when the Wizard was summoned to New York. The last GM who got summoned to New York never made it back.

The Wizard made it back.

And he came back with marching orders. The orders came from Jeb Junior. He's running Quincy Metro now. Cutbacks.

Massive cuts.

I've had to lay off before. I always fight it to some degree. "Maybe . . ." I began. The Wizard said, "No maybe. This is not a few heads. Jeb Junior wants to trim the workforce. Across the board. I'm talking about thirty-two people here alone." I thought, that's not a cut . . .

That's amputation.

"How can we run the station? Do you know what that will do to morale? We're starting to make headway. Is anyone aware of that? Our ratings are coming up!"

Disdain.

The Wizard shrugged, "I don't like it. But it's got to be done. Quincy Metro will survive. This is not new. Didn't CBS survive? Didn't NBC survive? They both had major staff cuts."

I couldn't stop it.

The Wizard had a list of the newsroom staff. The head of technical joined us. The head of sales too. It was quiet. It was dark.

Let the slaughter begin.

It began that day and lasted all week. We argued over favorites. Over procedures. Over how much or how little notice to give. Corporate called from New York. No notice was to be given. Lay off the employee. He or she has to leave the building immediately.

Mean.

It was a mean process. We discussed nonunion staffers first. They were slain without a blindfold. We laid off secretaries, mailroom workers, supervisors, security guards. Account assistants. Some had been with WKBA for ten to fifteen years.

Mean.

We talked about on-air talent. Who would be renewed and who would not? Whose contract would be bought out and whose would not? Hazel Morriette.

Dragon Diva.

Old man Quincy had been her protection. Heard that Jeb Junior couldn't stand her. Her contract had three months left. The word was stop negotiations now. No renewal. She's history. And being a woman over forty in this business, God help her.

Reporter openings.

The Wizard said no new hires. We were to stretch the talent we had. Then Holly's name came up. She still had time left on her deal. But would they keep her after that?

I waited.

The Wizard said, "Keep her. She's pretty good and we've got her on the cheap."

When it came to the writers, the last person hired was Kenya. Last hired, first fired. I argued, "But she's a good writer."

"She's got the least seniority," the Wizard said. "She's young. She'll find another job."

Save her.

The Wizard said what I knew. There was a union problem. There was a clause in the writers' contract. It said if layoffs are made out of seniority, double severance has to be paid.

That's a stiff penalty.

That's what would happen if we kept Kenya and cut someone with more seniority. "How," he said, "could we justify paying a penalty when we're suppose to be cutting expenses?"

I couldn't save Kenya.

Then we turned to technical. The technical union had signed a contract last year. Unfortunately, they gave up their seniority clause. In exchange they got a higher raise. Four percent instead of two percent. Bargaining.

It would haunt them.

"Alexandra Harbor . . . Meg Rippley . . . Jack Simpson . . . Harold Witt . . ."

What?

"All of those people are at the top of the seniority list," I said. "What happened to last hired, first fired?" It was then explained to me. They all made the most money. They cost the most for health care benefits and 401(k) plans. Younger employees worked cheaper.

I made a desperate attempt.

"Look, if you lay off both women photographers it will look sexist. I'm sure Jeb Junior wouldn't want a lawsuit, would he?" I waited. I prayed that I could save one of them.

"Okay."

The Wizard agreed. He remembered my lawsuit threat, which won me the news director job. "We'll keep one of them. Let's keep . . ."

"I don't want to know," I said.

I had a headache. My throat was dry. I managed to also save Vera. Everyone liked her. She was always helping people.

Then came the ultimate.

The Wizard asked me to stay after the other managers left. I heard the door slam. I looked him dead in the eye. Was he now going to fire me?

"You've done a great job."

Yes. Yes. C'mon. What are you going to do? "Denise," he said, "I was skeptical about you at first. But you have good news ideas. You have leadership qualities. I misjudged you because Mitch said a lot of negative things about you. He was wrong."

And?

"And I'm telling you this because when I was in New York, when I met with Jeb Junior, there was another person there. It was Mitch Saleen. Jeb Junior will announce that Mitch will be hired as the new vice president of the owned-and-operated stations. He'll be the senior manager over all the stations—including WKBA.

The Godfather was coming back.

"Apparently, Mitch and Jeb Junior have mutual friends. They've all become very close party buddies I hear. I've got friends in Corporate. I'm protected. I'll protect you. I think you've got talent and guts. But I wanted you to know about Mitch. We both have to watch our backs with him."

The Godfather.

I thanked the Wizard. I smiled. But my insides were erupting with rage. Mitch was coming back? And in a huge position of power too? Mitch had run the station into the ground, hadn't he? Yet he was being rewarded.

The ladder of success.

Mitch is *failing up the ladder*. I can't hardly climb the ladder. They keep shaking it. Mitch will be back. A bigger, badder Godfather than before. The Wizard said he'd protect me.

So what?

I sat in my office and thought. I'd proved that I could run a news operation. I'd brought up the ratings. I had proved that you could do journalistically sound stories and win over an audience. I'd proved that you could lead without berating. Without game playing. I'd saved some jobs.

The Wizard offered to save mine.

But why go there? I'd done everything I'd said I would. I was proud of what I'd done. I was tired. Tired of constantly proving myself. Tired of working twice as hard for three quarters the pay and half the recognition.

Fed up.

I was tired. I just didn't want to do it anymore. Slowly my anger left. I turned on my computer. I fired off a letter to the Wizard. It said . . .

"It is with mixed emotions that I submit my letter of resignation . . ."

Beans

Photographer/Technician

For the umpteenth time, and it burned me up each time, I walked pass the bathroom that's supposed to be "ours." The sign "MEN" glared at me, and I felt tired, mixed with anger, and I just stared at the sign.

I was fed up, with nothing especially, and everything in particular. Were we so afraid, so eager not to make waves, that for years we had put up with having a bathroom with a urinal in it? Did we tell ourselves, every day, that it didn't matter that the door said "MEN" when we were clearly women? How many people, technical managers, building managers, had lied to Alex and me about changing the bathroom? Promises made, and not kept, or did they just think we weren't important enough to matter?

Today I walked into the newsroom, that's when I heard the news. Bad news, I think, travels faster than the speed of light. People were getting laid off; one at a time, they were being called into the office. It was ugly, not well thought out, because each person was being tapped on his or her shoulder. How hard is that, and cruel, like waiting for punishment as a kid. The network wants to get slim, but it was never fat like some of the other networks.

By the end of the day, so many of us, the veterans, were gone. I wonder, Why am I still here? Why didn't I get the ax, and why do I feel bad that I still have a job? It's not my fault, but I feel so helpless, and nervous too. Goddammit, I know that television has changed, that people are watching cable more than regular networks. I know that the Internet is pulling a ton of people away, and where there are less viewers there's less money. But we are talking about people with families, with more than ten years on the job. Doesn't that count, and what price is put on that loyalty?

Alex, said to me, not shaken, but a bit angry, and with a whole hell of a lot of shock, "Well, I'll be good goddamn. Who would have thought they'd get rid of me? Beans, you'll have to hold down the fort by yourself, girl!"

Alex had a box in her hand; it contained the belongings she'd kept in her locker. She looked a bit teary-eyed; without a doubt, I surely was. Alex turned to go. I stuttered, "Wa-wa-wait!" I stopped, calmed myself, and said, "Let's keep in touch, no matter what, let's keep in touch."

"Shit yeah, girl," Alex said. Then she put down her box and hugged me. I felt her stiffen, and I drew back. "What, Alex?"

She nodded toward the bathroom, and then Alex said, "Beans, I sure hate that we never got that bathroom fixed."

I turned and stared at the door; the longer I looked, the madder I got. Then I looked at Alex, and I knew what we needed to do. I walked over to our unit, the one Alex and I rode together in for years. I pulled out two hammers from the tool box we kept there to fix things, and there was something Alex and I needed to fix, together.

I handed her a hammer, and she looked confused, confused until I

pointed at the door with the sign that said "MEN." We walked over together, side by side, and we went into the bathroom and we went to
work.

Together we hammered and slugged at that ancient, dried-up urinal and it just popped and came apart with ease. It was like it was dying all along and had been waiting for us, Alex and me, to put it out of
its misery. But we were putting ourselves out of a misery, a misery that
we'd kept for too long. And we hit crazy like at first, then softer as each
piece crumbled.

When we finished and looked at the pile of chalky porcelain, we
laughed. Alex and I laughed, then she said, "Wait! C'mon!" Alex took
my hand and we stood outside the door, then she pointed at the sign.
I took the forked end of my hammer, loosened the plate, and popped
it off. Alex went over to her box, fished around, and pulled out a black
marker. She wrote on the door, in big letters, "WOMEN." Then we
stepped back and admired our work, before we hugged.

Bye-Bye

Holly
Reporter/Anchor

Webster, who sharpened the tools that we use to express ourselves, defines the word "change" as: *to make or become different in some way.* The layoffs at WKBA forever altered us all emotionally, physically, and spiritually. Survivors of what would become known as the "Monday Massacre" felt a measure of guilt. We talked about it. Some who survived wondered, why not me?

And although the company payroll decreased, our workload and obligations as journalists did not. Physically we all carried the extra burden of delivering as good a news product as we could without nearly the same amount of heads and hands.

Of course, too, morale was again low. My father says that in human nature's cupboard, spirit is the most fragile dish. But he also says with time, there's healing.

The Motown Sweeps party never got off the ground. Instead it turned into a good-bye party that was held several weeks later. It had taken a while to agree to have a party and let the bitterness settle a bit.

We picked a restaurant in Navy Pier. WKBA staffers had made the owner rich over the years and he kindly gave us a back room with a heart-thumping view of Lake Michigan's silky blue waters. The night of the party that view was fabulous. The stars twinkled like holiday fireworks, and their reflections were majestic flickers of light skimming off the waves.

The mood was surprisingly festive. Most of the thirty-two people who were laid off, we called them "the kicked in the behinds," they did show up. And "the left behinds," as we called ourselves, we were glad to see them.

Rock agreed to be the DJ for the bash. He came dressed as James Brown in what had to be the tightest two-piece suit I'd ever seen. I'll bet his balls were squeezed beige by the iron-ribbed strands of the lime green polyester suit. And he had a hat with a brim that was so wide it deserved its own parking space.

"Holly, would you believe I was the coolest dude in the place in this once?" Rock laughed, styling.

"Nope!"

"Aww, you youngster. You don't know nothin' 'bout this kind of styling and profiling!" Then Rock cocked the hat to the left and slapped on a vintage J.B. cut, "Papa's Got A Brand New Bag."

As it turns out, Rock landed a job with the Chicago Bulls as video-tape coordinator. He was being well paid to shoot and edit game tape for team strategy meetings.

I looked around the swank restaurant and everyone was having a good time. I was glad to hear that many people had job leads, a few even had new jobs already.

I saw Dragon Diva sitting in a corner. When I entered the restaurant foyer, I'd heard that she was the first to arrive. She was clearly on her way to getting drunk and her eyes were teary. She looked like hell. The odds of her landing an anchor spot at her current salary and at her age were slim to none. I breezed passed Dragon Diva and didn't say a word. I was content to let her stew in her own out-of-style nastiness.

I spotted Alex . . . Beans . . . Kenya . . . and Denise at another table, kitty-corner to the picture window, sipping champagne. Alex had been laid off and had decided to go to film school, a passion long ignored.

After the layoffs—thirty-two people in our shop and some twenty-five more at each of the other owned-and-operated stations nation-wide—the company stock eventually skyrocketed. Wall Street seems to like companies that downsize.

Quincy Metro's stock went from a low of sixteen dollars a share to fifty-two dollars a share. Beans had up and quit, cashing in all she had salted away, and was now starting her own production company. Tonight she had her new camera resting on her leg. Beans had volunteered to shoot the party and put together a tape for people who wanted one for old times' sake.

Kenya got laid off too, but quickly, she landed a job. Now she works for the *Chicago Reporter*, an award-winning news magazine that focuses on race and poverty through investigative pieces. On the sly, Kenya had been floating her résumé around and had gotten a hit. The pay at the *Chicago Reporter* wasn't great, Kenya said, but the work and the people were second to none in talent, positive attitude, and industry accolades. The hours were reasonable too and Kenya would have more time to spend with her family.

Denise had decided to take a time-out. But her ability to bring up WKBA's ratings was not overlooked by industry watchers. Denise had two huge job offers at rival networks out of state. She considered the offers, but eventually decided to turn them down. Denise said she wanted to stay in Chicago with Perry. She planned to relax for a few months, and then maybe try her hand at writing a book.

When the shake-up had first hit the papers, all the shops were buzzing about who got laid off and Denise's abrupt resignation. I got a call from a news director across town. He offered me a weekday anchor spot.

I explained that I had more than a month left on my WKBA deal and they most surely wouldn't let me out of my contract, not one minute early. But still he said that they would wait for me, and the initial money we talked about was more than double my current salary. I was thrilled especially when my future station sent a dozen red roses with a card that said, *You're well worth the wait.*

"Hey look, everybody, it's the rising star!" Beans said warmly, giving me a hug before she began shooting me.

"Hey-hey, Miss Thang is here!" Alex joked next, as we embraced. We didn't see each other every day anymore and we missed one another. "Are you back here stirring up trouble, Alex?"

"And ya know that 'cause that's the way it is!"

"Just give me a starring role when you make that first movie, that's all," I said, sashaying my hips. I hugged Denise.

"Shoot," Kenya smiled, waiting to hug me next. "We all need to be in the party scene. I want to be in the center muggin' for the camera just like the folk on Soul Train."

"Uh-uh," Alex said before taking a deep sip of champagne. "You youngsters don't know what a real old school Soul Train line was like!"

"Please," I said. "You can't out-jam us. No way."

"I agree with Alex," Denise said, draining the last of her bubbly out of a flute glass.

"Seeing is believing!" I laughed as I filled my glass with champagne and began bopping to the music. "If Rock ever puts on a real cut instead of this old tired stuff we just might be able to determine who is bad and who is not."

"Oh no, she did not." Alex nudged Denise. "Hear that? No respect."

"What?" I laughed.

"R-E-S-P-E-C-T," Denise said. "Aretha Franklin. Before your time, madam."

"Yeah," Alex cracked. "All your music has base lines and rifts sampled from our old songs. Y'all wouldn't know a good dance record if you heard it."

Kenya challenged them. "Is that a fact?" And then she made a brisk move for the DJ booth where she whispered something in Rock's ear.

"What is she up to?" Denise said wistfully.

"I don't know," Beans said, swinging her head away from the camera's viewfinder, "but I'm getting it all on tape!"

Rock cocked his brim to the other side of his head and grabbed the mike. "We have a request! It's electric slide time. That's the hustle for you old disco folks and that's country line dancing for you Southern boys and girls—but add some funk!"

The heavy, Caribbean beat of a popular dance song began pulsing inside the room—"It's Electric!" Then the singer rattled off a contagious, breathy scat and people started getting out on the dance floor. Kenya was showing two of our former coworkers how to do the Electric Slide. Beans had anchored a spot in front and was down on one knee panning the dance floor.

Now all of us were out there doing the basic moves—four steps left, then back right, stop, lean forward, swing hips up and back, turn . . . and start again. Some people, like Alex and me, already knew the dance. Alex was freestyling and throwing all kinds of boogie moves into her slide.

"Oh you can go?" I laughed. "I'm with y'all," Denise said from my other side. We were both keeping up with Alex. Kenya was in front taking the lead.

The entire floor was now full of people. Black and white. Employed. Unemployed. We were all dancing to the same music but as always some people were out of step and others were in synch; still a few decided to give up and step away, content to watch or cheer those remaining on.

We did the Slide five times that night and after the last time as the party began to end, Rock got on the mike. "Ho! Ho! Ho!"

We chanted back, "Ho! Ho! Ho!"

At the end of the night, people hugged and wished each other well. Kenya, Alex, Denise, and I huddled together and made a promise to try to have lunch once a month, a tradition of support, of networking with one another that was born out of our experience at WKBA. It was a promise we kept, a bond of friendship that we happily shared for many years to come.

Closing Credits

Yolanda Joe
Journalist/Author

For years I have been thinking about writing this book. Several times I started and stopped. Each idea was so very different. So you can imagine how the story has changed shape, voice, and purpose over time. I settled on this . . . which I present with great joy and relief. The people are fictional but the issues and attitudes *are real*.

To drive that point home, in the tradition of the WKBA newsroom, I say . . . What movie? *To Kill a Mockingbird*. What Character? Atticus. What line? "You never really understand a person until you climb into their skin and walk around in it." I hope I've enabled you to briefly walk around in the skin of a woman in broadcast news.

I want to thank all my friends and family who love and encourage me. Special hugs to my broadcast buddies for letting me bounce ideas and emotions off them. (Never reveal a source—never ID a mole.)

Cheers and high-fives to my agent and editor—they are two of the most special people on earth. And to the journalists who work in newsrooms around the country, continue to do your best and remember to always keep your head up. And the final out-cue is Peace and God Bless.